I0629348

HEARTWOOD

EMMA HARTLEY

HEARTWOOD
Copyright © 2025 by Emma Hartley

ISBN: 979-8-88653-411-5

Published by Satin Romance
An Imprint of Melange Books, LLC
White Bear Lake, MN 55110
www.satinromance.com

Names, characters, and incidents depicted in this book are products of
the author's imagination or are used fictitiously. Any resemblance to
actual events, locales, organizations, or persons, living or dead, is
entirely coincidental and beyond the intent of the author or the
publisher. No part of this book may be reproduced or transmitted in any
form or by any means, electronic or mechanical, including photocopying,
recording, or by any information storage and retrieval system, without
permission in writing from the publisher except for the use of brief
quotations in a book review or scholarly journal.

Published in the United States of America.

Cover Design by Ashley Redbird Designs

For Tony, whose love makes everything better.

*"Your task is not to seek for love,
but merely to seek and find all
the barriers within yourself
that you have built against it."*

— *RUMI*

*"What makes night within us
may leave stars."*

— *VICTOR HUGO*

ONE

Dust billowed up behind Alex's truck, as she sped along the winding gravel road. Her balding tires skidded on loose rocks as she took an unexpected turn, eliciting a swoop of excitement in Alex's stomach. The tape deck on her beater Chevy had been teetering on the edge of oblivion for months and had finally given out, leaving her alone with a useless box of early nineties cassettes from Goodwill and her own racing thoughts.

Earlier, she had received the strangest message on her voicemail—some guy rambling about Lost Lake and a cabin on Bear Road, how much work it needed, and how he was looking for a contractor. He'd sounded delightfully clueless. It had all the makings of a city boy trying to sell an old camp, but she'd find out for herself soon enough. He'd left an out-of-state number, most likely a cell phone, so it had gone to voicemail a few times when she'd called back. The reception out here was still spotty.

Alex's decision to drive out and see for herself hinged solely on a single unfortunate event. Her first job of the year had been cancelled on short notice, and she was scrambling to make up for it. Being the only female restoration contractor in the Western Adirondacks was no easy task. For the past four years, she'd worked tirelessly, producing high-quality restorations, all the while desperate to be taken seriously. Slowly, her reputation was growing, but it was a constant battle.

As she crested the hill towards the end of the gravel road, a nearly hidden driveway appeared. Obscured by brush and trees, the entrance was punctuated only by a rusty mailbox whose lid hung open unnaturally, like the mouth of a long-extinct animal. This must be it. Alex turned into the driveway, hitting a deep divot with her left tire. "Shit," she muttered. "This is out there." As her wary nature was starting to prickle a warning to turn back, a sparkling lake rose up from the cloud of dust trailing her. Stopping at the edge of the driveway, Alex took in the view. The camp was an unqualified disaster—*man, did it need serious work*—but the view was unparalleled. Two ancient pines stood at the top of the lot, framing the sloping, mossy way down to the lake. The far shore curved gently, leading Alex's gaze from the protected bay into the greater lake beyond. Misty, atmospheric blue mountains stood sentinel beyond, their ancient, rounded tops peeking out above the tree line, soft and dreamy. It was a million-dollar view.

Alex turned off the truck, reached across the seat to grab her tape measure, and looked out the window. A bear of a man sat in a dollhouse-sized chair, tipping back on two legs. With his feet on the porch railing and his arms crossed over his broad chest, he had been watching her. Curious, Alex met his gaze. She took in his muscular chest and arms, thinking they looked like they belonged on a linebacker, or maybe like the model Michelangelo wished he'd had. The guy's hair was sandy blonde and buzz cut, and his eyes were steel blue. His expression held intelligence and curiosity.

Alex was about to smile at him when the porch railing gave way to his brawn, splintering, and violently thrusting the man forward and nearly off the porch. Through sheer force of will, Alex kept herself from laughing aloud. The guy brushed off his pants, looking furious.

The truck door creaked loudly as Alex opened it, hopped out, and slammed it shut behind her. This was going to be fun.

Closing the distance between them, Alex called merrily, "What'd you do that for?" Her eyes glittered with unconcealed amusement.

"Shit," he muttered. Looking down at the shattered porch railing, the guy assessed the damage. "This place is completely rotten." He kicked a splintered baluster off the porch and onto the lawn.

Alex spread her arms wide, taking it all in, and said, "Are you kidding? It's a quintessential Adirondack-style camp. It's got great bones. Granted, it needs a little TLC."

Incredulous, he replied, "A little TLC? The entire porch needs to be ripped off."

Still ebullient, Alex said, "Roof needs replacing, too, from the look of it."

"I'm sorry." He squinted at her, looking baffled. "Who are you?"

The brightness went out of her eyes as she remembered herself. A woman contractor named Alex. Of course he didn't know who she was. Dully, she said, "You called and asked me to come over. I tried to call you back, but your cell doesn't work out here. I'm Alex."

"Alex?" The man still looked perplexed, until the realization hit him. "As in, Alex Taylor Construction?"

"Yes." Steeling herself, her voice hardened, as she glared at him. "Not what you expected, I presume."

Sheepishly, the guy said, "Um…"

"Mr. Anderson, right? Do you want me to look at the place or not?" Alex took a steadying breath, as she awaited his reply.

"Sure. Sorry. Please, call me Blake."

Alex scanned the property critically. "Well, Blake, you're right about one thing. The porch definitely needs to come off, but I might be able to save the structure of the porch roof." She climbed the porch stairs and poked her steel-toed boot into a punky board.

"You might as well get the full effect," Blake said, dismally, leading the way inside.

As Alex followed him through the front doorway, she was confronted with a behemoth fireplace gracing the center of the front room. It erased her annoyance in an instant as her inner preservationist took control of the situation.

"Whoa!" she exclaimed. "That's extraordinary. It's a pristine example of turn-of-the-century stonework. They laid each stone in like puzzle pieces." She caressed one of the stones as she spoke. She kneeled down and looked up the flue, smiling unabashedly. "What a work of art. You've got a gem of a place here."

"Really." Blake's voice dripped with sarcasm.

"Really," Alex replied, as she stood up, brushing soot off her hands and onto her jeans. "Did you inherit or buy?"

With barely concealed annoyance, Blake answered tersely. "I inherited it. My dad died about a month ago."

"Oh, I'm sorry." Turning to face him, Alex fixed him with a gaze of remorse for his loss.

Blake's features were marble. "Don't be," he said, harshly.

Alex's expression hardened again. What was his problem? Done with this game, she asked, "Do you want me to come back another time?"

"No. Let's get this over with."

She snapped, facing him and coming a little closer than she should have. "Get this over with? Let's get one thing straight, Mr. Anderson. I will not do a hack job on this place. Not for any reason. It's not the camp's fault, whatever else happened between you and your father."

He narrowed his eyes, ferocity simmering in his gaze. "I'd appreciate it if you didn't make assumptions about me or my feelings about this place."

"I don't need to. You clearly hate it here, you hate him, and he probably deserved it."

Every muscle in Blake's body was tense, as he said, "Trust me. He did."

"Fine." Her eyes were blazing now. "All I'm saying is I refuse to compromise on my standards. I can reproduce the original intent of the place, but I will not use some pressure-treated four-bys and call it a day. It's going to take time and money. If that doesn't work for you, play roulette with the assholes in the phonebook. Good luck."

She was turning away as Blake called, "Wait, I'm sorry."

She kept walking. Blake wouldn't have much luck booking a contractor this close to summer. He should jump at the chance to hire her.

Blake followed her outside, hopped off the porch where the railing used to be, and faced her on the lawn.

"Please wait. How much will it cost and how long will it take?"

"To do it right?" she countered.

"Yes," he acquiesced. "To do it right."

For a long moment, Alex regarded this strange man before her. Blake was even bigger up close, broad shouldered, definitely over six feet tall, and almost *too* fit. His eyes had a hard edge to them when he was being defensive, but now they were softening into defeat. There was something sadder than she'd seen in him a mere moment ago. Every word, every action to this point, had made it clear to her how much he hated the camp. He probably had legitimate reasons. Her heart squeezed a bit for the poor son-of-a-bitch.

Regardless, she kept her guard up, facing him authoritatively. Blake had finally deflated, which she was thankful for, not having been too fond of his blustery defensiveness. But as she stared him down, his plaintive, vulnerable expression tied her stomach in knots. His eyes appeared so much bluer outside than they had indoors. They were less the color of steel, as she'd first thought, and more the color of lightening, unusually clear and bright.

Kicking her toe into the dirt, she looked out at the water, trying not to feel petulant. This shit happened all the time. If she'd been a man, he wouldn't have questioned her. If she'd been a man, she wouldn't have had to justify her commitment to restoration. If she'd been a man, where would she be? The question wasn't worth the pain of the answer, so she pulled herself together.

"Do you actually want me to do the work?" she asked, defiantly.

"Yes, Alex. Please."

6

"We talking inside and out or just the obvious outdoor work?"

"Outdoor. Roof, porch, paint."

Done with his shit, she said, "For the exterior work, we're talking minimum thirty grand and six weeks of work. Materials are included in that estimate."

"How many in your crew?"

"Only me. I had a guy helping me out last year, but he was more trouble than he was worth. I only take a couple of jobs a summer. I have stuff lined up for July and August, but my June job fell through. You can have me now and I'll be done by the fourth."

"You'll get eaten alive working out here in June. It's almost black fly season."

"Occupational hazard." Alex turned away from the lake, looked up at the façade, peeling paint and all. Wistfully, Alex said, "I'd buy the place from you if I could, as is, and do the work on my own time. I'd live here. It's a great view. But I only started out a few years ago and haven't quite built up my bank accounts yet." Turning back to him, she mustered her most businesslike demeanor. "Well, what do you say? Do you want me?" Immediately she blushed, realizing she should've phrased her words differently. "I mean, do you want me to do the work or not?"

"Fine." The shadow of a smile played at his lips.

"Half now, half at completion. I take bank checks. I can give you a few days to get the money together, if you need it."

"I don't," he replied, hastily. "I brought cash."

"Cash?" she asked, incredulous.

Blake shrugged. "Yeah. Don't people use cash anymore?"

"Um, sure. I guess. Not often, though. Usually to buy gum or something."

"This would buy a lot of gum." Was that a glimmer of humor? He headed back into the camp.

Alex looked around the living room, as she followed him in. "Are you going to do the interior work yourself?"

"I guess. I need to get this done as fast as I can and sell it. I need to get back to my life."

Alex was curious. "Where is your life?" Her voice was soft. She shivered in the cold of the dark camp. Why hadn't he turned the furnace on?

"Chicago," he said as he grabbed his backpack from the living room floor. He reached into it and dug around.

Alex watched him, quizzically. "That's kind of far from here."

"Yeah. Exactly." He pulled a bulging white envelope from the backpack.

Eyes widening, Alex asked, "What do you do?" She shifted uncomfortably from foot to foot as he stared up at her.

"Do you always ask so many questions?" He stiffened and narrowed his eyes at her again.

She was prepared this time and asked coyly, "Are you always such a jerk?" Amused, she ran her hand along the stone mantel.

"So yes, then. You can't help it, can you?" Blake gave her a half-smile, as he removed a thick stack of bills from the envelope.

Alex sighed. "I guess not. You can, though," Alex said.

"I can what?" he asked, "Help being a jerk?"

"Yeah. Give it a try."

"Okay." He laughed, shaking his head. "I'll try, but I'm not promising anything."

As he counted out the money, Alex asked, "So, what do you do?"

"I deal drugs," he replied, glancing back up at her with a straight face.

If she'd had coffee in her mouth, she would have spit it across the room. Her horrorstruck expression was enough to restore Blake's smile.

"Kidding. I'm a physical therapist. I work with the Bears."

"As in, the Chicago Bears?"

"Yep, them. It's a pretty good living. And luckily, it's off-season right now, so it was less problematic for me to take time off for this." He waved his hand to indicate the cabin, then handed her a wad of cash.

Hesitantly, she reached out her hand and looked up at him. "This is weird. You know that, right?"

"Whatever. Take it or leave it. Do you want the job?"

"Yes. I love a challenge." She took the money, still reluctant. "Seriously, though, why cash?"

"Jesus. You don't give up." He looked incredulous. "I knew I'd need to gut this shithole, and I didn't want to deal with a bunch of banks and checks and bullshit. Cash is easier, and I've been saving up for ages." He gestured widely and added bitterly, "I consider this an investment."

"Thank you for explaining," Alex replied. "I try to be careful, you know. There's a lot of weirdos in the woods."

"Oh, I know there are," Blake said, in an exaggerated way, his eyebrows arched. "Are you going to count it?"

"I guess I should." Awkwardly, she stood in the dim, decrepit camp, counting the bills. No one had ever handed her this much cash before. The bills were all hundreds, but it still took a while.

When she was finally done, she pocketed the money

and said, "Okay. I'll get you a receipt and start work tomorrow. How much land here is yours?"

"Four acres straight back to the main road. Why?"

"Can I cut trees on the property?"

"Sure. Go nuts."

All business again, Alex said, "Okay. I'll order a dumpster so we have someplace to put all the wood from the porch."

"Can I fill it with shit from the house, too?" Blake asked, brightening.

"Definitely."

"Fantastic."

"Okay. See you tomorrow."

As Alex slammed the door of her truck, she shook her head. What had she gotten herself into? As she drove back down the mountain road to town, she decided Blake was an unusual man. He was sullen. He turned on a dime. He made gender assumptions. And worst of all, he seemed to be settling for her as a contractor.

Still, there was something else, something compelling about him. There was a sense of humor under all that bluster, and between angsty glares and broody frowns, she saw the glimmer of a good man beneath the taciturn façade.

Maybe the job wouldn't be fun, but it might be interesting. At least it was work, and she needed the money.

———

What was he thinking? Blake had just given fifteen thousand dollars to a diminutive wood sprite and watched her speed away in a beat-to-hell truck from 1986. Alex could so easily take that money and he'd never see her again. No receipt, like it never happened. Somehow, though, he trusted she wouldn't stiff him. Her independent spirit was refreshing. It took balls to be a female contractor in the middle of the woods. This was definitely a man's world, and she was alone in it.

Despite her size and her adorably cropped copper curls, which seemed to have a life force of their own, she was tough as nails and all business. The color of her eyes, however, lingered in his mind as she drove away. Their particular shade of forget-me-not blue was painfully familiar. It was the same shade his mother's eyes had been, so long ago.

As dust from the gravel driveway settled, the sound of Alex's tires slowly dissipated, and Blake was swallowed once more by the quiet of the lake. The woods blanketed all sound, muffling it from within. Birds called to each other, but they were so much a part of the place they didn't register as noise. Alex was gone. Blake was alone, and he needed to stay busy, to move forward, to get away from this damned place as fast as possible.

When he'd arrived a few hours ago, stepping into the front room was like falling into a black chasm. Without looking around, he'd gone to the phone table, dug out the phonebook, and called the numbers for local contractors. There were few choices, and Alex had been the only one with voicemail. After he left a message with his number, he sat on the porch and stared at the lake, not ready to face the ghosts awaiting him inside.

Now, holding his breath, Blake surveyed the cabin's dilapidated exterior again. *What a wreck.* The cleaning alone was a daunting prospect, but the dumpster would be a blessing. Everything that wasn't nailed down would go. Absolutely everything. Blake would pass a clean slate on to the new owners, erasing every last trace of his father.

Two weeks ago, Blake's blood had gone cold as he learned of his father's death. Aunt Sal, his mother's sister, had called to share the news. Dwight was finally dead. There was little to say about it, other than the fact. Sal wasn't sorry, Blake wasn't sorry, and neither of them feigned remorse for the loss. The conversation was short and to the point, mainly because Blake had ended the call quickly, before Sal could pepper him with questions or blanket him with sympathy. The realization, however, settled in like a hard frost. His father was dead, and work needed to be done.

For better or worse, Sal had always cared deeply about Blake, reassuring him as often as she could that he'd eventually be free of his psycho father's tyranny. She had even offered to adopt him after his mother died. In a characteristically cruel rebuff, however, his father had refused to relinquish custody. Instead, Dwight had kept the ten-year-old Blake around, because Blake assumed, with his mother dead, his father would've had no one left to abuse.

Over the years, Sal had tried so hard to help. Sometimes, she managed to convince Dwight to let Blake come and stay with her, but it was only ever to suit his own convenience that Dwight agreed. Seeing the love of a real family close up, only to be tossed into Hades again at the end of the stay, was a torture all its own. Blake grew to dread those trips, with their cruel glimpses of the perfect, peaceful life he couldn't have. Poor Sal. How could she have known being with her family only made Blake feel worse? Her best efforts hadn't made a difference in his world at all.

Guilt for pushing Sal away had gnawed at Blake for decades. Why was he so hard on her? She had tried her best, after all. Tried and failed. Would Dwight's death change anything? Blake doubted it could, but he should at least let her know he'd arrived. Out of habit, he reached into his pocket to retrieve his cell phone, but of course, as Alex had pointed out, there was no reception here. Somehow, there was still a scattering of remote places left in the world. This forsaken corner of the Adirondacks was definitely one of them.

Steeling himself, he walked back into the gloomy cabin. On his way to the landline, he paused in the living room to glare at the fireplace Alex had admired so much. To Blake, it was only a monument to misery. Fifteen years had passed since he'd left his father's home, yet here, time had stretched and warped, as though teetering on the event horizon of a black hole. Now that he was alone, oppressive memories crept out from every corner to mock him. His racing heart betrayed him, try as he might to ignore the voices of his past.

Disintegrating roller shades, once so adept at concealing the violence within those walls, hung impotently at the windows. They had grown tired and given in to the persistent sunlight edging defiantly through the cracks. Ferociously, Blake tore down the tattered roller shades and threw them out the front door. A pile of decrepit paper mounted on the front lawn as Blake worked his way through the downstairs. As the papers landed, clouds of dust billowed up, curling and eddying into the day's golden air like ghosts, and then dissipated in the breeze.

Natural light now entered the cabin, streaming through filthy windows, making the place seem less like a dungeon. It was a slight improvement. Blake's mood rallied incrementally.

Resuming the dreaded task of calling Sal, Blake sat at the phone table and dialed his aunt's number.

"Hey, Aunt Sal. It's Blake. I'm here."

"Hi, my boy. I've missed you. Is it absolutely horrible there?"

Blake steadied his breathing and answered, "Not that bad. It's fine, actually. I'm going to clean it up. I hired somebody to fix some things, and then I'll sell it."

"You'll make some money on it, I think. That's a beautiful piece of lake frontage. Are you sure you don't want to keep the place?"

"Oh, I'm sure," Blake replied, not bothering to conceal the bitter edge in his voice. "I'll sell it as soon as I can."

"Why don't you come over for dinner? It's only me and Sam. The kids are still at college."

"College, huh? That's crazy. Are they doing well?" Blake rubbed his eyes.

"Who knows." Sal's laugh reminded him of his mother's.

"Listen, I gotta go. I'll call you soon."

"Oh, no you don't," Sal said, knowing he was trying to get out of seeing her. "You're staying here and that is that. Come for dinner, sleep in Bunny's room, and we'll look after you. You certainly can't stay there."

"I need to be here, Sal. I can't drive back and forth every day. There's so much to do. I'll come for dinner soon, though."

"Okay, Blake, but the offer stands. I'm here."

He forced a softer tone. "Thanks, Aunt Sal. I appreciate it. See you soon." Blake hung up before she could say anything else.

Rubbing his face again, he tried to put the hurt in his aunt's voice out of his mind. There was barely enough time for his own emotional baggage right now, let alone anyone else's. He had too much to do but didn't know where to begin.

As he surveyed the rest of the cabin, one glance into

his father's darkened bedroom was all he could manage before a wave of nausea threatened to take him down. He closed the door again, blocking out the air of cruelty and decay, the foul remnants of a foul man.

Apprehensively, Blake approached the back hallway. Thick layers of off-white paint peeled from the walls above the wainscoting, revealing glimpses of the strangely bright greens and pinks of the past. The walls were so far off-white now that to use the word *white*, even modified, seemed a gross misrepresentation. Even the paint was trying to escape this place, flinging itself from the horror of its own existence. The bathroom off the hall was a lost cause, and Blake shuddered at the thought of what might be growing in that fetid biome.

As Blake reached the stairs to the second floor, he inclined his gaze upward, toward his childhood bedroom. Darkness tunneled to another closed door. Desperately, Blake fought his flight response, willing himself to calm down, willing himself to face this whatever lay beyond. Nothing could undo the past now. Blake put his hand on the battered newel post, began to take a step up, and faltered, as his racing heart betrayed him. *Enough.* He turned around and stormed back down the hallway, through the living room, and towards the screen door. It slapped like a shot against the outside wall, as he burst through.

Breathing fast, Blake looked down to discover his hands were balled into tight fists. Sweat had broken out over his entire body despite the chill air of the camp. The toothless, broken balustrade surrounding the front porch leered drunkenly at him. Rotten decking that shouldn't have borne his weight bowed precariously beneath him, as though the entire world would give way any moment.

Eventually, Blake's senses resurfaced through the

panic. Little by little his breathing slowed, and his muscles relaxed, as he mastered himself once more. The tightness in his chest had been overwhelming as he gazed up those stairs. It had trapped him, pinning him with his own fear. Outside, though, it was as it had always been. The brisk air and the whisper of the wind through pine needles eased some of his anxiety. The sparkling water of the lake teased him, flirting with him, drawing him out of himself and into its beauty. He walked down the overgrown path to the water's edge, with its shifting array of blues, and sat on a mossy boulder until his calm was fully restored.

He could do this. He could face this place, these memories, without breaking. He had to. He had faced worse in living through it, after all. His reaction was only natural. He could master his emotions and get through the next six weeks. Dwight, from the hell he had surely gone to, could not hurt him anymore. Blake had won the fight.

When Blake eventually forced himself back into the camp, he strode past the fireplace and entered the kitchen. He flipped the light switch, but what he saw made him wish he hadn't. This was a different breed of awful. He wished for a hazmat suit.

The counters were encrusted with layers of filth. The tattered linoleum floor was caked with grime. The refrigerator would be a horror all its own. Surrounded by mismatched chairs stood the same sturdy depression-era table Blake remembered. Its stout wooden legs seemed rooted to the floor, as though they had grown there and never been shifted. Telltale gashes crisscrossed its shellacked surface; evidence of the violence Blake's life had been plagued with. *We're twins*, Blake mused bitterly, running his hand along the scars.

Under the kitchen sink, Blake was shocked to find cleaning fluid and a scrub brush stuck in a tin bucket from the 1950s. The scrub brush was brand new, the tag still on it, and by the price he assumed it was only a few decades old. Blake went at it. He first scrubbed the kitchen counters. Then he moved on to the windowsills. He tore down the ancient, moth-eaten, formerly-gingham curtains, rods and all, and added them to the growing pile of detritus on the lawn. He scrubbed and washed, emptying bucket after bucket of filthy water down the drain. It was a purifying ritual, utterly satisfying.

After hours of cleaning, hunger crept up on Blake. All he had with him was crappy snack food left over from the drive. He hadn't touched the refrigerator yet—he would have to scour it before he would allow food in there—but it would have to wait.

With his keys and his backpack in hand, Blake headed to his car and drove to town. He ate at the first restaurant he saw and picked up some beer, food, cleaning supplies, and garbage bags at the general store. A few of their lackluster, premade dinners would last him at least a few days. He got a blanket and a pillow as well, knowing there was no way he could use what was in the cabin.

The all-purpose nature of stores in remote places fascinated him. It was too far for people to drive to a big-box store, so the little stores had everything they thought you'd need. It was one of the few things he appreciated about the place where he'd grown up.

Back at the cabin, Blake tackled the fridge and then the bathroom. For hours, he channeled his unhappiness and anger into a dervish of scouring and scrubbing. Well after midnight, when he'd finally exhausted his manic energy, he grabbed a beer and drank it on the porch. Racing silver clouds obscured the stars and the cold sapped away his body heat. Every exhale floated off to collect with the low fog rolling over the lake. Blake finished his beer, tossed the bottle into the hulking pile of debris on the lawn, and walked to his car.

Trying not to think too hard, he unpackaged the pillow and blankets, and lay down across the tight back seat. Maybe he was being stubborn, but he refused to sleep in his father's cabin. *No fucking way.* The cold he could handle. The ghosts were another story. It was going to be a long, uncomfortable night.

As he lay awake, staring through the rear window at the fissures between clouds, glimpsing an occasional star, his thoughts turned involuntarily back to Dwight. For years, Blake would lay awake, staring at that same sky, trying to block out Dwight's cruel voice, the clatter of upturned furniture and breaking glass, the muffled sounds of his mother crying downstairs.

In the mornings, she'd hide her bruises and pretend all was well. Blake had no baseline for what a normal family life was like, but in his heart, he knew this was not it. He tried to be strong for her anyway. He fought impotently against the torrent of insults Dwight would unleash on her for the slightest misstep, but it was like talking to a wall. The bastard had ignored him entirely, like Blake didn't exist. Dwight waited until nighttime to unleash his physical cruelty. Until the end, that is. The violence had escalated fiercely in the end.

Dwight's cruelty against Blake, however, had begun almost the moment his mother had died. When Blake was at his most vulnerable, having finally confessed his deep sadness to his father, the man had turned on him viciously. Blake still bore the scars of that first assault, and those of all the subsequent attacks. They were etched into his back like a topographical map. He could see himself cowering in the corner. Calling out to empty space. Begging for the pain to stop. Begging for his father to stop.

Catching sight of his father's face reflected in the bedroom mirror, contorted in hatred and anger as he landed blow after blow.

"*You little bastard.*" His father's voice echoed through time, cold and cruel. "*You coward. Cry, little baby. Go on. Cry. It won't bring her back.*"

Blake choked back the lump he hadn't realized was in his throat, as he wrestled himself for control. Of course, coming back here wouldn't be easy, but this was torture. *I should've sold the fucking place and been done with it. Why am I doing this to myself? I don't have anything to prove. I've healed. I've moved on.* The faded memory of his mother drove the lies from his mind. He had come back here for her, not for his father. He was desperate, whether he wanted to admit it or not, for some kind of closure. Fighting the flood of heartache, Blake beat back the memories, one by one.

Even now that Blake was free of his father, he knew he wasn't free. The idea of setting down roots or having his own children someday set off a death spiral in every relationship he chanced. It was for the best. No good could come from getting attached anyway. That had been proven to him early on. Life was a game everyone lost in the end.

Sleep evaded Blake for hours, as he tried to settle his body and his mind. It proved an impossible task.

TWO

Morning found Blake's car cocooned in a shroud of frost. Half-frozen, cramped, and miserable, he awoke disconcerted, got out, and stretched his back. A volcanic shower and some coffee would've been nice after the shitty night's sleep, but the shower alone would have to do. He cranked up the camp's feeble furnace and ran the water hot, then thawed himself out, little by little, thankful he'd cleaned the bathroom the night before. The grime had been decades thick. Why would anyone want to live like this? It did fit his father, though—filthy shower, filthy soul. Some epithet.

As Blake got out of the shower, he realized he'd failed to bring or to buy a towel. He swore and grabbed his t-shirt from the day before to dry himself off. He dressed, brushed his teeth, and headed out to the living room, where he discovered Alex kicking the door to get his attention. When he opened it, Alex smiled widely and held up two coffee cups and a pastry bag.

"Morning," she chirped.

"My saving angel. How did you know I was desperate

for coffee? Did you bring me a towel, too?" He narrowed his eyes in a mock-seductive smile.

Perplexed, Alex answered, "No towel, only caffeine and sugar." Alex roundly ignored Blake's tone and didn't flirt back.

They sat down on the front steps, facing the foggy lake. All business, Alex handed Blake a cup of black coffee.

"I've been thinking about it," she said. "We might move faster and more efficiently as a team. The weather this time of year is still pretty unpredictable. This way, we can do the outside on nice days and work inside on rainy days. Same price, same timeframe. Maybe we can get the roof and porch done before the black flies hit too hard. Sugar?"

"Yes, honey?"

"Oh, my God. Do you want sugar?" Alex shook her head at his bad pun.

"No, only milk or cream or whatever."

Alex handed him the creamers, still shaking her head, but the hint of a smile tugged at her lips. She dumped sugar in her own cup and stirred it, then added some cream and put the lid back on. She opened the waxed bag stamped with the logo of the local bakery and sniffed it, smiling. She held it out to Blake.

Donuts. "Angel," he repeated, and smiled.

Alex frowned again, but Blake didn't mind. He took a cinnamon donut from the bag and bit into it with relish. "Damn, that's a good donut," he muttered through the crumbs.

"Sure beats the chain stores," Alex agreed, stuffing her own mouth.

Eventually, she looked at him expectantly and asked, "So?"

"So what?"

Exasperated, she asked, "So what do you think about the team plan?"

"Oh, that. Sure. I don't know what the hell I'm doing, though, so be gentle." Again, he tried out a flirtatious tone.

And again, Alex ignored him.

"You're obviously strong," she continued. "That'll help. I can usually rig things up myself, but it sure is nice to have some help. We'll get the place shipshape by July, inside and out."

"Good. It's settled. Do we start with the roof?"

Alex laughed. "Good lord, no. The roof is the last of the outside work."

"Right. Like I said, be gentle."

Alex bit into another donut with obvious zeal. Her determined expression was only interrupted by a sigh of contentment elicited by the sugar. In Blake's experience, women flirted with him in almost every context, and he had learned to read them pretty clearly, whether it was chatty or lusty or somewhere in between. Alex, however, was showing an unusual immunity to his charms. Of course it was for the best, considering he didn't do the relationship thing, but he sure enjoyed the company of a beautiful woman now and then.

Alex, despite her scruffy exterior, was definitely beautiful. Her skin was milky and smooth, the bridge of her nose dusted with pale golden freckles. Her mouth was gorgeous, with full, pouty lips, yet without a hint of petulance. Her heart-shaped face was augmented by her bouncy halo of russet curls, the color women paid serious money for. But here this tiny beauty was, in the middle of nowhere, seemingly unaware of how perfect she was. She was so real, so honest. And she was completely ignoring him. What a turn on. Blake pushed these thoughts away as fast as he could, but it wasn't easy.

"No," she continued, oblivious to his train of thought. "We'll start by demoing the bottom half of the porch. None of this can be saved. The dumpster will be here by noon. I'll take measurements beforehand, so I know what to put back where. Man, these donuts are good. They're from the little bakery in Edison."

"*Good* is an understatement." He had finished his second and was deeply considering grabbing a third.

"Glad you like." She finally smiled at him full force, her rosy cheeks now sprinkled with cinnamon and powdered sugar.

As they finished their breakfast, the frost melted from the grass and the angle of the sun grew higher. The camp faced west, so the sun was rising behind them, lighting up the far side of the lake with all its fresh, budding green, in a most picturesque way. The carpet of evergreens beyond was breathtaking. Steam rose off the water and condensed in the cool air, hovering like the soul of the lake, desperate for escape.

"So pretty," Alex stated, mesmerized by the scene.

"Yeah. It is. I spent a lot of time outside when I was a kid. It's the only thing from those days I miss."

"Chicago isn't exactly brimming with nature's beauty," Alex said, sarcastically.

"The lake is nice, I guess. I run along it every day. It's a different kind of pretty." A lot like the women, Blake thought, cultivated rather than natural. He wasn't about to say it aloud, though.

"Do you like your work?" she asked.

"Yeah. The guys are cool, and the work is rewarding. They push themselves hard and need trainers and therapists to help them do it safely. That's where I come in.

Plus, I don't need a gym membership. Every piece of equipment I could ever ask for is right there."

"Nice. I don't need a gym either." Alex gestured sarcastically to her truck full of tools.

Blake still couldn't picture her doing all this work. Bundled in layers, with a men's work vest over it all, Alex wasn't exactly the picture of strength. She looked more like an unassuming college art student who liked indie rock. Without thinking, Blake reached out to brush some powdered sugar from her cheek. She flinched, but only slightly, her eyes widening. She recovered her composure immediately.

She wiped her face on her flannel sleeve. "I'm a messy eater, sorry."

"Thanks for the breakfast. It was really nice of you."

"Any time. I figured you wouldn't have much in the way of food here. I made us sandwiches for lunch, too."

"Full-service treatment," said Blake. "I appreciate it. Thanks."

"They're only sandwiches, Blake. No trouble at all."

They stood up and surveyed the porch. Alex went to get her tape measure and notebook from the truck. She strapped on her tool belt, which was obviously made for a man's circumference. There was a sizable distance between the manufacturer's holes and the one she had punched as far toward the middle as she could. The long tail of the belt was tucked in and tied in a loop, so it didn't get in her way. Even so, the belt sat on her hips at an angle that Blake found wildly distracting.

She measured everything twice, calling out numbers to Blake, who wrote them down in her notepad. Then after she drew out some plans, she handed him a pair of safety glasses and a sledgehammer.

He grinned. "Where first?"

"Well, we don't want the porch roof to fall on our heads, so we'll remove the corner supports after I prop up the roof tomorrow. In the meantime, we can demo the railings, steps, and floorboards. While you get started on that, I'll set up the ladders so I can examine the roof. Let's see if we can save it."

While Blake started to bash away at the rotten wood railing, Alex climbed up her ladder and perched along the edge of the porch roof.

"It looks sturdy enough." She crawled out onto it. "The eaves are sound," she called down to him. "I'll strip the shingles and replace the boards. I'm so glad. Framing out a roof is a huge pain in the ass." She scampered back down the ladder to grab her shingle lifter.

Blake tried hard not to watch her as she went past, but she paused beside him for a moment.

"When I strip the shingles," she said gently, "they're going to fall off the edge of the roof. Grab a tarp from the truck and put it down. That'll catch everything and we can dump it later."

"Yes, ma'am." He followed her directions and called, "All clear."

"Thanks."

For the next two hours, they worked, demolishing the effects of wear and time and the elements. Blake forgot about everything as he smashed up the railings, then moved on to lifting floorboards with a crowbar. It was wonderfully cathartic.

When Alex finally came down for a break, the shingles were off, and she was beaming.

"I was right, the roof is salvageable."

Blake returned her smile, his heart racing from the vigorous work. "Awesome," he replied.

"I got all the shingles off and measured the sections of

board I need to replace. Now I know how much roof felt we need over the wood and how many square feet of shingles to order."

"That's good, I guess. Better than having to replace the whole thing." Blake had no idea what he was talking about.

Alex looked around and surveyed his work. "Damn, you're moving fast. This would have taken me twice as long. Keep up the good work. I made a long list of what I need from the lumberyard, since I don't want to make a thousand trips to town, but I'm going to do a little more now, since I'm on a roll. This time, I don't want you anywhere near the edge of the porch—the rotten plywood is coming down. Work on that end, okay?"

"Yes, boss," Blake said, nodding. Alex narrowed her eyes at him before ascending the ladder once more.

Alex pried the rotten boards off the roof, starting at the far end and working her way back to the ladder. The boards slid off the roof with a bang. Blake looked up through the new hole in the porch roof in wonder at this toy-sized carpenter girl silhouetted by sky and sun and pine trees, a rugged little angel. When she caught him staring at her, she waved and smiled. His heart tugged uncomfortably as he waved back, but he forced himself back to work.

Blake and Alex removed most of the rotten wood from the porch, leaving exposed framework below. It looked sound enough, but what did he know? When everything was down to joists, Alex took final measurements on the base of the porch. She checked all the joists and sills for rot, then wrote down some more notes.

"We definitely have to replace a few joists and the north-facing sill. We can use pressure-treated for them since they're hidden. Do you want me to replace every-thing or only what's rotten?"

"Just what's rotten, I think. The rest looks solid enough."

"My feeling exactly. Now I've got a pretty comprehen-sive list of what we need from the lumberyard. They'll have to deliver it, so the sooner we get the order in, the better. I'm going to use tree posts for the corner posts, cross beams, banisters, and balustrades, in keeping with the original look of the place. We'll use white pine or cedar for the floor, unless you wanted to do composite decking. It's pricier, but it looks nice, and no one gets sliv-ers. It also lasts forever. Your choice."

"I thought you didn't like to use materials that don't match the historical integrity of the period." He was being cheeky.

"I don't, usually. Composite decking is where I make exceptions. I like to think that if such an awesome material was around back when these places were built, people would've used it."

"You're probably right, but wood is fine."

Alex hesitated a moment then asked, "Do you want to stay and work, or do you want to ride down to the lumberyard with me? We can eat lunch on the way."

Relieved to take a break, Blake eagerly answered, "I'll come, if that's okay. I could use a break."

"Cool. I'll hit the can, and then we can go."

"My can is your can," he said, with mock chivalry, bowing and gesturing into the camp.

She gave him an inscrutable look that might've contained a slight smile, and climbed up into the front door since there was no longer much of a porch floor to stand on. She was pretty graceful about it.

They rode down to the lumberyard a few towns away.

It was a glorious day, with the sun shining, the trees leafing out, and the cool air of the mountains entertaining a slight spring warmth.

The proprietor of the lumberyard greeted Alex by name. "Well, well, well. If it isn't Alex Taylor. Who's your beau, beautiful?"

"He's not my beau, Joe. He's a client. We're fixing up his place so he can sell it. Here's what we need." She placed her neatly written list on his grimy desk.

They settled everything up. She bought nails for her nail gun and corner braces for the new joists. She gave Joe the address of the camp and told him if he could have it there tomorrow morning, he would have her undying fealty. They bantered back and forth, and he ultimately agreed to the timetable.

"Need anything else in town, Blake?" Alex asked on their way out of the lumber yard. "It's a pain in the ass to get down here all the time. You mentioned a towel."

"Thanks for asking. I used my t-shirt to dry off this morning, so yes, I need a towel. How about that place?" He pointed to a sprawling general store.

"Good as anything," she replied, sarcastically.

As they entered the store, Alex donned a baseball cap sporting a trout's head on one side and its tail on the other.

"That will spark a new fashion trend," Blake said, eliciting a coy look from the ridiculous looking Alex.

"It's very becoming, isn't it." She spun around like a model.

"The species suits you."

Laughing, Alex took off the hat and put it on the hook. Together, they made their way through the dark labyrinth of the store. Rows of tchotchkes, moose stuffed animals, and souvenir snow globes awaited summer tourists. The craft section of the store was occupied by a couple of retired women debating the merits of wool versus acrylic yarn. Alex's eyes danced with mirth as she whispered to Blake, "I like wool for socks, but prefer a blend for hats. It holds its shape better."

Blake's eyebrows rose. *Did she actually knit?*

"Winters are long," Alex said, seeming to read his mind.

Finally, a randomized selection of homewares stretched out towards the rear of the store. Blake browsed the towel selection, which was augmented by some cheapo beach towels in a surprising array of colors and patterns. He held up one with sharks on it.

Alex commented, "I wouldn't have pegged you for a shark. More of a clownfish."

Indignant, Blake retorted, "No way. Sleek, aggressive, and ravenous. That's me."

"Watch out, little fishies."

Blake made a chomping motion with his hands and said, "Snap."

To his own surprise, he chased after Alex with chomping hands and she yipped like a little kid as she got away from him.

"Dork," she teased, rounding an aisle.

They both laughed. Alex's eyes glittered, and Blake's heart seized up. He tried to stay cool as he paid for the towel. As they walked out, however, he nearly took her by the hand. It seemed a natural reflex, but he stopped himself in time. Luckily, she didn't notice. *What was it about her?*

When had he ever been so carefree with a woman? Not one example came to mind. But Alex was so natural and cute and funny, it was easy to be himself. Somehow, in twenty-four hours, he'd let down his guard. What an idiot he was. It was time to rein in his feelings, whatever they were, and be more reserved. Alex was in his employ, after all.

Blake kept quiet on the way back to the truck. Alex looked pensive, but he didn't know what to say. They drove in increasingly awkward silence and returned to the cabin. Alex got straight to work, plugging in her extra battery chargers for the cordless drills, assembling her work bench, and clearing some of the debris away. The dumpster arrived shortly thereafter, so they took the better part of an hour to haul all the rotten porch wood and roller shades over to the dumpster and tossed it all in the open back. Blake was glad to see it all go.

———

Blake's manner had gone all frosty after their shopping adventure. Had she been too silly? Didn't he take her seriously anymore? This was how things went as a female contractor, and it made her furious. Men always judged her by a different standard than they judged each other. If it had been some bro acting all goofy, they would chalk it up to building camaraderie. With her, though, it meant she was frivolous. It rankled.

She hurled a last piece of the rotten porch wood into the dumpster with more force than was necessary. It struck the metal with a loud bang.

"You okay?" Blake asked, from behind her.

Startled, she turned around to find Blake, his brow crinkled in concern. It was kind of sweet.

"Yeah. I'm fine. Not too much more I can do without wood." Alex stared into the debris in the dumpster. "Let's take a look around and make a game plan for the interior."

"Just the downstairs. Upstairs isn't a concern."

Alex looked at him, quizzically. "Okay, boss."

They walked together back to the cabin, clambered up onto the porch joists, and swung in through the open front door.

Alex went into the kitchen and crossed her arms over her chest. She eyed the room critically. "Are we keeping the kitchen cabinets, or are you replacing them, too?"

"They're awful, but I was going to keep them."

Alex considered. It wouldn't be her choice, but it wasn't her money. "If we put new counters on and paint the doors, we'll be able to get away with it. Want me to pick something out and put the order in for a counter?"

"Sure."

"I'll measure later." Alex put her hands on her hips and scrutinized the rest of the room. "Appliances?"

"They are pretty gruesome, aren't they?" Blake looked disgusted.

"Yeah. I won't lie. They should go in the dumpster."

"Fine." His dad had actually lived in this shithole? Had used this kitchen? Alex had seen it yesterday and had been horrified. Blake must have been up all-night cleaning it. She looked down and said, "The floor is shit, too. Shall we rip it up?"

Blake looked down and nodded.

"Luckily, it's not asbestos tile," Alex said. "Those are smaller. These were made in the sixties. Probably wood underneath. Let's look."

She went back out to the truck and grabbed the same tool she'd used to remove all the shingles from the porch roof. After edging it under the aluminum ribbon dividing the kitchen from the hallway, she shoved, prying up the ribbon. It lifted easily, so she grabbed it, taking the time to catch the three nails that had been tacking it down, and handed everything to Blake. Then, she slid the edge of the tool under the first floor tile, at an angle, and shoved again with her foot. It scraped enough tile away to reveal the hardwood floor. The linoleum tiles had been thoroughly glued to it.

"Nice. They really glued 'em down. That'll be fun."

"Can't we take them off?"

Blake was adorably clueless.

"Of course we can, but it'll be a huge pain in the ass. Then we'll go through like a million scraping discs on the floor sander to get rid of the glue. The wood looks really nice, though, same as the other rooms. Maybe we could hit the whole downstairs with the sander and refinish the entire floor. It sure would look good. Buyers will come in and catch that gleam of fresh poly. They'll fall all over themselves and hand you an extra hundred grand."

"Fabulous. The wood is a mess in the other rooms, too. It's all pretty beat up."

"It's okay. Adds character." That's what they say about scars, Alex thought, her heart sinking a little farther. She took a deep breath and said, "Well, we can add a lighting fixture, too, and that's the kitchen."

"What, the single bulb hanging from a wire won't be appealing to a buyer?" Blake quipped.

If he was trying to ease some of the tension between them, it wasn't going to work. She was too tired and too depressed to play along. "I have something that will work," she said, ignoring his tone, and moved along to the dining room. "Those walls should come down. They're made of this rotten cardboard they used to use in seasonal places. We can put up sheetrock instead. Luckily, the pine paneling is nice in the living room. I like how the shellac yellowed as it aged."

32

"There's knotty pine paneling in the downstairs bedroom, too."

"Good. That saves us a little work. Can I see?"

Blake hesitated for a second, before he acquiesced. "Sure. Come on."

Alex caught a glimpse of the same sadness she'd noticed yesterday, before Blake had recovered his cool composure. Some part of her wanted to reach out and comfort him, but it would be inappropriate. Instead, she followed him into the bedroom.

———

Last night, Blake couldn't face Dwight's bedroom. He wasn't sure he was ready now, but Alex was here to do a job. It was what it was. When he opened the door, the stale, awful smell hit him first. He hesitated and said, "I can clean this up first before we go in. It's bad."

Alex peered in around him, crinkling her nose. Her expression darkened, as though she'd been formulating an opinion about the man who had lived here, and this confirmed it. She seemed to understand. "I am going to help you clear this right now."

"I can't do that to you. It's pretty awful." Blake felt guilty even showing her this mess.

"Listen," she said, sternly, facing him down. "I've been in camps all over the Adirondacks and I've seen it all. Shit that's been gathering in corners for fifty years. Dead animals, nests of mice and squirrels, bat colonies, you name it. Nothing will shock me. And I am not judging you," she added, noticing his pained expression.

"I know you're not," he said, teetering between nausea and surrender. He was utterly vulnerable before this woman and her no-nonsense approach. His macho shit wouldn't fly with her, and she didn't seem in the mood for his excuses. "Okay," he decided. "If you're sure."

"Hell yes," she answered, staring into the abyss of Dwight's bedroom.

"Thank you, Alex. I'll get some trash bags."

Together, they took every loose object and tossed it into trash bags—clothes, old hunting magazines, rusted tools, Dwight's belts. Blake nearly had a heart attack when he opened the closet to find all those belts hanging there, implements of torture no one but him would recognize as such. Was Blake's blood still on them? He was on the verge of a panic attack as he shoved the belts into the depths of a garbage bag.

Alex, however, was oblivious. Luckily, all she seemed to notice was the structure of the camp.

As they worked, she said, "This room is solid. Nice walls. Ceiling needs to be repainted. Otherwise, it's in good shape."

She must have caught a glimpse of his expression of disgust as he looked around the room.

"You wanna start hauling these bags to the dumpster?" she asked.

"Yeah," he said, desperate for some fresh air.

Alex put some plywood down over the porch joists to act as a bridge to the stairs, since they'd already removed the decking.

Bag by bag, they cleared the entire room. Blake hauled out the bed frame, the mattress, the dresser, and the wardrobe, his muscles straining at the latter.

"Can I help you with that piece?" she asked. "It looks heavy."

"No. I got it."

He hauled every bit of furniture outside, relishing the cracking sound the wood made as it splintered against the metal walls of the dumpster. Piece by piece, he was getting rid of his father. Alex didn't comment, as she helped him remove the trash and clean out the room.

They opened the windows to get rid of the stale, musty smell they had unearthed by moving all of Dwight's rotten things. At least he hadn't died in the camp. Dwight had been found outside, half-decomposed, by a wayward hiker. Somehow, he had spared Blake that particular mess.

After the bedroom was clear, they moved back to the dining room.

"Let's get rid of all this too," Blake said eagerly.

"What will you sit on? Where will you eat? Keep the kitchen table and chairs, at least for a couple weeks. I'll haul them out to the dump for you when we're done. Deal?"

"Deal."

Maybe she thought he was being unreasonable with his deep purge. So what if she did. It all had to go. They hauled out papers and piles of crap, broken dishes, and a ghost of a hutch. The room looked bigger already. Blake still hadn't been upstairs, but it could wait.

At the end of that very long day, the pair had stripped every room on the bottom floor of its contents. They had even started tearing down wallboard. Alex used the house phone to call the lumberyard, leaving a message to add sheetrock to the order, as well as mud and screws and tape. That way, they could sheetrock on rainy days.

When they finally collapsed against the living room wall, Alex surveyed the space looking satisfied. "This will work out perfectly," she said, stifling a yawn. "Everything will be here tomorrow. We'll start by propping the porch roof. Then, the sill and those couple of joists, and eventually we move on to the decking. You happy?"

Blake was worn out, physically and emotionally, but

having Alex here made it less harrowing, somehow. The work of exorcising Dwight was therapeutic. "Yeah. It's nice to see it all go. I appreciate your work ethic, by the way. It's pretty late."

"Yeah, well, I get on a roll. You know how it is."

"Can I take you out for dinner?" Despite having asked, he wasn't sure it was a good idea.

She must have picked up on his hesitation. "No, thanks. You should think about ordering your new stove and fridge. They'll take a while to get here. They've got an Internet connection at the bakery and at McGill's Bar. Do you have a laptop with you?"

"Yeah. Thanks."

"Okay. See you tomorrow."

Alex strode away. Although he didn't blame her for not wanting to keep him company tonight, he kind of wished she had. Admittedly, it was better this way, for he wasn't exactly feeling congenial. Somehow, capering around the general store with Alex had sent him into a maudlin mood. A fun, genuine person like her certainly didn't deserve to be toyed with by a fuckup like him. The sound of her truck receded into nothingness.

Depressed, he grabbed a premade dinner from the fridge, didn't bother to heat it up, and ate at the miserable kitchen table. After, he walked down to the water's edge. The lake was calm and glassy, reflecting the riotous number of stars overhead. The bullhead lilies were sending up their buds, and by July the lake's edge would be a bustling ecosystem of frogs and dragonflies and flowers, a floating wonderland garden.

A loon's lonely call sounded in the distance, stirring Blake's memories uncomfortably. It was his deepest desire to be a kinder, more accessible man, but was it even possible? Was he too broken to let himself feel...what? Love? Is love what he wanted? The eviscerating pain of losing the only person he had ever loved had left him utterly destroyed. His mom couldn't protect herself, she couldn't protect him, and then she was gone. Blake's heart had died with her. To examine his own vulnerability was to admit to the gaping hole where his heart should be, the abyss left by his loss.

He had sealed it all off, walled it all in, and the fortifications had held. For twenty-two years. Until now. In Alex's wake, the slightest tremor shuddered through his armor. It absolutely terrified him. The loon called out again into the darkness and again, the call went unanswered.

THREE

B lake awoke stiff and miserable from another frigid night's sleep in his car. He stumbled out and stretched, dug his sweats and sneakers out of the trunk, and went for a run. Following the path he'd run as a teenager, Blake jogged up the gravel drive and along the main road, pushing himself as fast as he could go. He stopped and did some pull ups on a tree branch, some pushups in a mossy glen, and then sprinted back toward the cabin. The sound of a pickup approaching startled him, and he feared it was Alex. He was right.

She beeped her horn a few times and rolled down her window. "Keep up the good work," she yelled, her face ablaze with good humor, her curls wild in the wind. Then she gunned it.

The taillights of Alex's truck disappeared around a bend in the road. She hadn't offered him a ride—why should she? But she had laughed her ass off as she drove away. Why did this bother him so much? Did he want her to baby him? Mildly annoyed, with himself more than Alex, he upped his pace. By the time he arrived, she was already setting up her work area in anticipation of the lumber delivery. His heart was pounding and he was drenched in sweat. Alex, on the other hand, was fresh-faced and downright giddy.

Panting, Blake said, "Thanks for the ride."

Feigning innocence, Alex replied, "I thought you were exercising. A ride would've been cheating."

Shaking his head, and forcing himself not to scowl, Blake said, "I'm going to go take a shower."

"Good. Looks like you could use it." She smiled at him again, unabashedly amused, and resumed her work.

A few minutes later, Blake emerged from the camp, drying his head with the shark towel.

"I still think you should have gone with the clown-fish," Alex said, smiling mischievously.

Although encouraging this camaraderie was a terrible idea, Blake couldn't help it. "Watch out, little fishies," he said, coiling the towel and snapping at her. Alex jumped out of his way playfully, trying not to giggle. Something seemed to release a little between them, as the goodwill of the previous day seeped back into their atmosphere. Blake hung his towel over a tree branch to dry in the breeze.

Alex went to the truck and turned towards him bearing a pastry bag and two large cups of coffee. "Breakfast?"

"Angel."

With the porch in ruins, they sat side by side on the tailgate of her truck and ate together in the dewy morning sunshine. Today's offering was ham and cheese croissants.

"So, about yesterday at the store," she said, soberly, halfway through her croissant. "I apologize. It wasn't exactly professional of me." Alex swung her legs nervously, like a little kid in a too-big chair.

Blake felt terrible. She had picked up on his awful

change of mood. "I was having fun with you, too. It's me who should apologize. I didn't mean to get all down and quiet after. It's just, I'm not used to, you know, acting care-free or silly with anyone. I didn't even act like that when I was a kid. It's unfamiliar territory."

Without hesitating, Alex asked, "Why didn't you get to act like a kid when you were a kid?"

"You really do ask too many questions," he replied darkly, looking back down at his breakfast. "Just trust me. I didn't." He finished the croissant in two more bites. It was as good as anything he'd gotten in Chicago.

When he looked back up, Alex's expression was thoughtful. "Is that why you started playing sports and exercising so much?"

Blake was floored she had put it together so fast. "That's exactly why. It was my only way to escape. I ran. I hiked. I played every sport I could sign up for. Anything that meant I wasn't here."

She reached out and put her hand on his arm, her blue eyes misty. "It sounds terrible. I'm sorry."

Blake shifted his arm and her hand fell away. Turning towards her, he said, "Listen, Alex. Ground rule. You don't need to feel bad for me. Lots of people have shitty childhoods. Plenty have it way worse. I don't want pity. Never have, never will." This was a speech he'd given over and over, to teachers, social workers, his aunt, every girl who had ever liked him in high school. It was well rehearsed, and it usually worked.

Alex, however, swallowed hard. Her expression was hurt but transformed almost instantly to a frozen mask. It was her all business face. Crumpling the pastry bag, she hopped off the tailgate.

"My apologies," she said, her voice sharp-edged.

"Won't happen again." She strode toward the torn up porch and straightened up her tools a little more.

———

Why couldn't she act like all the bro contractors out there? Why did she have to get all chummy and thoughtful with people? Couldn't she just talk about sports or the weather? Here she was bringing breakfast and coffee to this guy in the woods, feeling bad for him and his sorry lot. Instead, she should look at him like he looked at her. It was a job, he was a client, and that was it.

Something about him couldn't let her do that, though. She did feel bad for him. That rathole of a bedroom yesterday proved it. The expression on Blake's face when he opened the cupboard to all those belts had hit her like a truck. He was a broken little kid again, with all the fear and grief and whatever else had been in his life. She couldn't blame him for wanting to get this job done as fast as humanly possible and leave this place in the cold, dead past.

Isn't that what everyone tries to do after experiences like that?

Alex ran an extension cord out the bedroom window and plugged in her saw. She put up a little pop-up tent over it, just in case it rained, which was always a possibility. As she was slowing down and wondering what else she could do to stay out of Blake's way, she heard the sound of a large truck approaching. Alex's eyes lit up, her annoyance dissipating. She clapped like a little girl and skipped toward the truck.

The truck beeped as it backed up to unload. Luckily there was a lot of space to the side of her truck on the gravel driveway. The crane lifted pallet after pallet of materials off the truck. Alex sweetly thanked the driver and signed the payload receipt. Smiling, she turned to Blake, the unpleasantness of their earlier exchange forgotten in the shining light of fresh construction materials.

"Let's get the sheetrock into the cabin," she said. "It can't stay out here in the elements. Can we put it in the first-floor bedroom to keep it out of the way?"

"Sure." His expression was unreadable.

Blake walked over to the pallet containing the sheetrock, lifted three sheets at a time and hoisted them over his head.

"Holy shit," Alex whispered. He unloaded three boards to her one, getting the job done in record time. He may not be emotionally available, but he sure was strong.

"What's next?" He wiped perspiration from his forehead.

"Next, we prop the roof so we can remove the corner posts. Then we'll remove the rotten sill and lay the new one in."

They worked hard, helping each other with the most strenuous tasks. One corner at a time, Alex set up the jacks and lifted the porch roof just enough to prop it up with long, heavy four by fours. Each corner took over an hour, as they had to get rid of the old beams and make sure everything was secure.

Eventually, they stopped for a breath. "What time is it?" she asked.

He squinted at the sky for a moment, as though looking for the answer. "Looks like one," he said, authoritatively.

Alex rolled her eyes and dug out her phone. It was exactly one o'clock.

"How did you know by the sky?" she asked, mystified.

Blake laughed. "I had looked at my phone, like, a minute ago. Sorry."

Alex cracked a smile. "Lunch?"

With a pained look, Blake said, "You brought lunch for me again?"

"I did," she replied, sheepishly.

"Thanks, Alex."

"Let me wash my hands. I really need a good soak."

"I'll join you," he said, and Alex raised her eyebrows. He quickly added, "At the sink. I meant at the sink. Not in a tub. Why are you looking at me like that?"

Alex's couldn't help grinning as Blake dug himself another hole.

On the mossy lawn by the lake, they lay down a canvas painting tarp and set up lunch, picnic style. Alex had brought some locally brewed sarsaparilla sodas for them, and Blake took out his Swiss Army knife to pop the top on hers. Alex tried not to laugh, as she grabbed his bottle and twisted. The cap popped right off into her hand. She handed the soda to him, looking smug. Blake shook his head.

After lunch, they continued their work until nightfall.

The next day, they replaced the rotten sill and began laying the decking. It was time consuming, as Alex had to cut every piece precisely to fit. By the end of the following day, the boards all lay flat and attractive next to each other, their ends perfectly aligned.

Things were moving along faster than Alex could believe. The next day, Alex wanted to put in the corner posts. She didn't want any nasty surprises if one of the temporary support posts gave way. Blake was an eager, focused worker, helping her get the beams cut to length and waterproofed on the top and bottom. When they were finally ready, together, Blake and Alex stood and shimmied the giant tree rounds into place, two at the corners of the porch, and two framing the stairs at the center. Alex secured the posts to the decking, pleased with how everything looked. When they had four posts up, they carefully removed the temporary supports, and the roof settled into place. Blake looked amazed. "I can't believe that worked. It looks like a porch again."

"Yep," she agreed, exhausted. They backed away from the camp to get the full effect.

"Well, holy shit," he said, bemusedly. "This is incredible."

"I agree. We work fast. This much work would've taken me several weeks alone, or with my idiot assistant from last summer. You're great help. I'd hire you in a minute if you ever decide to change career paths."

Blake crossed his arms over his barrel chest and made a face of disgust. "And live in the woods for the rest of my life, like a beaver?" he said. "Thanks, but I'll pass."

Alex staggered backwards, his words landing like a blow. "Wow," she said, breathless. "This work is my passion. I'm putting these historic places back together, one by one, with integrity. Fuck you, if you can't see that."

Blake looked sorry, his eyes had gone wide and remorseful. "Jesus, Alex. I'm so sorry, I didn't mean…"

"Whatever. But I'd rather be a beaver than a total prick. See you tomorrow."

"Alex, wait," Blake called after her, as she stomped toward her truck.

Before he could reach her, she sped off.

In the rearview mirror Alex saw Blake kick a piece of wood across the lawn. She didn't care if he was mad. As she drove, Alex could barely see through her tears. She roughly wiped them away with her sleeve. What the fuck was wrong with her? She never cried. Was she really so hurt by Blake's careless comment? Of course he wouldn't want to live in the woods. He hated it here. She'd known that about him from the beginning. So, why did it hurt so badly?

Beaver...He thought she was a beaver. That's what stung.

How could Blake know the time and energy and skill she'd invested in the work she did? She'd never told him about her training, college, her passions, her reasons for doing this work. Why should she? And why should she care if he never understood? He was a client, and she was an employee. It was simple math.

Trees sped by as she ruefully analyzed why his comment hurt so much. She didn't need to prove anything to him, and she shouldn't care what he thought of her. The sad truth, however, began to bubble up. Maybe a part of her enjoyed Blake's company. Maybe she even wanted to impress him, a little. What an embarrassing admission.

Alex needed to get a grip. Blake was off limits, even for friendship. He lived in Chicago, for fuck's sake. Romantically, he was way out of her league. He wasn't even her type, if she had a type. He was too sporty. Too cold. Too gorgeous. There were so many things about him that she found incompatible. For instance, he went running every morning before they started working. Sure did look good doing it, too.

All this needed to end. She would stop thinking about him. She wasn't interested in a relationship. She didn't need friends, and frankly, she had no investment in Blake's erroneous opinion of her. It didn't fucking matter. In a few weeks, he'd be gone, and she would go back to her normal, boring, Blake-free life.

Alex cried even harder.

———

After she'd left, Blake had felt terrible. How could he hurt her like that? Wasn't it enough he was keeping her at arm's length? He had to go and be a total asshole too? She was absolutely right. He was a prick. Alex deserved people in her life who would be kind and loving and treat her like the absolute gem she was. The sooner he could get out of this place, out of her life, the better.

Blake cleaned the lawn of all wood waste, put the remaining detritus in the dumpster, and swept the porch. Maybe if Alex returned tomorrow to a squeaky-clean work site, it would mend their rift. He went to town for some food, bottled water, instant coffee, and more cleaning supplies. He ate a crappy dinner and went out to the car, where he lay awake for hours, trying not to think about the past.

The next morning, Blake went for a run, showered, and waited for Alex. He waited patiently, but still, she didn't come. No Alex, no coffee, no donuts. Maybe she was done with him. He couldn't blame her if she was. His heart sank lower and lower as the moments tripped over themselves.

By nine, he'd resolved to go to town and look for her, when he finally heard her truck. A surge of elation swept through him, making him breathless. He was nervous but excited to see her. She parked, got out carrying neither coffee nor donuts, and went around to open the tailgate. It was full of denuded tree trunks, all of a similar diameter. Alex's chainsaw was off to one side. Had she been out in the woods cutting down trees all morning? He was afraid to ask. And to his dismay, Alex didn't say a word. She didn't greet Blake. She didn't make eye contact. Instead, she grabbed a few trees, hoisted them onto her shoulder, and brought them to the saw under the tent. There, she started cutting smaller diameter tree rounds into lengths and stacking them on the porch.

Blake didn't know what to do, so he brought over the rest of the trees. He desperately wanted to make things better between them. He'd fucked up and it was time to apologize in earnest. After he dropped off the last trees, he knelt down on one knee, nearby to where she was working. As she finished a cut on her saw, she turned and walked straight into him, tripping over his bent knee, and dropping the cut wood onto the ground as he caught her.

"What the fuck are you doing?" she yelled, as she struggled to extricate herself from his arms.

He grasped her shoulders and easily stood her upright. Then, he took her hands in his. "Alex, I'm so sorry. I didn't mean to be so insulting yesterday. Please forgive me."

She took her hands back and glared at him. "Get up, Blake," she said, her tone angry.

"Please, hear me out. I spent my whole childhood longing to get out of here. Dreaming every day of a different life, a million miles away. I had to. It was my only source of hope. So, it's a real shift for me to think about anyone actually *wanting* to live here. I need you to know that I deeply respect what you do, Alex. In fact, I think you're a magician."

"Oh, really." She crossed her arms over her chest and glared at him with cool annoyance.

"Yes," he said, supplicating himself further. "A wonderful magician who can magically forgive the idiot still kneeling in her path."

She looked down at him, her expression fierce. Her hair framed her face, her curls imbued with wild energy that seemed to feed off her anger.

Finally, she put out her hand and said, "Oh, get up, Blake. Just try not to be a dickhead."

Bowing his head in apology, he said, "I will try not to be a dickhead." Then he took her hand and stood up.

"Fine. Now, stop milling around pretending to work and grab a drill. I'll show you what to do."

Alex set up a clamp vise on the porch and attached a crazy looking thing to the end of her drill. "This is called a lumberjack bit, believe it or not, and it makes a perfectly round tenon that fits into holes on the top and bottom railings. This is a game changer. People used to have to cut each end by hand. Now, the work zips by." She clamped a baluster into the vise and put on her goggles. Bracing herself, she positioned her drill on the end of the log and started the drill. Within a minute, she had shaved the entire end down like it was in a pencil sharpener, only with a rounded end.

"That is so cool," Blake said, in awe.

"Glad you approve. Now you do that to every piece I cut, both ends. I'll set up the shave horse and pull all the bark off the pieces. Then, eventually, we can assemble the railing. This is time consuming. Don't let the drill overheat, by the way. It's okay to give it a second between."

They spent the remainder of the morning cutting tenons on both ends of every log, and shaving bark off, one log at a time, all to maintain the Adirondack style of the original porch. The long pieces would run between the posts of the porch, with a low post between for stability. The short pieces would fit between the railings. Alex cut mortises into two long logs and constructed a full railing so Blake could see how all the pieces fit together.

Amazed, Blake said, "This is going to look awesome. Who knew we could transform this place into a desirable piece of property? You *are* a magician."

Alex beamed. How she had forgiven him was beyond his understanding, but he was thankful. Blake's stomach rumbled. It was well past lunch time.

"I made lunch today," he said. "I went to the store last night and got us some provisions. Will you eat with me again?"

"Sure," she agreed, indulgently.

Blake had gotten pasta salad and sandwich meat, as well as good bread from a local bakery they had at the store. He grabbed the sandwiches he'd made earlier and set out everything on the porch where they enjoyed their repast. They didn't say much, but then again, their mouths were full the whole time. Carpentry works up an appetite.

When Alex was done, she looked up. "I'd like to get the roof put back together before it rains. Let's do it now and finish the railing tomorrow or the next day."

"Whatever you say, boss."

They stacked up all the logs they'd finished so far, so they would stay dry. Alex put up her ladder and one for Blake. Together, they wrangled full sheets of plywood up onto the porch roof. Alex slid them into place and nailed them down with a massive nail gun. Her triceps bulged under the strain of its weight, but she handled it gracefully.

After each of the plywood boards was nailed down, Alex lay the roof felt.

"You okay with heights?" she asked.

"Not the best, not the worst," he answered, honestly. "But this isn't too high. What can I do?"

"I'll show you how to use a nail gun and we'll start shingling. I'll start the row along the bottom, and you work behind me, overlapping the next layer and staggering the shingles."

"Yes, boss," he said, smiling.

Together, they nailed the asphalt shingles into place, starting at the bottom and working across and eventually up. Blake learned how to overlap them properly, working hard and fast with Alex's auxiliary and smaller nail gun. They got halfway before nightfall.

She climbed down and started putting tools away. "I'm beat." She leaned against her truck.

"You work hard, Alex. I can't even imagine how you do this kind of stuff alone. Wood and tree trunks and nail guns are heavy."

"I'm resourceful. Pulleys, leverage, the truck's power —I always find a way. But I admit, your help has been welcome."

"Thank you. I couldn't be happier with this."

He put out his hand, which she regarded with suspicion for a moment, before taking it in her own for a handshake.

"Well, you are paying me." She winked at him and turned to leave. Over her shoulder, she called, "See you in the morning."

Blake made a frozen pizza for dinner. Bachelor food had never been his thing, but needs must. Back in Chicago, he had a massive modern kitchen in which to hone his self-taught cooking skills. He missed the taste of real food, although he had to admit, Alex's donuts were scrumptious.

After he ate the pizza, he walked outside and sat on the edge of the new porch. He swung his legs and gazed up at the stars. With every load of rotten wood they'd hauled to the dumpster, less and less of his father's presence remained to weigh him down. Maybe he'd try to sleep indoors tonight. The living room floor had to be better than the car.

More and more stars appeared, glimmering bright, ribboning across the sky, as the Milky Way came into focus. The magnitude of the cosmos splayed itself out, crystal clear, above him in this semi-wilderness. It almost overwhelmed Blake. It was all so vast. Looking back in time millions, billions of years, was humbling. The universe had had a violent beginning, and it had turned out all right. Wasn't that a comfort, of sorts?

Blake, in the face of the vastness, was nothing but a tiny child, all alone, after all. His ancient loneliness was such a part of him from the very beginning. He had always been alone, with the exception of his mom, for the short time he'd had her. Loneliness was a habit, now, recited over decades, reinforced by his choices to live alone, rely on no one, and form no attachments. Recently, however, an unfamiliar kind of longing had begun to wear away at the loneliness. There were fissures in his armor, and they threatened to crack into chasms, as Blake finally admitted to himself that he longed for more. He longed for company. For care. For connection. Blake longed for someone like Alex to share his life with. Beautiful, enigmatic, feisty Alex.

Alex showed up at seven, right as Blake got out of the shower. He had left the front door open for her, but she hadn't come in. Instead, he heard her tossing her tools around in preparation for the day's work.

He walked out onto the porch where Alex held up two cups.

"Coffee?"

"Angel."

They sat dangling their feet off the front porch as Alex explained her game plan.

"It's due to rain around one, so I want to finish the shingling on the porch roof. We should make it if we work solidly. Then we'll switch to the inside and try to lift that awful kitchen floor. I brought my sander and some scraping disks. Will you help me get the sander out of the truck? Otherwise, I need to put up the ramp, which takes time."

"Of course."

After they finished the last of the donuts and coffee, they retrieved the sander. Alex backed the truck up to the open edge of the porch and put down the tailgate. They walked the sander out, taking care not to gash up the carefully laid decking. Once it was inside, they got all the disks and tools out of the back of the pick-up and stretched a tarp over it. Alex drove the truck back to the driveway and they began shingling without delay. She had estimated correctly. They nailed the last shingles under the flashing right as raindrops began to pelt them.

"It might be a pretty good storm." Alex smiled, her damp curls already plastered to her forehead.

Inside, Blake retrieved the shark towel and handed it to her. "Sorry, it's all I have."

"Thanks."

She dried off her hair, removed her sweatshirt, which was soaked through, and put it on the back of one of the remaining dining room chairs. She shivered in her thin t-shirt.

Blake took the towel back to the bathroom and got her a dry sweatshirt out of his duffle bag. "I don't want you to be cold."

She regarded him quizzically before stretching out her hand to accept the sweatshirt. She put it on and laughed, as it came down to her knees. She was more attractive than ever. He tried—and failed—to ignore her, but his heart ached at the sight. It was unbelievably sexy.

"Thanks, Blake," Alex said, pushing up the sleeves. "I

won't be able to work in this, but I'll warm up fast. I can't imagine how stupid I look."

Blake swallowed hard. "You definitely don't look stupid." He regretted saying it, and looked away, embarrassed, before she could read his thoughts.

Blake had made sandwiches again. They sat at the kitchen table to eat as thunder cracked and wind lashed the trees.

Alex smiled broadly, looking out the window. "Man, I love a good storm."

"Why?"

"Power. It's the awesome power of nature and I can't get enough of it." Alex looked like she might add something, but she decided against it.

Blake said, quietly, "I think I know what you mean."

Alex was a force of nature, but she also possessed a profound loveliness, a tender vulnerability. Beneath her powerful personality lay something delicate, almost fragile. Blake had no idea how to handle her kind of beauty.

Now, her milky skin glowed, lit by the stormy, blueish light filtering in from the window. Golden, her freckles stood out in contrast against it. Her cheeks had an ethereal glow, and it all broke his heart. Alex looked up from her sandwich and met his gaze, catching him as he stared. Furious with himself for these flights of fancy, he tried to mask his attentions with conversation.

"You must use a good sunblock," he said, as Alex sipped her drink.

Alex almost spit out her seltzer. "What? That's not what you were thinking, is it?"

Trying to recover his flustered state, he said, "I was looking at your skin. It's so pale and I thought it might be hard to keep it from burning, with your job outside and all. It was stupid. Sorry."

"It's not stupid. You're right, but I've never had anyone ask me about it before. Sorry to laugh. I do use a forty SPF sunblock every morning, to answer your question. I burn easily. Thus, the freckles."

"I like the freckles."

"Right. Because we all want to look like Raggedy Ann."

"No, because they're unique. Like you," he added, softly.

She leaned in and squinted at him. "You didn't put any hallucinogenic drugs in the sandwiches, did you?"

"Sorry," he said, embarrassed. "You done? I can take the plate." She nodded, and he brought her plate to the sink. He hadn't meant to sound like such an idiot, but what was he supposed to say to a woman like Alex? He had never met anyone like her. He had only dated—and he used the term *dating* in its most casual form—high-maintenance, fashionable women. They wore makeup. They liked to talk about their appearances. They wore expensive clothes and shoes. Their wiles worked on him, but they could only hold his attention for a matter of days or weeks. Ultimately, he would move on.

His most recent companion, Veronica, had been the anthesis of Alex. She had come on to him at a Bears event, mistaking him for a player. Beautiful, with sleek raven hair and bright brown eyes, the tight black dress she wore showed off her curves in all the right places, and her expensive heels made her look elegant. Her beauty, however, had been quickly diminished, as Blake noted her ill-concealed disappointment at learning he was a mere physical therapist. He had the stature and bearing of a football player, six-two and very muscular, so people were often misled on that point.

Veronica talked to him for a moment, to be polite, all

the while glancing around the room, looking for a better prospect. Finding none, she settled on him that evening. They had seen each other a couple times, but her over-done manner and her way of losing the thread of their conversation as she primped and posed made him sad. He ended it with her over the phone, not even bothering to put the effort into a breakup date, like he usually did. She didn't seem to care at all.

Alex was different. She was so *herself*. He appreciated her feisty independence and her strength. She would also call him out if he didn't focus on the work they had to do, so he snapped out of his reverie. He washed up the dishes and table and got ready for whatever task she set before him.

Removing floor tiles proved to be awful, hard, unre-warding work. It was slow-going and annoying, requiring a perfect, exact angle to pop the tiles. He worked from the hall-side doorway and Alex worked from the dining room doorway. Ideally, they would meet in the middle. Alex took off Blake's sweatshirt after a mere five minutes of work.

Lifting the floor took forever, and as the rain plum-meted down, drenching the whole world outside. Inside, they grunted and swore over their exertions. By seven, every tile was lifted, and they were beat.

"Holy shit, that sucks," he stated emphatically, as the last of the tiles came off.

"Why, yes. Yes, it does suck. But now it's done. Tomor-row, we sand. That's more fun. If you're good, I'll let you use the sander." She winked at him, then blushed deeply and looked away.

They bagged all the tile, shop vacced the floor, and washed up. As Alex dried her hands, Blake took a beer out of the fridge and offered it to her.

She looked at it, skeptically. "Um, no thanks. I'm good."

"Don't drink?"

"I need to go home and go to sleep. Another time. I promise." She grabbed her damp sweatshirt from the chair and put it over her arm.

"Got it. Sleep sounds pretty good, actually."

He put the beer back and closed the fridge, then walked Alex out to the front door, where they stood side-by-side, looking at the wild storm.

"You okay driving in this weather?"

"Yeah. Thanks for asking. I've got food in my slow cooker, so I should head out. Here goes nothing." She took a running start, jumped off the porch, and ran to her truck.

In another moment, she was gone.

Blake brought a chair out to the porch so he could watch the storm for a while. A fire would've been pleasant, but the rain had soaked all the wood. For a little while longer, he sat on the porch, trying to absorb whatever magic Alex perceived in the power of the weather. For him, though, it was soaking everything to the bone. As the light continued to fade, he was forcefully reminded of the night his mother had died. It had been an awful, stormy night, just like this one. He'd gone to sleep, never imagining that his mother's good night kiss would be her last. Now, feeling the ghost of her lips on his cheek, Blake's psyche balanced on the edge. Tears filled his eyes. He couldn't give in to that memory. He couldn't let it suck him down.

Blake stood violently, the chair tipping over and hitting the porch floor. "Fuck this," he yelled at the ghosts. He grabbed his coat, wallet, and keys, and he headed to his car, unwilling to spend another night alone, eating a goddamn frozen pizza. Maybe the bar in Edison would have some food. At the very least, there might be sports on the TV.

Thankfully, he was right on both counts. He ordered a full-sized salad, a burger with fries, and a lager. Then, he settled in at the bar, fixing his attention on the screen above.

"You got Wi-Fi?" he asked the bartender.

"That's the other bar in town. Sorry, buddy."

Blake leaned and stretched against the back of the tall stool. "That's okay. How long is the rain going to last?"

"Do I look like a meteorologist?"

Taken aback, Blake replied, "Nope."

"Nope. No clue. Sorry."

After a pause, "I've heard it's supposed to stop tonight," slurred a voice to his left.

Blake hadn't noticed the woman sitting a couple of stools away. Tall and slender, she was probably in her late forties, but her face had a weathered edge to it from hard, fast living. When she smiled, deep lines crinkled at the corners of her made-up eyes. She leaned over and put out her hand. Blake leaned over as well and shook it.

"I'm Darla." She tried to look seductive.

"Blake. Good to meet you."

"Where you in from, 'cause you're obviously not from here?"

"Chicago." He decided not to tell her he had actually grown up here.

It would require too much explaining, and although Blake didn't wish to be rude, he didn't feel like talking to her. Keeping his answers as short as possible, he hoped she'd get the hint, but she didn't. Instead, she ordered a Tequila Sunrise and drank more than half of it in her first sip. When she finished that, she moved a stool closer to

Blake and ordered a tequila shot. She chased it with a cheapo beer out of a glass which had someone else's lipstick on it. She didn't even notice.

Blake assumed she'd been there a while. He tried to watch the game and eat his dinner, but Darla kept talking. She told him about herself, her house, her husband, her ex-husband, her good-for-nothing kid. She finally asked him if he wanted to drive her home, since she was so drunk.

"I think you'd be better off taking a taxi." He signaled the bartender for his check.

"Taxi? You really are from the city. We don't do taxis here. We rely on the kindness of friends."

"Then I guess you'd better call a friend." He hadn't intended to sound like an asshole.

The bartender stifled a laugh into a cough as he took the money Blake had set on the counter.

"Keep the change."

Turning his back on the stunned Darla, Blake stalked out into the rain, wishing he hadn't bothered to go out after all. Darla was clearly too drunk to drive, but if he offered her a ride, she would try to pinch him for money, or worse, for sex. He didn't have the heart to deal with her, so he kept walking, hoping she would be okay. As he approached his car, however, he was consumed with a deep sense of guilt. If something happened to her, he wouldn't be able to forgive himself.

Growling to himself, he turned around, strode into the bar, and walked right up to the drunken woman. "I will give you a ride, on one condition."

"What's that, honey?"

"Now it's two conditions. First, don't call me honey. I am *not* your honey. I just don't want you wrapping your-self around a fucking tree driving home inebriated.

Second, don't talk on the way home. I've had enough for one night. How far do you live?"

"She's not far, man," said the bartender, who sported a look of relief. "Thanks, or I would've had to do it at the end of my shift."

"No problem. Come on, Darla. Let's get you home."

When they pulled up to Darla's house, the rain had stopped, as Darla had predicted it would. Blake got out and opened her door for her, as was his habit. He regretted it immediately, as an equally drunken man in a dirty shirt toppled out of the ramshackle cabin and confronted Blake with a shotgun.

The man, clearly Darla's husband, shouted obscenities in Blake's face, accusing him of all manner of transgressions, some of which Blake understood, some of which he didn't. By this time, Darla had staggered out of the car. Blake shut the door and tried to walk to his side of the car, but the drunken husband stood in his way. This time, the man pumped the shotgun and aimed it squarely in Blake's face.

Blake stared into the man's bleary eyes, and quick as lightening, he grasped the barrel of the shotgun, aiming it into the trees beyond, and kicked the man in the groin. The shotgun went off, luckily blasting into the trees, and the man groaned. Screaming, Darla ran to her husband, asking him if he was okay. Then she turned on Blake, who by this time had had exactly enough of the scene. He got in his car, still holding the shotgun by the barrel as the couple yelled and waved their fists at him. He squealed out of their driveway and returned to the bar.

"You could've warned me, buddy," Blake called to the bartender, as he stormed back into the bar.

Everyone in the joint turned to stare at the big,

imposing man with the icy blue eyes, holding a shotgun. A woman screamed.

"Darla's husband tried to kill me," Blake continued, unperturbed. He slammed the shotgun on the bar, turned around, and walked away. "No good deed goes unpunished," he muttered, as he left.

He couldn't wait to tell Alex about this.

FOUR

lex arrived the next morning with homemade egg sandwiches for breakfast, looking apologetic. "I wasn't in the mood for donuts, Blake. Sorry. I hope you like eggs." She thrust a sandwich at him, all wrapped up neatly in waxed paper.

"You cooked for me?" He didn't bother to mask his surprise.

"A woman of many talents," she replied.

Alex wasn't her usual spunky self this morning. He looked at her as they ate their sandwiches and drank coffee.

"You okay?" he asked.

"Yeah, why?"

"You don't look like yourself this morning."

Alex raised her eyebrows and asked, "Who do I look like, exactly?"

"You know what I mean."

"Yeah. Didn't sleep too well. I'll perk up after the infusion of caffeine. How are you?"

"You would not believe the night I had."

Blake told her all about the inebriated Darla, how the shotgun had been brandished in his face and gone off as he had removed it from her drunken husband's grip, and how Blake had then carried said shotgun into the bar and laid it on the counter.

"I still don't know why I did it. Maybe I wanted the bartender to know he shouldn't send innocent people into a lion's den."

"Were you going to fuck her if Russel hadn't been there?"

"You know these people?"

Alex sighed, "Of course I know these people. There aren't a ton of folks who live here year-round, and even fewer watering holes."

"I wouldn't have fucked Darla with a ten-foot pole," he shouted.

"That sounds uncomfortable."

"Why would you ask me that?" he asked, seething at the turn of the conversation.

"That's why most guys drive her home," Alex said, matter-of-factly. "It's a fifty-fifty shot if Russel will be there. If not, she's usually good to go."

"I can't believe you think that low of me. I was driving her home because she would've wrapped herself around a tree if I hadn't."

"Yeah. She's been in quite a few accidents. Well, I'm glad you escaped. Russ doesn't have the best aim."

"I wrestled the fucking firearm out of that drunken lout's hands as the gun went off. I can't believe you don't think this is a big deal. And how could you think I would've fucked Darla?"

"Settle down, Blake. I'm teasing you. It's like a hazing,

around these parts. She gives it up to any and all. Sorry you found out the hard way."

"This place is batshit crazy. This kind of insanity is why I hate it here."

"Do you hate it? Really?" Alex looked serious.

"Yeah. I fucking do." He was still brimming with surliness. "The reason people end up getting abused or kicked around is because everyone writes it off. 'Oh, she's like that when she's drunk.' Or, 'Oh, he beats his wife, but only when she deserves it. Fuck that.'"

Sobering perceptibly, Alex said, "You're absolutely right, Blake. I never thought about it like that. Sorry to make light of your experience." She fixed him with her widest baby-blues and laid a hand on his tense forearm. "You okay?"

He glared at her. "You're still laughing at me."

"Honey, the whole town is probably laughing at you by now, striding into the bar with Russel's shotgun. How very cowboy of you." Her eyes glittered with mirth.

Only then did Blake see the humor of his actions. He'd been played, and good.

A little smile peeked through his stormy façade.

Alex patted him on the arm. "Holy shit." She squeezed his forearm. "You do work out. Will you drive *me* home tonight?" She winked at his stunned expression and sprang out of her seat before he could catch her. They chased each other around the lawn for a minute like puppies, slipping in the muddy spots and taunting each other.

When they finally settled down to the work of the day, she showed Blake how to use the sander.

"If you can do the floors, I can finish the porch and start on the stairs. Deal?"

"Deal."

"Shop-vac it all when you're done. Twice."

"Yes, boss."

They worked on separate jobs all day and by the early evening, there were some stairs on the porch, and the floors inside the cabin were smooth as satin. Blake had worked with the floor sander all day, enjoying the raw power of it. Standing back, they surveyed their work.

Alex said, "I'll take that beer now, Blake. If you're still offering."

"Coming right up."

"You did great with the sander. You didn't get too many dips from keeping it in the same place for too long. Most newbies have a hard time with it. It helps that you're strong as an ox, though."

"Thanks. It was kind of a blast to use. All that power. I had it under control. The kitchen looks incredible. It's so different."

"Better than a facelift."

"Yep. I'll drink to that."

They clinked bottles and drank.

Alex looked at the living room floor, a pensive smile at her lips.

"What are you thinking?" Blake asked.

She sat down cross-legged on the freshly sanded floor. She set down her beer, leaned over onto her elbow, and ran her other hand along its smooth surface.

"How much do you know about wood?" she asked. Then she blushed at the double connotation, and he smiled.

"It comes from trees?" Blake parried, unsure where the conversation was heading.

Still serious, Alex said, "Of course. But look at these lines here. Do you see the grain?"

"Yes." He sat down and traced some of the wood's tight pattern.

"This is old-growth, forest-grown wood. It's dense and strong. All these old places are made out of it. It's called heartwood because it comes from the center of a tree's growth. It's stronger than the outer part of the tree because the rings are so close together."

"Oh." Blake felt a sudden tightness in his chest at her sweet face in this rare unguarded moment.

"New wood isn't strong like this. They grow trees too fast now, with so much light and so much water on tree farms, that the growth rings are wide and separated. The trees are growing fast, but nowhere near as strong as their forbearers. The old forest-grown trees had to compete for water and light. They grew slow, but strong. Dense. Their heartwood is evidence of their struggle for survival."

"I didn't know that," Blake said, softly, mesmerized.

"Yeah, well, it isn't something a person who doesn't work with old wood would ever know."

They sat in silence for a moment as Alex drained her beer. Then, without warning, she hopped up, set the empty bottle on the kitchen counter, and headed out the door.

"Well, 'til tomorrow. Oh, and there's a surprise in your fridge. Look in there before you go braving the wild bars of Edison again."

Before he could thank her, she was gone. In his fridge, wrapped neatly in tin foil and hidden in a vegetable drawer, was a roast with potatoes and carrots. It smelled divine. He silently thanked her and immediately heated it up in the ancient oven.

Woman of many talents, indeed. Blake took his first bite, and it was every bit as delicious as it smelled. When he finished the dinner, he cleaned up and turned off the lights. He sat on the front porch once more, this time in total darkness, letting the stars come into focus. They reminded him of some poem he couldn't remember fully, something about love and the firmament. If he had the goddamn Internet, he would Google it. Although, if he had the Internet, he wouldn't, under any circumstances, be sitting alone in the freezing cold night air, waxing philosophical about the stars and sixteenth century poetry.

With a deep sigh, he went in, lay his blankets on the freshly sanded and twice-vacuumed floor, with its warm, woody scent. He fell asleep thinking of Alex and heartwood and the infinite stars. Perhaps it was because of this, that Blake dreamed of her.

Standing on the camp's roof, her hair was ablaze in the sunshine, as she held her nail gun aloft. Balanced in one hand like a cowgirl's pistol, the nail gun gleamed in the light. A wicked smile spread across dream Alex's face.

"Come and get it, Blake," she cooed, brandishing the nail gun.

The dream version of him moved closer, only to have her take aim at his chest.

He awoke to the thudding of his heart. Or was that the thudding of her truck door closing outside? He came to, gathered his bedding into the closet, and went to the front door. There she stood, no nail gun in sight, her smile bright as day.

Blake opened the door as she cheerfully lifted the donut bag and coffee.

"Angel." He shook his head and joined her on the porch once more.

They worked all day, and then the next, and the next. Days passed by quickly. Alex and Blake always ate lunch together, bantering more and more as time and comfort progressed. Tirelessly, they worked. Alex demonstrated what she wanted Blake to do each day, and he was never afraid to ask her questions if he wasn't sure what to tackle next.

They'd worked through the first weekend, by mutual agreement, not wanting to lose momentum. Progress seemed slower since the dramatic porch restoration. The railings were finally up but still needed to be stained. Alex wanted to be sure the wood was nice and dry, and there had been some intermittent rain.

The next weekend, Blake finally succumbed to his aunt's request to have him over for dinner. So, on Sunday, he drove the hour to her house. She lived in a slightly larger town, by Adirondack standards, this one boasting a vintage movie theater which was in no way hip, and a real grocery store. Blake stopped there and bought flowers for Sal and beer for Sam, Aunt Sal's husband. Blake had never called him Uncle Sam because it sounded kind of stupid. And although he'd never said so, Blake suspected Sam appreciated the courtesy.

Their place looked exactly the same as it always had, and the sight made Blake's stomach lurch. He couldn't do this. Why had he agreed to come here? He didn't want to see his aunt's face, so like that of his mother's. Nor did he want to hear her sympathetic voice, so unlike his father's. It was all too painful. On the verge of turning around, Blake's heart stopped in earnest when Sal came out onto the steps. There she was, unchanged but for the grey at her temples. She was as pretty as he remembered, and every bit as beautiful as his mother had been, for they were twins.

Blake hated himself for rejecting Sal. She had wanted

so badly to make his life all right and so desperately to keep him safe. That she had failed miserably on both counts didn't mean she deserved his harsh judgement. Maybe he needed to explain to Sal how seeing her caused him physical discomfort, and that being with her reminded him, excruciatingly, of all he had lost, of the family he'd never been granted. Or maybe not.

Smiling, she came down the steps off the screened-in front porch. Trying to rally, for her sake and for the sake of his mother's memory, he pushed all the pain of the past back inside and walked forward to meet her. He handed her the flowers, and she hugged him, with tears in her eyes.

"Let me look at you, Blake. I've missed you terribly. Come. Tell me all about your new life in Chicago."

"It's hardly new, Aunt Sal. I've been there for five years."

"Well, to me it's new because I haven't seen you in seven. Your graduation from grad school was the last time, I believe. Wasn't it?"

"Yes." He felt guilty.

"Honey, I'm not trying to make you feel bad. I love you and I know you've been out there forging your own way. I'm very proud of you, Blake. Your mom would be, too."

The word *mom* hit his solar plexus like a taser. He couldn't breathe.

"I forgot something in the car," he managed to say, and turned back.

How could a thirty-two-year-old man still react to the word *mom* like that? He was a fucking adult, for goodness sake. It was time to get a grip.

He grabbed the beer from the passenger seat and headed back up, meeting with Aunt Sal's outstretched arm. She wound it around him, and they headed inside to greet Sam. Blake stretched out the beer and Sam took it with a grateful smile.

"Thank you, Blake. You haven't changed a bit. Maybe a little wider, if you know what I mean." He patted Blake's bicep. "You've been hitting the iron hard, huh?"

"Yeah. I gotta' keep fit for work. The guys expect me to be in top physical shape, like they are. I can't be a hypocrite."

"I guess not. Well, you look good. Want a cold one?" He tilted the six pack toward Blake.

"Sure. Thanks, Sam. How are you guys?"

"We're good. Sit down," Aunt Sal said. "We put out a cheeseball for you."

And there it was, in all its orange glory, the almond-covered cheeseball of all his childhood holiday nightmares.

"Thanks, you shouldn't have." Blake tried to sound gracious.

He stole a glance at the mantel clock. It was only a bit after four. This was going to be a long evening. Little in this place had changed. The polyester sectional, as well as the other furniture in the room, was from the late 80s, and since it still worked fine, it would probably outlive all of them. Permanent fixtures.

Defeated, Blake sat down.

"The Bears, huh?" Sam handed him a beer. "Congratulations."

"Thanks. It's a good gig." They clinked bottles. Blake took a long swallow.

Sam sat forward on the edge of the couch. "I bet," he said. "Do you get to watch from the sidelines? People would kill for that view."

Blake settled himself into the couch cushions. It was

the most comfortable place he'd sat in two weeks. "Most games, we're on the sidelines with the guys, reminding them to stretch, getting ignored in the heat of the game. It's afterwards where we do most of our work. They push themselves harder than most people can imagine. It's good to be there for them."

"Sounds incredible. You worked hard for it, Blake. Nice going. Do you think you'll stay?"

"Yeah, I guess. I can't imagine a better gig."

Aunt Sal came back into the room with a platter of black olives, celery, and crackers. There was peanut butter on the celery. Blake suppressed another flashback to a thanksgiving before his mom had died. It was one of so few he'd been able to get away from Dwight for. His aunt's generosity had inspired him then and it inspired him now. He thanked Sal again and took a cracker. Sal sat down in the brown plaid armchair across from him and seemed to be preparing herself to talk to him.

Here we go. Blake tensed again, as he recognized the warning signs of a reprimand.

Then, the mood seemed to pass Sal by, and she joined the chitchat with him and Sam instead.

"Still no girlfriend, I assume." She tried to look innocent.

"Still no girlfriend, Aunt Sal. Not my thing."

"Lots of men your age come out of the closet. It's encouraged these days, even out here in the Adirondacks." She folded her hands in her lap.

Blake choked on the black olives he had put in his mouth and gulped down some beer to keep himself from coughing.

"That's not what I meant by *not my thing*," he said.

"We understand. Right, Sam?"

"Right. Bunny explained everything to us a couple of years ago. We live in modern times. Anything goes."

Sal nodded in agreement. "We only want you to be happy."

Only the earnest expression on her face prevented Blake from annoyance.

He took a deep breath. "Thank you for your concern. I'm happy enough. I honestly am. I date women, from time to time. As a matter of fact, there's someone I'm interested in now. We'll see how it goes."

"Oh," Sal said. "Well, in that case, good luck with your new gal."

"Thanks." Blake was unable to disguise his discomfort.

Hopefully, that was all Aunt Sal had wanted to address. It was always something. Grades, college applications, girls, now guys. She tried so hard.

After hors d'oeuvres and a dish of local gossip he tried to tune out, they headed to the dinner table. Sal had made a mystery casserole and an iceberg salad. Blake was thankful she hadn't tried anything unusual. Then, as he placed his napkin in his lap, the bomb dropped.

"Your father left you the camp, only because he was too lazy to do anything else, but he had a tax bill on it stretching back quite a few years."

His heart sank. "What are we talking?"

"Twenty thousand. You might be able to negotiate."

Blake's heart sank. That would mean the rest of his savings. "Why didn't you tell me this before? I've put, like, fifteen grand into the place and have it in the middle of a full rehab. Seriously. You should've told me." Blake did nothing to disguise his frustration.

"I didn't tell you because I didn't know. Judy down at City Hall told me last week. How am I supposed to get a hold of you? You don't communicate, Blake. I tried calling but no one answered. I figured I'd tell you in person. Sorry."

"Don't worry about it. We disconnected the phone when we started doing work in that room. Besides, it's not your fault my dad didn't care about anyone but himself."

"He honestly didn't," Sal agreed, sadly. "He was a total son-of-a-bitch."

That he was. In spades. This new development didn't shock Blake. In fact, he should have expected it from the man who had tormented him and his mother and ruined his life. How had Dwight gotten away with it all? It seemed uncanny how no one had ever called him out. No one had ever arrested him. No one had stopped him.

Unable to contain the hurt of it any longer, Blake lashed out. "Sal, how could you let my mother stay with him? I've never understood it." His knuckles had gone white as he gripped his fork and knife.

Crickets. Blake could hear actual crickets chirping outside, in the vacuum of silence between him and Sal. A dam within him finally cracked. He had never confronted his aunt with these questions. He'd remained quiet his whole life, but he couldn't stay quiet any longer. He had to speak his truth. His aunt sat in stricken silence, her cornflower blue eyes brimming with tears.

"I mean," Blake continued, "You loved her. I know you did. So why didn't you get her away from him?"

"Blake," Sal's voice quavered, "I talked to her before she married him. I tried so hard to talk sense into her. Then once she realized what a monster he was, I tried to help her get away from him. He always came and took her back, and your mother always went. She said he'd kill us all if she didn't. Then, after you came along, her only goal in life was to protect you."

"Protect me?" Blake raised his voice, his heart racing.

"How exactly did she end up protecting me? No one protected me, and now the bastard fucker is dead. And you know what? I'm thrilled. He can't hurt anyone again. Ever. Him being dead doesn't bring her back, though, and it doesn't answer the question that has been eating me alive for two decades. Why, Sal? Why didn't she leave?"

Tears streamed down Sal's face, her fork still poised in midair, fingers trembling. Her chest convulsed with a suppressed sob.

Sam, interjected, "We know how hard it was for you, Blake. We tried to adopt you. We tried so hard. Dwight had an iron hold on you that the law wouldn't touch, and it's not fair to blame Sal."

His soft-spoken words did nothing to assuage Blake's inner rage.

"I've gotta go. I'm sorry, Sal. Thank you both for the dinner." He stood, pushed his chair back loudly, and tossed his napkin on the placemat.

As he left their home, Aunt Sal called out for him. "Blake, please. Come back. Blake."

Sal's voice broke on his name, splintering in the cold air, and his heart was screaming. Hot tears pricked his eyes. He pounded the hood of his car, got in, and peeled out before they could come after him.

The rain-swept trees bent and shuddered in the fury of the storm. Blake's heart was a mirror of that fury. Sal and Sam had given so much and tried so hard, but instead of gratitude, he had this grudge, this monumental chip on his shoulder he couldn't seem to find his way clear of. They loved him so much and this was the best he could give back.

A guttural roar, an animal sound that would've scared off the deer and birds within miles, burst from within him. He pounded the steering wheel, unable to let go of the pain of it all, unable to move past it. Yet, the fact was, Blake was angrier at himself than he was at anyone else.

With a stone of remorse firmly lodged in his chest, he drove back to his father's camp and lay down on the floor to sleep. Instead, he lay awake for hours, hating everything he'd been through and everything he'd put Sal and Sam through. He never should've come back.

FIVE

orning was rough. Blake roused himself from troubled sleep, sore from sleeping on the floor, and starving, as all he'd eaten the night before was a couple of olives and a cracker.

Bedding folded, shower complete, Blake took a moment to examine himself in the tiny patch he'd wiped clear on the foggy bathroom mirror. Icy eyes stared back at him—in them, he found his father's cruelty, his penchant for hurting others.

Squeezing his eyes shut and leaning his head against the glass, Blake pushed all the heartache and hurt back down. He was a survivor. He had come this far in life. He had forced himself through worse and he could do this too. He turned off the light and got dressed, dreading Alex's arrival, fervently wishing it wasn't Monday. He wasn't up for her bubbly morning banter. Not today.

She arrived soon after, sporting her usual smile, and divided up the donuts and coffee, as was their ritual. Blake failed to realize he hadn't greeted her in his usual way until Alex interrupted his moody silence. She asked him, "What's wrong, Blake?"

He couldn't begin to describe it, so he settled on, "I slept badly." It was part of the truth, after all.

"Sorry to hear it. You need the day off?" Her concern was making everything feel worse. He wanted her to stop paying attention to him and get on with the work.

"No, I'm fine. What's on tap for today?" he asked, trying not to sound surly.

"I've worked up a schedule for indoor jobs since there'll be showers midday. I'll scrape and paint the bedroom ceiling. You can finish tearing out the wallboard in the dining room and kitchen. That should take us a couple of hours. Then we'll regroup."

He nodded, thankful her plan would keep them in separate places.

A few hours into the day, however, Blake heard a creak from somewhere above his head. He froze in sudden fear, listening. Was there an animal trapped upstairs? He still hadn't gone up there. He had successfully avoided it for weeks, but when he heard the sound again, this time louder, he knew exactly what had happened. What the fuck was she thinking, going up there? Hadn't he told her not to?

Furiously, Blake stalked up the stairs, feeling the walls close in on him, as he used to. He tried to regulate his breathing, but it was an effort. With a shaking hand, he pushed open the door to the second-story bedroom—his childhood bedroom—full of ancient terror and pain. His face contorted in anger, aimed at Alex across the room. Wide-eyed, she stood staring at the bloodstained, twin-sized mattress dominating the scene. Her face was drained of color and frozen in total fear. When she looked up at him standing in the doorway, she gasped. She clearly hadn't heard him come up the stairs.

"What are you doing up here?" Blake asked her, in a dangerously low voice, unable to conceal his fury. He took an angry step into the room and stared Alex down.

———

"I-I wanted to know why there was water damage on the ceiling downstairs," she stammered. "If I needed to fix anything up here." She was trembling, her heart was beating furiously.

"You shouldn't be up here. You should've asked me if you could come up."

"We've been working together for weeks. I didn't even think of asking. This is my job, Blake." Her voice was unsteady, betraying her panic. "I'm just doing my job." Tears filled her eyes. Terror gripped her.

Simmering with aggression, Blake was blocking the doorway. There was no way out of this darkened space. And Alex, a cornered animal, imagined what horrors had produced the brownish stains on the mattress before her. Was it blood? It looked like dried blood. There was so much of it. The stained mattress loomed between them now, making her nauseous and dizzy, as she took a step back. Tears streaked down her face as she tried not to sob. Her legs were shaking.

What would he do to her? Had she misread him so completely? Would he attack her? She couldn't go through that again. She'd throw herself out the fucking window first. Jesus, no one even knew where she was.

In Alex's full-blown panic, Blake's face melded with that of the attacker, ten years before, as the memory strangled her. Physical and torturous, consuming. She could feel his weight compressing the air from her lungs, the fear, the inevitable, unbearable, unspeakable pain.

Unable to breathe, Alex backed herself against the dormer window, desperate to escape.

———

Blake was horrified, as this vivacious woman disintegrated before his eyes. Usually so cavalier, so strong, so feisty, he could barely recognize her. Who was this, shrinking in fear, tears flowing? Didn't she trust him? Weren't they becoming friends, or at least colleagues? She'd brought him donuts only hours ago.

Understanding hit him like a blow to the gut. *He* was the threat. *He* was terrorizing her. She had seen that mattress and then he blazed in all angry and crazy, only thinking of himself, as usual. Now, she looked like a cornered animal. It almost killed him. He needed to fix this, quickly.

"Alex," he said, calmly, his anger instantly replaced by compassion. "Listen to me. I'm not going to hurt you."

"Don't come any closer," she said, her voice almost a whimper.

Blake was in agony. "I am so sorry, Alex. I had no idea I was scaring you. This room is full of horrible memories for me. No one has ever been up here. I didn't mean to freak you out. Come down when you're ready. Preferably by the stairs, Alex."

He turned and left her, knowing she needed to master herself before she could face him again. Halfway down the stairs, he heard her sink to the floor and sob her heart out. Her grief, her pain, her loss, her vulnerability, her anger—Blake recognized them all. His heart constricted within as he listened, regret for hurting her raged in his breast. He sank to the stairs and buried his face in his hands.

Only someone who had been deeply hurt would react like that. All this time, he'd assumed Alex was simply a happy-go-lucky person, that there was no way she could relate to what he'd experienced. But whatever she had been through to warrant this kind of reaction must have been unbearable.

Blake's stomach turned as it dawned on him what kind of trauma it probably was. He wanted to scream, to tear out the heart of the man who had hurt her. But today, Blake had been the monster. He'd been the one to terrorize her, and he was consumed with grief over it. Without any idea how to make it better, he stood up, went to the fridge, and got out two beers. They were going to need them.

When Alex finally came downstairs, she looked spent. A tangle of curls sprang from her head. Her eyes were red-rimmed and puffy and bluer than blue, and she had wrapped her arms around herself in a subconsciously protective gesture. Still trembling, she refused to look him in the eyes.

He reached out and offered her a beer. Hesitating for a moment, finally meeting his sorrowful gaze, she took it. Blake left through the front door and sat down at the top of the new steps, looking out at the misty water. It smelled like rain. Alex followed him out and sat down, leaving some space between them.

"I owe you an explanation," he said. "I hadn't gone up there yet. I couldn't face it. I almost thought I'd be able to leave without ever going up those stairs again. When I saw you up there, I was so angry, but mostly angry at myself for being so weak."

"Blake, it's okay. I'm fine," Alex said, trying to make him feel better. It was so like her.

"No, Alex, it's not okay. I am so sorry for scaring you. But that room...Jesus." He swallowed hard and forced himself to continue. "That mattress was mine as a kid. It's where I slept. My father—"

"Don't," she interrupted. Her expression was stricken. "You don't have to tell me, Blake. I shouldn't have been up there."

"I want to tell you," he continued, vehemently. "I would never hurt you and I need you to know that. I need you to know that's not the kind of person I am. All the blood on the mattress...is mine." He set down his beer and took off his shirt.

Countless raised scars shone livid white on his broad back, each one a memory of pain and abuse.

Alex gasped. "Jesus. Your own father did that to you?"

"My fucking bastard father."

"Oh, God, Blake. I am so sorry. I know you don't want to hear that, but I am. No kid should ever have to go through that." Tears filled her eyes.

"Remember, I don't want pity. Don't feel sorry for me." He turned to face her and said, "Please accept my apology, Alex. I never meant to scare you. Please know I'd never hurt you in a million years."

Alex nodded her head. "I know." Then, she hesitated, her hands still trembling, as she held her beer tightly to her chest. "I'm afraid I can't show you my scars," she said, soft as a whisper. "They're of a somewhat different nature."

His heart felt like it had been sliced to ribbons with razor blades. Who could hurt this precious person? It killed him to think of. "I'm so sorry, Alex." Blake said, his voice low and gentle.

"See? What else is there to say? When I say 'I'm sorry,' to you, you get angry and tell me you don't want my pity, but I feel that way too. I don't want your pity." That innate ferocity he loved about her bubbled up as she spoke. "But I am sorry. I'm sorry your own father hurt you. I'm sorry for all of it. And I'm angry. For both of us."

All he wanted was to reach out and take her hand. To hold her and cry together about how awful it all was. But he couldn't reach out. Instead, he stared out at the water.

"We deserved better," he muttered.

"We really did. I was only sixteen. I was out on a first date with a guy I liked. He was a little older. I don't know why I went. He...He..."

Anguished, Blake turned to face Alex. "You don't need to tell me."

"No. I need to say it. I fucking hate never saying it. He raped me. He destroyed something in me, and I hated myself for it for years. I still sort of do. I knew he had a reputation for being pushy, but I didn't know that's what it meant. I put myself in that situation."

"He was a monster. It was not your fault."

"Like hell it wasn't. I should have known. I should have stopped him."

"Are you saying it was my fault that my father beat the shit out of me? That he abused me? I was smaller than him. I was younger than him. I didn't have anywhere to go. And what you're saying is it was my fault for being here? For not trying harder to stop him?"

"Jesus. Of course not." Her eyes were wide with shock.

"Sorry, but if that logic doesn't work for me, it doesn't work for you. We were hurt by rotten, evil fuckers, and it had nothing to do with us and everything to do with them. Hate yourself, love yourself, whatever. But don't you *ever* say it was your fault."

Alex was stone still. Although Blake could feel her staring at his profile, his gaze remained fixed on the water beyond. Its surface was pebbled with falling raindrops. He hunched over, defeated, as he, too, relived the worst moments of his life. They were a matched set.

"I didn't mean to scare you," he said, as broken as he'd ever been. "I didn't mean to bring up such horrific memories. I'm so sorry. It's this place. I should never have come back. I should've demolished it and moved on. Too much pain resides within these walls for anyone else to live a happy life here."

"Destroying the place wouldn't destroy the pain, Blake," she said softly. "That pain is also a big a part of you. Of me. I'm sorry I didn't trust you wouldn't hurt me. I know you wouldn't. I saw the stains and I was wondering if they were actually blood, and then I saw you standing there so angry, and all rational thought drained away and I was suddenly consumed by fear. I fucking hate that fear. I hate how he did that to me. I've been fighting it for years. Pain and fear. How do you get rid of pain and fear?"

"I don't know." Blake shook his head. "Nothing I've found can undo what's been done. These bastards marked us, Alex. We won't ever be the same as if they hadn't."

Alex was silent a moment beside him. Then, she said, "I always thought if I could put enough things back together, I'd get over it. I fix old, broken places. I put life back into them. I put the heart back into them." Her voice trembled, but she continued. "And somehow, maybe, I thought that would put the heart back into me. Heal me." Her voice broke as the tears came again.

Blake desperately wanted to comfort her, to hold her. He put out his arm and asked, "May I?" Alex nodded and he wound his arm around her. He scooted closer to her and enveloped her in his arms. She sobbed into him, as he held her tight. He'd hold her for as long as she wanted him to.

A few moments passed and a cold wind blew, spattering them with raindrops. Alex suddenly laughed.

"What?" Blake released her from his embrace.

"You must be freezing. Here. Put this back on." She handed him his shirt.

He put it back on, then picked up his beer and finished it. After standing up, he put out his hand. Alex took it and he lifted her to her feet.

"Let's go get drunk," he said. "I've had enough for one day."

"God, that sounds good," Alex said, laughing a little through her grief.

"Let me grab my keys," Blake said, heading for the cabin door.

"It's okay, I'll drive." She stepped out into the rain. He grabbed his wallet and coat and left the cabin behind.

They drove down the long, winding mountain road toward the village. Like many of the towns in the Adirondacks, Edison consisted of a single main road with a lake on one side and establishments on the other. Alex parked the truck on the road in front of a dive called Ricky's. The front end of Ricky's was a pizzeria, complete with Formica booth tables and red gingham curtains. The back room, however, was a gloomy bar with pool tables and TVs. It wasn't quaint. It was a utilitarian space, devoid of any character other than darkness. They took an empty booth in the front end and ordered pepperoni pizza and Saranac lager, the local brew.

Alex still looked rough.

Jesus. She's been through it. Men are horrible. He deplored upsetting her. How could she have known not to go up there? What a fucking mess.

———

Blake's dismal expression tortured Alex. How could his father have hurt him like that? What kind of psycho could do that to a child? Had Blake ever let himself love another person? Was he too damaged to open up like that? Was she? Where had his mother been during all this? Alex was brimming with questions she didn't dare ask.

Squeezing back her racing thoughts was physically painful and it must have shown on her face.

"What is it?" he asked her.

"A thousand questions I don't think you want me to ask."

"Fuck it." He threw up his hands. "Go ahead. What could be worse than what you saw earlier?"

Alex shifted in her seat, looking down at her clenched hands. "Your mom? What happened to her?"

"Wow. You managed to find the one and only thing that is actually worse."

"Goddamn it." She met his gaze with an anguished look. "I told you, you didn't want me to ask."

Blake laughed, mirthlessly. "You were right."

"Never mind," Alex replied, miserably.

She looked out the window, at the lake across the street. The sky had finally cleared a little and the water glimmered in the setting sun. It was so pretty it hurt to look at.

"Her name was Caroline," Blake said softly. The anguish in his voice was palpable. "She died when I was ten. My dad killed her, I think."

"What?" Alex cried. "Do you mean metaphorically?"

"Yes. Although, I don't know. I mean, sometimes I thought he would kill me. I could feel it. He hated me."

"Why?" Alex asked, desperate to understand.

"I don't know. He was seriously fucked up. He was violent and deranged, and he used to beat Mom up pretty bad. His father was a bastard, too, from what I understand, so he learned from the best."

Alex knew what Blake was thinking. "You aren't like that," she said vehemently.

"No?" he asked, disbelief dripping from his voice. "You thought so earlier."

"That was a shitty coincidence." She gripped the edge of the table, her knuckles turning white with the strain.

"Hmm. I disagree. I genuinely upset you." He crossed his arms and leaned back in the booth.

"Bastards like your dad do it on purpose. They do it to exert power over others. That's not what happened today. You were angry because I was in your space. That's all."

"Our reactions under stress tell a lot about us," Blake said. "Don't they say that most abusers were abused when they were kids?"

Her chest constricted with pain at his statement. "That's not who you are, Blake. You're gentle and kind."

"Am I? I was furious at you for being up there. I felt exposed. You weren't supposed to see that shit. I didn't want to have to explain all this to you. To anyone. And then I saw your face and realized it wasn't about me in that moment. It was about you and your anguish and your experiences. God, Alex. I'm so sorry."

His pained expression said it all. He had finally let his mask fall away, finally let her see the man he was, and he was utterly beautiful. But he was also sensitive, kind, and as broken as she was. And now that Alex saw through the façade, she was surprised to see how deeply he cared for her. His clear, blue eyes caught the light streaming through the window, and she was suddenly thankful to him for finally being honest.

"What makes us think we have to hide our pain?" she said, quietly. "Why do we feel ashamed about what other people did to us? You're right. We were in the wrong place at the wrong time, in the paths of madmen."

Blake nodded in agreement. "I wish acknowledging it made the pain go away," he added, sadly.

"Maybe I've tried so hard to forget the pain that I haven't let myself fully face what happened, grieve it, and then try to move past it. Pushing it down inside and locking it away for ten years certainly hasn't helped me at all."

Blake nodded again, his eyes ablaze with feeling. "My strategy was to run away and keep on running. Survival was all I could manage at first. Day to day. Then, little by little, I thought I'd outrun the pain. But I have never let myself get close to people. This was the true cost, I guess."

"You've never had a relationship?" Alex was looking at him in disbelief.

Blake thought about it a moment then answered, "If you're talking about the difference between physical intimacy and a relationship, I guess the answer is, no. Not really."

Alex nodded gravely. "I get that," she said, although she wished she didn't.

"Attachment wasn't something I wanted. I've always fucked with the lights out so I didn't have to explain my scars, my past to the women I've been with, and I've never been with any of them long."

"Then your dad died?"

"Then he died. It all came crashing in. I got a call from

my Aunt Sal, and she said I needed to come home. Home. As if that place was ever a home." He spat out the words like poison. "Sal tried to adopt me after my mother died, but my father wouldn't let her. She's tried to understand, to help me over the years, but she couldn't face what my dad did to me because it would've meant facing what he had done to her sister. She couldn't do it."

"It's such a nightmare," Alex said. "Did Sal ever see your scars?"

Blake looked at Alex, his expression couldn't hide his anguish. "Alex, you are the *only* person who has seen them, other than doctors over the years."

The gravity of this revelation hit her hard.

She swallowed and held his gaze. "Thank you."

"Thank you?" he replied, incredulously.

"Yes. Thank you for trusting me with your truth. I've never met a man who could understand my history, my pain, and if you hadn't been so honest, maybe I never would have."

Alex reached across the table and took his hand in hers. She was usually embarrassed by the rough calluses and the dirt-ingrained lines of her hardworking hands, but all her defenses had come crashing down today with Blake. He closed his eyes for a moment and hesitated, before turning his hand over in hers and holding it tight. They held hands across the table until the pizza came, and along with it, another round of beers.

They ate in silence for a while, until Alex asked, "How do you sleep in that cabin at night?"

Blake looked up, his expression darkening. "I sleep in the living room."

"What? On the floor?" How had she never asked? She'd never even thought about it.

"Yeah," he said, taking a swig of beer. "I *was* sleeping in the car."

"Shit."

"Yeah, well, Sal had asked me to stay with her, but I didn't want to. It would've meant a lot of driving and hours of questions every night. I couldn't face it."

An idea came to Alex, and she couldn't keep it inside. It was a perfect solution to the problems at hand. "Stay with me, Blake. I have extra room. Actually, I have five extra rooms," she added sheepishly.

"Five?" His eyebrows raised in disbelief.

"Yeah, I bought a huge, dilapidated Victorian a few years back and I've been restoring it, room by room. I'm almost done. Then, I'll flip it, I hope, and make enough money to buy a cabin on one of the lakes."

"That's awesome. Good for you." He grew pensive and went silent for a moment, considering. "Thanks for the offer, Alex, but I don't think I should."

"Please. The place is so big we'll never even see each other. Come and go as you please."

"Alex—"

"I insist, Blake." She took a deep breath. "I trust you."

———

Inside, Blake wrestled with himself. He and Alex had been working together for weeks, so it wasn't like they were strangers. Now, they even knew each other's darkest, most intimate secrets. Not to mention, it would be fucking awesome not to have to sleep on the living room floor, freezing his ass off every night. But on the other hand, it would be weird, wouldn't it? Blake never relied on anyone for anything. He never accepted help, even when it was offered. It was his way. But why?

He knew why.

"Please, Blake. Just say yes." Alex squeezed his hand, her eyes pleading with him.

"I can't, Alex. It's really kind, but unnecessary."

She wasn't about to let it go, however. "Listen to me. You were a zombie this morning and now I understand why. I can't have you using power tools on no sleep. You are staying at my house and that's final." Her curls always seemed redder when she was angry.

Blake fought the urge to say no. He fought and won. With a deep breath, he said, "Okay, boss. Thanks."

"Good. You're welcome. We can actually get drunk now—we won't have to drive anywhere. My house is around the corner."

Smiling bleakly, Blake said, "That is the best news I've heard all day."

He flagged down the waiter and ordered them double shots of whiskey.

Alex finally looked a little less stricken. The fear had dissipated, her grief was slowly drowning itself in whiskey, and her feisty side was returning, if not full force. The farther she let down her guard, the younger she seemed. And twenty-six was pretty young to begin with. Blake wanted nothing more than to look after her, and to join her on the slide into drunkenness.

Alex was a self-admitted lightweight, however, so after two beers and a couple of shots of whisky, she was pretty well toasted. To keep up, Blake ordered himself another double and regarded Alex. She was finally relaxed, her cheeks were rosy.

"Let's play pool," she said, after a while.

"Okay," Blake agreed. "Not much else to do around these parts anyway."

"Not unless you like skinny dipping in fifty-degree water," Alex said, smiling mischievously.

"Thanks." Blake laughed. "But I'll take pool."

They made their way back to the bar-end of Ricky's. A crowd of older men, some of whom knew Alex and waved, turned on their barstools to watch them.

Alex was awful at pool. She laughed at every missed shot, taunted him as he lined his up with unfailing precision, and sang along to every bad song on the radio. Blake found her delightful. They played a couple rounds, and he beat her easily every time.

"You're terrible at this, aren't you?" he teased.

"You gathered that, huh?" she said, laughing and leaning against the pool table. "I might not be very good at pool, but I have other talents." She actually winked at him.

Blake was astonished. Alex had been all business with him for weeks. She'd ignored all his early, awkward attempts at flirtation. Now, here she was, goofing around with him and flirting like they were normal people capable of normal interactions. It hit him hard.

A thrill of attraction flowed through him like lava, distracting him from a clear shot that would've won him the game. Instead, he knocked the eight ball into the corner pocket. Alex roared with laughter.

Blake shook his head and got them another round. Finally, as the drinks took effect, Blake started to feel lighter and less miserable about the day. It had been the point of coming to the bar, after all. That was the problem with being a big guy. It took quite a few drinks to hit him at all.

Alex took a sip of the light beer she'd asked for, not wanting any more whiskey, and lined up another shot that went wide. "Wanna mansplain what I'm doing wrong?" Alex asked, smiling.

Blake laughed. "You want me to?"

"Clearly, I have no idea what I'm doing," she said. She was even holding the pool cue wrong.

"With your permission, may I show you how to hold the cue?" Alex nodded. He came up next to her and held her hand in the proper position on the table. He guided her other hand on the handle of the cue. "Feel the balance?"

"Sure?" she said, not sounding sure at all.

"The rest is just math. Think about what angle the ball is at in relationship to the pocket and your force against the ball needs to mirror that angle." Together they drew back the cue and hit the ball, which went flying off the table.

"They make it look easy in the movies," moaned Alex, as she left his side to retrieve the cue ball. "Can we try again?" she asked, her eyes so big and vulnerable he would have given her anything in that moment.

"Of course, Alex." She came up beside him, put the ball down on the pool table and looked up at him expectantly. Blake wanted to kiss her. Instead, he moved to the other side of the pool table and said, "When you cut a piece of wood, how do you know what angle to cut it at?"

"I measure," she said, with complete assurance.

Blake nodded. "Exactly. You're forgetting to measure before you cut, so to speak. Look over here." He pointed to the green ball by the pocket. "Imagine cutting a piece of wood that makes a triangle between the cue ball, the green ball, and the pocket. Do you see it?"

Alex's eyes went wide, and she nodded.

"Okay," Blake continued. "You're just extending the other leg of the triangle with the pool cue. Visualize the apex of the triangle being on the green ball and aim the cue ball for it. Try it."

She lined up the shot, squinting so much it wrinkled her nose. "Relax, Alex," he said. She breathed in and out and her shoulders seemed to untense. She lined up the shot again. "Widen your angle by two degrees," he said, gesturing. She followed his instructions. "Whenever you're ready, you'll take the shot, letting the cue pass through the cue ball, metaphorically."

"Okay," she said. "Here goes."

Alex pulled back and decisively made the perfect shot. The green ball landed in the corner pocket with ease.

"Yes!" Blake yelled, filled with actual joy at her success.

Alex set the cue down on the table looking flabbergasted, then she jumped up and down and clapped her hands. "I did it!" she cried, running to his side and throwing her arms around him. "Thank you!"

Hesitantly, Blake hugged her back and said, "It's all simple math, after all. I knew you'd get it." Alex beamed at him.

They finished the game, during which she made two more flawless shots. Geometry was her language. Afterwards, she said, "Do you mind if we go? I hate peeing in bar restrooms. They're always gross."

Blake laughed and said, "No problem. Good game, by the way." He headed up to the bar to pay their tab, only to find Alex had already taken care of it.

"Why'd you do that?" he asked, incredulously. "This was going to be my treat."

"You get next time," she said, with a coy smile.

As they were leaving, Alex waved to a few of the old guys at the bar. They all had their antennae up, wondering who Blake was and if she was in safe hands. He found their protective nature endearing.

One white-bearded guy dressed in lumberjack plaid signaled for Alex to wait. He came up to her and whispered something in her ear. She shot a glance at Blake and kissed the old timer on the cheek.

"No worries, Stan. He's one of the good ones. Thanks for looking out for me, though."

Stan looked sternly at Blake. "You be good to her, now, son."

"Yes, sir, I will."

Stan fixed him with an intense gaze, searching Blake's face for something. Blake had no idea what. When the guy looked satisfied, he nodded and bid them goodnight.

Outside, the stars were putting on their nightly show and the air was cool and crisp. It was a refreshing contrast to the stuffy, dark bar. Alex took Blake's arm and wound hers through the crook in his elbow. She was so close he could smell her balsam shampoo and feel her warmth against him. It filled him with an unfamiliar and deeply unsettling sensation. What he was experiencing wasn't just simple attraction. He'd been attracted to Alex from the first minute he'd set eyes on her. This was something else. Something deeper. It terrified him.

They turned at the corner and walked along a short street, at the end of which was the base of a small mountain, with a creek rushing by. Only in the Adirondacks, Blake thought.

Then, Alex pointed. "That's mine," she said proudly. Her house was halfway down the block, but it looked more imposing than the mountain.

Three-stories tall, with Italianate windows and a mansard roof, it was set back on an enormous lot. The long driveway led to a carriage house bigger than most people's homes. The garden gate and fence were original —ornate, rusted Victorian wrought iron, done-up in scrolls and spires. They were gorgeous. The house glowed from the curtained windows. She had left some lights on, and Blake understood why.

Alex fetched her keys from the carabiner connecting them to her belt loop and opened the right side of a set of double doors onto the foyer. The heavily carved door swung open to reveal a grand staircase, complete with a hand-carved newel post and banister, all gleaming with care. The ceiling must have been ten feet tall, with elaborate crown molding along the edges, and a floral medallion in the center, hung with a vintage light fixture.

"This is incredible," Blake breathed, in awe.

Alex beamed. "You should've seen it when I bought it. It was literally falling apart. The roof had caved in. The staircase was a waterfall every time it rained. There was water damage everywhere, broken glass in the windows. Once I replaced the roof and dried everything out, I started restoring it, little by little. It seemed impossible, at first. Then, I started to see real progress."

"It's hard to believe. Your skill is off the charts, Alex."

Alex beamed. "This is what I do every weekend, every night, every spare moment of my life. I even learned how to make plaster. Real old-fashioned horsehair plaster. Did you know you can still buy horsehair?"

Blake laughed. "I didn't."

"Well, you can. I'm really proud of this place."

"You absolutely should be. Give me the full tour." He smiled at her.

Her enthusiasm was infectious.

"Okay, but before we start, I want you to know something." Alex teetered, but only slightly. Her cheeks were flushed and her eyes bright, but her speech wasn't slurred, and her smile was genuine. Gently, she reached out and put her hand on his arm. "I think you're a good guy, or I wouldn't have asked you here."

What was he supposed to say? He had no idea, so he nodded, touched.

She nodded back, adding, "I just wanted you to know." She suddenly looked uncomfortable and said, "I'm going to go pee, and then a tour."

While she was gone, Blake took in the space. He couldn't imagine a waterfall sweeping down those stairs. How had she brought it all back from the brink? It looked perfect now. Unscathed. Appearances were deceiving.

When Alex returned, she led him through the house, regaling him with the details of her restoration. With unwavering commitment and skill, she had returned each room to its former glory. And after having worked with her for a few weeks, Blake understood the amount of work and care she had invested in every detail here. He'd seen her invest the same level of care in the camp.

They climbed the grand staircase to the second floor. Alex pointed to a door and Blake opened it to reveal an ornate parlor. "This room," she patted the nearest wall, "was totally trashed. Squirrels had gotten in and made a nest in the fireplace. All the walls were covered with peeling wallpaper, and the plaster was basically a gut job. I took it down to the lath and re-plastered, I recreated all the crown molding and recast the plaster details. This single room took months. But look at it now." Alex beamed with pride. "Someone is going to love this place someday."

Incredulous, Blake asked, "Are you actually going to flip it? After all this work?"

"Of course I am. It was an investment. I only paid thirty thousand for it, since the city just wanted the tax money. They were about to tear it down. When it's done, I can sell it for a mint in this market. Someone will make it a bed and breakfast, and I can move wherever I like."

"Sweat equity," he said, understanding. His own success was based on the same notion.

"Yep."

Alex led him through the rest of the second floor, room by room as they talked.

"Will you stay in the Adirondacks?" he asked, looking at a glittering bedroom with stained glass windows.

"I think so. I'm from Lake Placid originally, so I've lived here my whole life, except during college. Even then, I didn't go too far."

"Where'd you go?"

"Skidmore, down in Saratoga Springs. It was cool. I studied sculpture and set design, thinking I'd run off to Hollywood to work on movies or something. But then I took an American Architecture class with this elderly professor who really loved old buildings. I loved that class. I started sitting with him in the cafeteria when I'd see him and we sort of got to be friends. After a while, he started inviting me to look at old houses with him. We'd also go to antique stores together and look for restoration items. Everything in Saratoga was priced too high, but out in the sticks, it all changed. People were happier to bargain with you."

"That's so cool," Blake said. "Do you still keep in touch with him?"

"Sadly, he died a couple of years ago. He was pretty old, and he only taught the Architecture class once a year, and only because the students loved him so much. He had that nutty professor air about him, all argyle sweaters and thick glasses, but he was truly brilliant. I think about him a lot. He helped make me who I am. When I graduated, he hooked me up with a local architectural restoration firm. That's how I got started in construction. I worked with them for a few years before I started my business."

Alex then took Blake by the hand and led him back into the hallway and up the stairs to the third floor. Her hand was warm and so small in his.

"And now, the pièce de résistance." When they reached the top of the stairs, she turned on the lights.

The third floor was a wide-open space, and the walls were angled to match the extravagant slant of the mansard roof outside. The ceiling, however, was unlike anything he'd ever seen. Stretching out above them was a plaster mural of the cosmos in deep blue, with golden constellations standing out in relief. It was breathtaking.

Mesmerized, Blake asked, "What on earth is this?" He slowly walked into the center of the room, staring at the ceiling.

"This ceiling was taken out of an old Tudor-style home in western New York, that had been damaged by fire. Some of my little spies told me about it, and when I went there, I found it in pieces in the driveway, ready for the dumpster. I had to have it. With permission, I put it in my truck. There were over two hundred crumbling pieces. I reassembled it here and filled in the gaps the best I could. Can you imagine what it took to make this ceiling in the first place?"

"I can't imagine how you preserved it. It must have been so fragile. This is incredible."

"Craziest puzzle I ever did. Construction adhesive helped. I tried to match the original colors when I repainted it. Then I put a few coats of matte polyurethane over it, and voila."

Blake lay down on the rug in the center of the room, folded his hands behind his head, and stared up at her work. She flopped down right beside him with her head on his shoulder, warm against his body. He put his arm around her and pulled her in close. She smelled like pizza and pine needles. His heart lurched, but he ignored how much he wanted to kiss her.

Finally, he said, "You're so passionate about the work you do. I'm so impressed by that. Your dedication and care are incredible."

"You don't think I'm a beaver?"

Shame burned Blake's cheeks as he recalled his hurtful comment. "No, Alex. You're an artist."

She swallowed hard. "Lots of things have been lost because people didn't care enough. Buildings of such great beauty hit with bulldozers, only to be replaced by shitty concrete skyscrapers. They did that to the old Penn Station in New York. It was a masterpiece. Then they tried to tear down Grand Central. Did you know that Jackie Kennedy Onassis saved it?"

"I didn't."

"Well," Alex stated proudly, "she did. Have you ever seen it?"

"No."

"You'd love it. I burst into tears the first time I saw it. It is beauty on such a scale it's hard to imagine. Why would anyone want to tear it down in the first place? Now, it's a World Heritage Site. There's a cosmos ceiling in there, too. When I heard about this busted up plaster ceiling, I realized I could have my own miniature Grand Central. And now I do. It's the only thing I'll really miss when I sell the place."

"It's a rare beauty, Alex. Just like you." He involuntarily kissed her on the head before he could think it through.

He didn't regret it, though, for her hair tasted of

balsam and rain. He wanted so badly to protect her, to hold her closer, to be the kind of man she deserved, but he contented himself with this moment.

———

The kiss seeped into Alex's psyche like melted caramel, drowning her in its heady delight. What did it mean? Blake didn't seem prone to displays of affection, but the walls between them had crashed into rubble today. And they'd been drinking, which always lubricated people's feelings a little.

Taking a chance, Alex turned into him, draped her arm across his broad chest, and breathed him in. Torn between dread at having this moment end and her fear of ruining it by doing anything Blake wouldn't want, she couldn't decide what to do next. Should she kiss him back? Frozen with indecision, she hesitated.

As she weighed the pros and cons of making a move, she realized she was tired of holding back. Tired of her never-ending internal conflict over intimacy. Tired of protecting something that had already been shattered. What was the point? The worst damage had already been done. Why should she be deprived of care and intimacy because a horrible person had hurt her? Right now, she wanted to kiss Blake. She had never wanted anything so badly.

Resolving to take charge of the moment, she leaned up on her elbow and said, "I need you to know something. I am not drunk."

Her vehemence startled Blake and his body tensed beside her.

"Okay. Thanks for the heads up." He turned his face to look down at her.

They held each other's longing gaze for a moment.

"I wanted you to know that this is not some drunken, spur-of-the-moment thing," she said, softly this time, her heart beating wildly.

"Okay," he breathed.

Beneath his shirt, Blake's heart beat a furious counterpoint to hers. Alex caressed his cheek, and he closed his eyes, drawing in a sharp breath at her touch. His trepidation was as obvious as her own. What was the point of keeping up their defenses after everything they'd learned about each other today? Blake's breathing grew shallow, the furrow between his eyebrows deepened.

She took him in, trying to impress the memory of Blake's face in her mind. She wanted to memorize every line, every contour of his expression, the delicate flutter of his eyelashes, before she let herself kiss him, for she knew that once she crossed this line, there would be no turning back.

———

When Alex caressed Blake's cheek, he almost cried. Not since his mother had any woman touched him so tenderly, so lovingly. There was no pretense to the way Alex moved through the world. She was honest, and this touch was an embodiment of that honesty. It contained all her care, all her regard, all her desire for connection. Whatever this was between them, she had galvanized it with her courage. She had allowed him to see this special place. She trusted him enough to let down her guard entirely. She had bridged the remaining space between them, and Blake's heart was breaking. It was all too much. He didn't deserve it.

He opened his eyes to find her close, her lips nearing

his. "May I kiss you?" she asked, her voice almost a whisper. Blake nodded, unable to speak. This would be the end of whatever their relationship had been, and the beginning of something terrifyingly new and unfamiliar. He should run now while he still could.

She bent in closer, balanced on one elbow and leaning over his chest, and her sweetness, her face, her exquisite frame, he couldn't leave. He didn't want to leave. He wanted to be in her embrace for the remainder of time.

And then her lips met his.

SIX

The first kiss is everything. It's a spring rain, the perfect sunrise, the feel of dewdrops between your toes, the stomach-dropping rush of a rollercoaster pulling you over a precipice.

As Blake looked at her, his expression unreadable, Alex took the risk. Leaning down ever so slowly, she brought her lips to his. The thrill their connection sent coursing through her body was transcendent.

At first, she was light as air against him, his own breath lingering on his lips. Had she stopped breathing? Had he? She kissed him deeper, feeling for any sign of hesitation from him, wanting to honor his need as much as her own. Balanced in this delicate space between desire and uncertainty, she pulled his lip between hers and tasted him. He was divine. His lips parted slightly as he began to kiss her back.

Slowly, he responded to her. He turned toward her, sliding his free hand around the back of her head. Gently as a dove's wingbeat, he pulled her into him and widened the kiss. It was skydiving, falling into a liquid joy—the connection between them was exquisite.

Longing, that dormant seed in the deepest part of Alex's being, germinated and grew, taking on a life of its own.

They kissed for an age. They came together, ancient barriers falling like glass from skyscraper windows, crashing to the ground in a million infinitesimal splinters. Alex pressed her body against Blake and ran her hand up his chest and over his shoulder, drawing him to her, relishing the sensation of his heat against hers. The world fell away, and Alex was content in this perfect kiss, beneath her mended stars.

They held each other afterwards, nestled together perfectly. Any awkward feeling dissipated. There was something between them, something worth exploring. As Alex relaxed into his strong embrace, she almost fell asleep. It had been an exhausting day, an epic emotional expenditure. Before Alex let herself surrender to her body's desperate need for sleep, she lifted herself regretfully from Blake's arms. She stroked his cheek once more and smiled sadly. She didn't want to leave his side, but she also couldn't stay.

"There's a bed and bathroom up here if you'd like to sleep under the stars. Otherwise, there's a bed in the guest room downstairs. If I don't go to sleep soon, I'll fall asleep on the floor right here and the whole point of this excursion was that I didn't want you to have to sleep on the floor anymore."

Blake looked tired, too. "Thanks, Alex. I'd love to sleep up here. I appreciate it."

"No worries. I'm glad you agreed to stay. I really like you, Blake. You're a great guy."

"I really like you, too, Alex." He smiled sheepishly.

"Great. I'm glad we've established the fact we like each other." She paused awkwardly and then burst into giggles. "There are fresh toothbrushes and toothpaste in the top drawer in the bathroom, and towels in the closet. See you bright and early."

They stood up stiffly and regarded each other shyly for a moment. Then, Alex surged forward and hugged Blake tightly. He only hesitated a fraction of a moment before he hugged her back. Before she could think about it, she tipped her head back and their lips met once more in a goodnight kiss.

Blake pulled her in tight, placed his hand at the back of her head, and kissed her passionately. The first kiss had been her lead, but this was all him. Her body tensed and then relaxed against him. The longing that had sprung to life within her before was doubled, fuel poured over her flames. It was an unfamiliar but welcomed sensation. Blake was so strong, yet so gentle, and he held her to him like something precious.

They parted once more, leaving Alex with an intense ache inside that seemed to demand that they come back together, like the elemental pull of magnets, longing to connect.

Alex whispered goodnight and forced herself to go downstairs. After she locked the front door, she poured herself a glass of water, popped a couple ibuprofen, and promptly went to sleep.

———

Blake brushed his teeth and lay awake, staring at Alex's cosmos for a while, wondering what he'd gotten himself into. He was relieved Alex hadn't offered her own bed as one of the options, unlike so many of the women he'd known in Chicago. He wanted to take things slow with her, and he knew they weren't there yet.

Also, the fact remained, he didn't live here. He didn't plan to live here. He had always hated it here. His life was a thousand miles away in Chicago and it was a pretty good life, he had to admit. He had built it himself from nothing and he answered to no one.

There was something special about Alex, though. He had seen it from the start. Her spirit, her drive, her bearing, they were all so different from anyone he'd ever known. No woman had ever stirred him like this before, and although he was terrified, he wanted to explore their connection. The last thing on earth he wanted to do, however, was to hurt her. He had to tread carefully, for her heart was as fragile as his own.

Sleep finally fragmented his thoughts and took him under. The spill of morning light onto his bed was a shock, equal only to finding Alex on the bed as well, smiling at him, holding two steaming cups of coffee.

"Good morning," she whispered.

He blinked back sleep, rubbed his face, and blearily said, "What time is it?"

"Nine-thirty." She sounded amused. "I haven't slept this late in, well, ever. Maybe college, I guess. Did you sleep well?"

"Yeah. Once I was out, that was it. Feels like time barely passed."

"That's the best kind of sleep, if you ask me."

He sat up in bed and accepted the cup of coffee. "Thank you, Alex."

"You're welcome. Breakfast is all done downstairs, whenever you're ready." She shyly glanced at his face and started to stand.

Before she could leave him, Blake took her hand and kissed it. "Angel."

———

A lump rose in her throat and the threat of tears stung. She squeezed his hand in return, smiled wistfully, and left him to get ready. What was she thinking? This man was a client, first of all, and lived in Chicago, second of all. He was never going to move here, and she would certainly never move there. He would be gone forever, in a matter of weeks.

I can't do this. I can't. Alex scurried down the stairs and paced around the kitchen, draped in a mantel of thin eastern sunlight, as she tried to muster the courage she would need to tell him it was all a mistake. Things between them could never work out. It would be easy to blame it on the drinks.

Then, she stopped herself. What if they followed through on their feelings? What if their connection needed to be explored, even if he did leave in the end? Maybe it was part of their path towards healing their old wounds. She could be a realist, right? As long as she prepared herself for the definitive eventuality of him leaving her, it would be okay. She repeated this lie to herself as she sat down at the breakfast bar in the sunshine, trying and failing to calm her racing heart.

Blake came down fifteen minutes later, looking like something out of a magazine. He was gorgeous. His unshaven face had enough rugged scruff to kick his good looks over the top. The mountains agreed with his constitution. It was something else, though, that made him so irresistible this morning. There was something in his eyes she hadn't seen before, and it gripped her by the guts.

He walked directly over to her and fixed her with an intense look before he leaned down to kiss her.

"I'm thankful you had a toothbrush for me," he said, as he released her.

She swayed a little, dazed.

"Are you okay?" he asked.

"Yeah. I made eggs, bacon, and toast. Nothing fancy, I'm afraid."

"Smells perfect. Another home-cooked meal. Thank you."

He made himself a plate and sat across from her, the sunlight hitting him from behind and gilding his silhouette. Alex wanted to cry, he was so lovely.

Instead, she said, "Blake, I've been thinking. We need to talk."

———

Blake's heart sank in him like an anchor. His expression froze.

"Oh?" he managed to say, dreading the words she might utter.

Why had he let himself become so vulnerable?

"We, um…we seem to like each other's company, right?" Alex looked as uncomfortable as he felt.

"Right," he replied, hesitantly.

"But we still have to work together. Maybe we need to have a rule that while we work, we focus on work. Is that okay with you?"

She looked horribly nervous. Blake admired what courage it took her to say these words, to enter into this relationship, whatever it might become. They were each treading uncharted waters, and each of them had personal struggles to surmount, but they would be brave. Together.

He set down his fork, stood up again, and walked around the breakfast bar to her. Taking both her hands in his, he brought them to his heart.

"I have no idea what I'm doing here. I've never once let myself feel so connected to anybody. I don't want to hurt you, and I don't want to get hurt. It took a lot of courage for you to lay out that rule, and I promise I'll abide by it. I have a request as well."

Alex was still trembling, her pulse racing as fast as a hummingbird's wings.

"What?"

"That you keep being honest with me, and I'll keep being honest with you."

"That's it?" she asked, her voice cracking.

"That's it," he said.

She burst out with a cry of relief, unable to hold back tears. "I seriously thought you were about to tell me it was all over and that it was a horrible mistake and that you never wanted to see me again."

"Alex, that's what I thought you were going to tell me. Wanna know why? Because we're a mess. We're broken, fucked-up people who've been kicked around and have forgotten how to trust. But I'm ready to be a mess together, for however long, in whatever way you want." He mustered all of his strength and said, "I'm yours."

She threw her arms around him, holding his body close to hers.

Knowing someone could feel the raised scars etched in his skin below his shirt would ordinarily have been enough to send him into a panic. Not with Alex, though. They would be courageous together, come what may.

Grasping her by the shoulders, he pulled her from their embrace and kissed her once more. Her strong biceps tensed beneath his hands, her back went rigid. Then, she melted. Her warm mouth yielded, her tension dissolved. Blake stretched his hands down under her rear and pulled her against his body. The attraction between them crackled like electricity. He didn't want to let her go.

After a moment, with a pained expression, Alex said, breathlessly, "Blake, we have work to do. Eat your eggs."

"Okay, boss," he said, reluctantly, pleased that Alex looked like she wanted anything other than to stop.

They finished breakfast and headed over to the camp. He looked out the window as they drove and it dawned on him that her house was the only one like it.

"Why is your Victorian house, with all its frills, set in the middle of the Adirondacks? Doesn't seem to fit."

"Didn't I tell you? It's the Edison house."

Blake's eyebrows raised. "As in, the guy the town's named for?"

"Yep. Building that crazy ornate house was the only way he could lure his wife out to the boondocks every summer. She demanded an exact replica of the home the couple shared in Troy. If you go down one of the residential streets, Wisteria Court or something crazy like that, you'll find the exact same house. This was the summer house, but everything was done to the nines."

"That is so crazy. They came up here and she carried on as though nothing had changed? People are insane."

"That, Blake, is the honest truth," Alex laughed. "People are insane."

"Do you know how it ended up in such a state of disrepair?"

"I guess the descendants abandoned it when they couldn't sell it, back in the nineteen-sixties. Most people don't come to the Adirondacks to buy a high Victorian-style house, so it went derelict. I bought it from the town. They had reclaimed the property to account for back taxes or something. That's why it was such a steal —they were planning on torching it, but they held an auction first to see if anyone wanted it. Thirty thousand was the reserve price and I was the only bidder. Lucky me."

"Well, I hope you took before and after pictures. You could work anywhere in the world with a portfolio like that."

"I did. I have a whole online portfolio detailing the process. I figured it would be novel reading when I'm old." She smiled as she drove, looking content that Blake liked her work.

When they got to the camp, they divided up the tasks. Alex said she wanted to do a little sanding on the porch stairs before she stained them, and that Blake could keep tearing out the wallboard. Then she paused, as though mustering her resolve.

"With your permission, I would like to clear out the upstairs for you. I don't have any link to that space, but for you it represents the worst times of your life." Before he could protest, she put up her hand. "Please, don't say no to me. I want to do this. I'll take care of it, and you never have to go up there again."

A lump appeared in Blake's throat as her words hit him. He was touched by her fierce resolve to protect him from further pain. He couldn't accept this level of care, it was so unfamiliar to him.

"Alex. You don't have to do that. Some of that furniture is heavy. I'll take care of it."

Folding her hands over her chest she said in her sassiest tone, "Have you met me? I am stronger than I look. If I need help, I'll let you know."

"But—" he started.

"But nothing. I'm working on the space alone and

that's final. I'm assuming you're not saving any of it, right?"

"Right…"

"Well, then don't be stubborn. Let me do it. I'll throw most of it out of the window and into the dumpster. Deal?"

She wanted to do this for him. Why should he say no? Pride? That was plain stupid. Fear? What did he have left to fear? "Okay. Thank you, Alex. But don't hurt yourself. If something is too big, yell."

———

Alex worked outside before the rain started again, and then she headed upstairs. She hesitated at the closed door, but only for a moment. Turning the handle, she took a deep breath and went in.

There it was, on the floor, the filthy, bloodstained mattress that had been the only place for young, terrorized, bleeding Blake to sleep. It filled her with rage and sadness to picture that hurt little boy, cowering against such cruelty. She couldn't understand his father's motivation. Why did he hate Blake and his mother enough to torture them? What could fuel that kind of brutality?

These thoughts swirled in her head as she stared at that horrid object and all its implications. Enough. Alex opened the big double-hung window overlooking the dumpster and stuffed the mattress out into the rain-soaked universe.

Next, there was a side table, a small desk, and a dresser with a mirror. She took the drawer out of the side table, examined it for contents, and finding none she threw it out the window as well. It splintered satisfyingly as it hit the dumpster's edge. She broke the legs off the desk and hurled it and the side table out as well, as both were empty.

In the drawers of the dresser, she found a couple stray tube socks and that was all. One drawer at a time, she tossed out the window into the dumpster. She got her screwdriver out of her tool belt and pulled the dresser away from the wall to remove the large mirror. After unscrewing one side and then the other, she pulled the mirror off the back of the dresser and lay it on the floor, face down. Even she wasn't bold enough to throw a mirror out the window.

Only then, in the dim light of the room, as the rain fell steadily outside, did she notice the corner of a piece of paper sticking out from between the mirror glass and its wooden frame. Her heart stopped.

"What have we here?"

She reached down and gently tugged at the corner of the piece of paper, dislodging it from its hiding place. She examined it by the light of the window. It was a thin, yellowed envelope with Blake's name written on it.

Instinctively, Alex knew it was from Blake's mother.

SEVEN

aybe Blake knew about it already. Maybe he had forgotten its existence. Or maybe she had found something of great significance.

Gingerly, she held the envelope in her palms like an offering, so as not to disturb it any further, and headed back downstairs.

"Um, Blake?"

"Alex? What's up?" He put down the crowbar, shook off the wallboard dust from his arms and shoulders, and came over to her.

"You need to see something. I found it upstairs, tucked between the glass of your dresser mirror and the wooden backing. Blake," she fixed him with a compassionate gaze, "I think it's from your mother."

All color drained from his stunned face. He looked from Alex down to the letter laying limp as a dead bird in her hands, and back to her face.

"My mother? Why would you say that? How do you know it's from her?"

"I didn't open it. I just know. It's the writing. It's a woman's writing."

Blake could not process it. "But how?"

"It looked like it had been tucked back there forever. A tiny part of the corner stuck out from behind the glass. Maybe she thought you'd notice it while you looked in the mirror."

He turned away from her. Maybe he was trying to shield her from his confusion and anger and loss. He went outside to the front porch and sat down heavily upon one of the dining room chairs. She followed. Bending forward, he leaned his head in his hands, his elbows resting on his knees.

"I never looked in that mirror, Alex. Never. Every time I caught my reflection in that glass, it showed me this beaten, defeated, red-eyed, wimpy kid getting the shit beat out of him by his hateful father. I couldn't face myself after he had hurt me. I hated myself. I literally avoided that mirror my entire life because all it reflected back to me was pain. Now you're telling me that this letter has been perched there all along?"

"I don't know."

Alex was panicking. She hadn't thought this through. She had only wanted to show Blake what she'd found. Part of her wished she had hidden it from him to save him from this anguish, but that wouldn't have been the right thing to do either.

"I'm so sorry. I didn't think before I showed you."

"I'm not upset with you. You did the right thing." He looked up at her with tortured eyes.

She sat in the chair next to him and threaded her arm through his, nestling her head on his shoulder.

"I'm here. Whatever you want me to do, I'll do. Tell me what you need."

Blake reached out. Slowly, Alex handed him the age-yellowed missive. He held it tentatively for a moment, examining it.

He looked at both sides, scrutinizing the handwriting. "It's from her. You were right."

With a steadying breath, he opened the letter and began to read it aloud, maybe to make it seem real, for the situation felt anything but.

"My darling boy, Blake,
I want to begin by telling you how much I
love you."

Blake choked back a sob. Tears filled his eyes. The hand that held the letter trembled. "Jesus, Alex. I can't."

She took the letter from him and read.

"My darling boy, Blake,
I want to begin by telling you how much I
love you. You are such a beautiful, kind, and
smart kid, and I'm so thankful to have you in my
life. Without you, I don't know what I would do.
Things have gotten bad with Dwight lately. He
has been crueler than usual. I desperately fear
that he has learned of a truth that I have not yet
shared with you, but when I do, it shall make all
the difference in the world. In the meantime, I
need you to stay strong and know that I love you
and that I am working hard to get us away from

Dwight. He is not a good man, as you well know, and I'm sorry that I ever put you in his reach. I'm sorry we couldn't get away from him sooner. I tried.

I'm leaving you this letter, though, because I'm even more afraid than usual. I need you to know that if anything should happen to me, there's a man you must see. His name is Jacob Blackwell, and when you tell him my name, he will know the truth. If you must go on your own, wait for a night when Dwight is out and take his money box out of the hiding place under the kitchen sink. Lift the bottom board and you will find it. Then run, my love. Run far and fast, for his hatred will never afford you a moment's peace. Be strong, little dove. I love you more than anything, and someday, the angels will bring us back together.

All my love,
Mom "

Alex finished the letter with a shaking voice, tears streaming down her cheeks. She chanced a look at Blake, who sat hunched over next to her, his back heaving in silent sobs of agony. She dared not move, dared not touch him. She knew instinctively that he would push her away if she said or did anything. So she sat inert as Blake's broken heart became her own.

Eventually, his body calmed. He stood up, crossed the porch, and headed out into the rain. Helplessly, she watched him go.

This was devastating. The letter had shattered him. The simple fact that it was his mom's writing would've been enough, but knowing all this pain might've been prevented, that his mother had indeed had a plan to get him out of there? It was too much. And what was the part about the man with answers who would know her name? What the fuck did that mean? Alex mulled that one over for a few moments as she stared out into the rain. Why would a strange man have anything to do with it, and more importantly, why had she hidden it from Blake? Who was Jacob Blackwell and why would he have answers?

Holy shit. Alex jumped up. *Holy shit. That other man is Blake's real father. Dwight found out and what? Did he kill his wife? Had Blake come to that conclusion yet, or was he out there wandering around, still in shock?*

She re-read the letter, and her conclusion felt correct. She went into the house, in a daze, and located a yellowed phonebook in the kitchen drawer. Then, she sat down on the floor by the phone in the empty dining room. She looked up Jacob Blackwell and found only one. Her heart raced as she impulsively dialed the number.

A woman's voice answered.

Alex hesitated and then said, "Hi, ma'am. My name is Alex Taylor, from Alex Taylor Construction. How are you this afternoon?"

"Fine," the other woman answered. "How may I help you, Ms. Taylor?"

"I'm looking for someone named Jacob Blackwell, and this is the number that was listed."

"He's right here. Hold on one moment."

Alex heard the woman cover the receiver and call for Jacob.

A moment later, a man's deep voice said, "Hello. Jacob Blackwell speaking."

"Hi, Mr. Blackwell. You don't know me, and this is strange and rather awkward, but today I was helping my friend Blake Anderson clean out his late father's home, when we came across a letter from Blake's mother, Caroline. In it, she said you'd know what it was about. I think you'd better come out here, if you don't mind. There seems to be a lot of unanswered questions."

Alex heard a sharp intake of breath and Jacob paused for a long moment.

Before he could deny her request, Alex pleaded, "Please, sir. Blake deserves to know the truth, and he deserves to hear it from you."

"I'll come out now. Where are you?"

Alex gave him directions. "Thank you, Mr. Blackwell."

"Be there soon." He hung up.

It was a risk, she knew, but this was a horrible day for Blake, and he might as well get it all over with as soon as possible. The truth was always preferable, she hoped.

Blake was still gone when Jacob Blackwell arrived almost an hour later.

"Where is he?"

"Finding her letter was a real shock. He's out trying to clear his head, I think. He'll be back soon, I'm sure. Thank you for coming."

She examined this striking man. Tall and built like a grizzly, he seemed to take up most of the space in the room. His icy-blue eyes were the same color and shape as

Blake's. Jacob really was his biological father. She knew this with certainty, still in a state of bewilderment. Looking at him, it couldn't be more obvious. They were almost twins, despite the age gap.

"Can I offer you a drink?" Alex asked, unsure what else to say.

"No, thanks."

She stared at him for another moment, then asked, "So, what do you do?"

"I'm an attorney. I do pretty much anything anyone needs up here. It's good work."

"Was that your wife on the phone?"

"Yes. We got married fourteen years ago."

Alex didn't press.

Blake walked in, soaked to the bone, and stared from Alex to the strange man standing next to the fireplace. It must have been like looking into a mirror, yet Blake had still failed to make the connection.

"Blake, I'm Jacob Blackwell."

Blake stared for a moment at Jacob, still stunned. "Jacob Blackwell? From the letter?"

"Yes. I knew your mother, long ago. Blake, I know this may come as a shock to you, but I have a feeling, based on the letter and our, um, physical likeness, that I'm... Jesus. How do I say this? It appears that I'm your father."

"What are you talking about?" Blake asked, still in a state of disbelief. Then he turned on Alex. "Did you call him?" His tone was low, and rage simmered behind his gaze.

Alex held her ground, standing as tall as her five-foot-three-inch frame would allow.

"Yes, Blake, I did."

"You had no right to do that, Alex. No right."

"But I did it anyway. And here he is. Now you never

have to wonder. You never have to think about it. And I can die someday, content, knowing that the bastard who raised you wasn't your real father. You are nothing like him and you never will be." She spoke loudly, with vehemence, tears threatening to spill again. "Be mad at me, never speak to me again, blame me for everything, I don't care. I will never regret calling him. After a lifetime of pain, you deserved to know the truth."

Jacob stared at Alex with his mouth agape. "Blake didn't know you called me?"

"No. We read the letter and then he left. I decided in the moment, and you can hate me, too, if you want. The truth is more important than my delicate feelings."

Alex turned around and stomped into the kitchen, setting Caroline's letter on the counter. Her body was rigid and tense, still in battle mode, flooded with the strength it had taken to stand her ground. After opening the fridge, she took out a can of seltzer and drank half of it down in one breath.

Then she grabbed her bag off the counter, stormed through the living room. "You know where to find me, Blake, if you decide you want to. Your call. Jacob, thank you for being an honest man. Good luck, gentlemen."

The screen door slapped shut behind her as she left the stunned men behind. She climbed into her truck and drove away.

The uneven gravel driveway leading away from the cabin seemed endless. As she pulled out onto the main road, the trees seemed to close in around her, trapping her with her own thoughts, her own remorse. Alex had staved off tears through sheer willpower while she'd stood her ground with Blake and Jacob. But now, as she drove, her headlights made a weak tunnel of light through the dense woods and the full weight of her actions weighed heavily upon her heart. The look on Blake's face as he realized she'd called Jacob, wasn't one of anger. It was one of betrayal. Impulsively, she had let her own penchant for action make the decision for someone else's life. It was unfair. She'd placed both men in a terribly awkward position, foisting the truth on them without their input or consent. With that impetuous action, she had undermined the tentative trust she and Blake had finally found in each other.

As she realized the full impact of her choice to call Jacob, Alex sank deeper into regret. What had she done?

———

"I'm sorry. She called me and I came, thinking you wanted me here."

"I was still in shock about finding this long-lost letter from my mother. I hadn't figured it out yet. I hadn't read into the letter in the same way Alex did. Man, she's incredibly smart. I don't know how she put it all together so fast."

Jacob exhaled a long breath and said, "Well, I certainly never expected this when I woke up today."

"Me neither. My mother's been dead for twenty-two years."

"I know," Jacob said, softly. "I remember reading her obituary and feeling a deep sense of loss, even though we had not seen each other in so long."

Blake steadied his nerves. "Well, since you're here, you might as well tell me everything you can."

They sat down on the remaining dining room chairs which had been placed against the living room wall.

"I met your mom when I was doing some legal work for her sister. Caroline came with Sal, and I couldn't believe the two of them. What beauties. Like a Doublemint commercial. You're probably too young to know what that is."

"The twins and the gum. Go on."

"Well, before they left, I gave your mother a business card and told her to call me if she needed anything. She had been recently married and realized she'd made a grave mistake. She called me not long after and we met in secret. We hit it off right away. Caroline was so kind and so funny. She came in a few weeks later with bruises all up and down her arms and chest, and I drew up the divorce papers for her. Dwight refused to sign them. She begged and pleaded with him, but he wouldn't let her go. She and I hatched a plan to run away together. I desperately wanted to get her away from him. I'd fallen for her, and I thought she felt the same. We made love." Jacob paused for a moment. "I never saw her again. At the time, I didn't understand what had happened. I was so insecure. I thought she'd changed her mind and gone back to her husband. I waited for her for so long."

Blake sat still, but Jacob's posture changed little by little. He seemed to deflate. He slumped forward, leaned his elbows on his knees, clasped his hands.

"I thought she'd left me. I assumed she never wanted to see me again. I tried to call her, but the number was disconnected. I tried to talk to Sal, but she didn't even know about your mom and me in the first place. It was a dead end. I don't know if Dwight found out or was noticing she was gone more than usual, but my guess, in retrospect, is that he put her on lockdown. I let Caroline go, believing, or making myself believe it was what she wanted. It was the biggest mistake of my life."

"Then?"

"Then your friend called me today. Out of the blue. I'm

married now. Fourteen years. It took me ages to get over your mom. My wife answered the phone today. I'll explain everything to her. She's a good woman. I know she'll understand."

"Did you know about me?"

"No." Jacob looked bewildered. "Caroline and I were only together a handful of times before your dad, I mean, Dwight locked her away. But when Alex told me your last name was Anderson and that your mother had left a letter with my name in it saying I would have answers, it clicked. I knew it was true. And look at us, Blake. You know it's true, too."

Blake drew in a breath and shook his head. He had no idea what to do or say.

"Thank you for your time, Mr. Blackwell. I appreciate it."

"I know this is a lot to take in, Blake. The past never quite dies, does it?"

"I guess not."

"Here's my card. Please call me, Blake. I..." Jacob's voice cracked as he handed the card over to Blake. "I never imagined I would have a son."

Blake accepted the card and Jacob's strong handshake, unsure how to feel.

After Jacob left, Blake sat back down on the porch, his mind reeling. How could this be happening? He replayed Jacob's story, trying to project himself into the past, trying to understand everything in the light of this new information.

Eventually, he went to the kitchen and retrieved his mother's letter from where Alex had left it on the counter. Reading it over and over, he desperately tried to figure out what his mom must have meant. His father was not his father. That alone was a bombshell. Why hadn't she told him? His whole life would've been different.

She had known she was in danger. Did this mean his father—man, he was going to have to stop calling Dwight his father, for never had there been a person who was less of a father—did this mean Dwight had found out and actually killed his mother?

Holy shit. How would I even figure that out now?

Angels would bring them back together? *What, like in heaven?* This was the strangest, most cryptic letter he had ever seen.

He tried to put himself into his mother's position. Caroline had married a man who turned out to be a miserable, abusive fucker. Desperate to leave him, she fell in love with someone else, someone kind, and got pregnant. Then, pregnant with Blake, the child of a man not her husband, she tried to get away and Dwight stopped her. He was domineering and possessive—he wouldn't let his pregnant wife out of his sight. For ten years, she plotted getting away from him. If Dwight had somehow found out that Blake wasn't his son and gone ballistic, he easily could've killed Caroline. He certainly had it in him. If that was the case, no wonder Dwight had hated Blake so much. No wonder every strike of the man's belt had felt personal, as though fueled by true, unadulterated hatred. Blake wasn't his son.

Everything Blake had based his world upon, every decision, was rooted in his desire not to be like his father. He had constructed a life with zero attachments, so he didn't run the risk of hurting anyone. His fear that somehow Dwight's cruelty was genetic and would surface in Blake's personality or relationships had driven Blake to shut himself off, wall himself up, and take zero risks with his own emotions. His mind was reeling. It was all a lie.

His whole life was based on this one horrible secret. Desolate and alone, he didn't know what to do next.

Then he pictured Alex. Precious, beautiful, brilliant Alex. Her fierce expression had masked her hurt as she'd defended her choice to call Jacob. True, Blake had been furious with her. Whether or not she'd made the right decision, however, she didn't deserve his irascibility. As usual, he was angry about the circumstances, and she happened to be in his path. Just like Aunt Sal.

Blake's remorse was palpable. He needed to do better. He needed to make amends with both of them, and he would begin this instant with Alex. He'd vowed to himself not to hurt her, and he intended to stay true to that promise.

As he was about to head out the door and drive to her house, he remembered something else from the letter. He turned around, headed into the kitchen, opened the cabinet door beneath the sink, and squatted down. Beneath the cleaning supplies he'd stored there, he found a rusty nail toward the back of the shelf, sticking up about half an inch. He tugged on it lightly, but it didn't budge. The shelf lifted slightly when he pulled on it harder. After adjusting his grip, he pressed his fingers into the narrow gap he'd created. He had enough leverage to pry out the shelf.

Below, laying against the raw wood floor, where the drainpipe led out of the camp and into the septic tank, lay the money box his mother had written about. *Alex should be here to see this crazy shit.* The last thing he wanted was to open the box by himself. Retrieving her number from the phonebook, he dialed it on the landline. The antique rotary phone took an eternity to use as the dial slowly returned to its starting point after each number. No answer.

"Fuck it," he murmured, and slammed the phone down on the receiver.

He owed Alex more than a phone call, anyway. After retrieving his jacket and keys, Blake stormed out the door, leaving the secrets of the money box behind. He stopped at the general store to buy Alex flowers, but they didn't have any. Instead, he bought a six-pack of beer and a bag of oranges and sped to her house.

He parked in front of her gate and strode to the door. He rang the bell and knocked furiously. Then he waited, shifting his weight from side to side, desperately hoping she would answer.

She did. Her shadow passed by the transom window and Blake's heart leapt. As Alex opened the door, she gaped at him with unconcealed surprise. In loose fitting sweatpants and a thin white t-shirt, her hair still wet from a shower, Alex looked like she was on her way to bed. Never had a woman looked more exquisite.

"Blake," she said, looking down self-consciously, "I honestly didn't expect you."

"Alex, I'm sorry. I'm sorry I got so angry with you. None of this, in any way, is your fault. I was shaken and upset, and then Jacob was there and if you hadn't called him, I don't think I ever would have. You were right. The truth is always better. Please, please accept my apology." He thrust out the beer and the oranges as peace offerings.

"Beer and oranges?" she asked, looking puzzled.

"They didn't have flowers," Blake said, as though it was an adequate explanation.

"Of course. Because the next logical step from flowers is beer and oranges. Even Emily Post says so." Cracking a smile, she accepted the offerings and invited him in.

"I found the box."

Alex stopped walking and looked at him. "Which box?"

"Dwight's money box under the sink."

Her eyebrows raised. "Oh, my goodness, I'd forgotten about that. What did you do?"

"Nothing. I left it there."

Alex looked astonished. "You didn't open it!?"

"No."

"Why?" she pressed. "Aren't you burning to see what's inside?"

"Yes," he admitted.

"Then why did you wait?"

"Because, Alex, the second I lifted the board that had concealed my salvation for so many years, I realized I didn't want to be there alone. I don't want to be alone. I wanted to share that crazy, unlikely moment with someone." He paused. "With you, Alex."

"Oh."

"I didn't mean to be horrible to you earlier. I am trying so hard to figure my shit out right now, and it keeps getting weirder and weirder, but I promise I will try harder not to be angry with you for anything."

Instead of looking thankful or relieved, as Blake had expected her to, Alex looked miserable.

"I called Jacob Blackwell, Blake. I fucked up. I know I said I wasn't sorry, but I am. I had no right to call him. I should have handled it all differently. I should've waited for you to come home, then discussed the situation with you and left it up to you to call him." Her eyes shone in the lamplight, deep wells of cerulean. Blake could tell she felt awful. "I shouldn't have taken it upon myself to do that. It wasn't my place."

"Your place? What does that even mean? In this life, isn't it your place to stop a hemorrhaging person from bleeding to death? Alex, I've been hemorrhaging emotionally my whole life. All this time, I've kept myself from getting close to people because I was afraid I'd be like him. I was terrified the second I let anyone close, I would hurt them the way he hurt me and Mom. I thought it was genetic, that I was damaged, that I didn't deserve to love anyone. But he's not my father. He's not my father." Blake's eyes were filled with tears of joy. "Knowing that... just knowing that I was in the path of a madman for all those years but not connected to him by blood is everything. Understanding that Dwight and I had no more in common than spatial proximity has saved my life, Alex. I don't have to be afraid of becoming like him anymore. Because of your courage and action, I'm free. You have nothing to be sorry for, angel. Nothing in the world."

He threw his arms around her and held her close. Alex had waited in stunned silence during this soliloquy. Still holding the beer and oranges, she stood awkwardly, her arms outstretched as Blake bear-hugged her. When he let her go, she held up her full hands and smiled. He laughed and took the beer and oranges from her. He set them on the floor and cupped her face in his hands. "May I kiss you, Alex?"

Her cheeks were flushed, and her eyes were bright. Alex nodded her head and said, "I'd like that."

He bent down to kiss her, and it was like putting pieces of the broken world back together. She leaned into him and kissed him back, putting one hand on the back of his head and the other around his waist. Her heart beat against him, between them, as though they were sharing the same blood.

Blake pulled away for a moment and questioned her with his look.

"What?" She was breathing heavily, cheeks flushed.

"Alex, you are in control. Always tell me what to do, when to stop, what you like. Promise."

"I promise. Now kiss me again."

He did exactly as he was told.

———

Blake was a phenomenal kisser. Tender and caring, yet hot as hell. He could read her and responded to every nuanced movement she made. He was a physical therapist, after all. Maybe his deep, professional understanding of the body had perks in his personal life. Then, she remembered he was kissing her, and she came back to the moment.

When their lips parted, Alex cleared her throat and looked at him. "I'm really glad you're not angry with me and that you're doing okay. It was a crazy day. I'm guessing you must be hungry."

Blake's expression told her he was probably hungry for more than dinner, but she had food cooking on the stovetop. "Now that you mention it, I really am," he admitted. "Something smells good."

She handed him one of the beers and carried the rest, along with the oranges, into the kitchen. Then, she opened a beer for herself, raised it, and said, "To the weirdest Monday ever." They clinked bottles and Blake laughed.

Together, they finished cooking dinner, carefully tending to the vegetables and meat, and steaming rice. They dined at the breakfast bar as the sky finally cleared and gave way to a riot of crimson and gold. Afterwards, they built a fire in the living room fireplace, an extravagance of marble and gilt wood.

In the soft firelight, they held each other. Blake leaned back on the sofa and Alex lay against him, enveloped in his powerful arms. Being held by Blake felt so natural. It was the perfect balance between comfort and desire. The scent of him, the feel of his skin, the warmth of his body against hers, she couldn't get enough of this compelling, sensitive, attractive man. He was everything she hadn't known she wanted. It was terrifying.

"You know what, Alex?" Blake said, interrupting her thoughts.

"What, Blake?" She turned toward him, like a plant towards the sun.

"If it hadn't been for Dwight, we would never have met. I mean, if my mom had lived, let's say, and gotten away from him, or if she had managed to run away with Jacob, I never would've inherited Dwight's camp, and therefore I never would have hired you, and we wouldn't be here together right now."

"I guess that's true. Leave it to you to find the silver lining in all the misery you faced with him. That's not easy." The process of overcoming trauma was something she still hadn't quite mastered. Years of therapy had helped her intimacy issues, but some piece of her was still broken inside. Her body stiffened up at the thought.

Reading her body language, Blake said, "Baby steps. You'll get there, Alex. And so will I. Healing is a process, right?"

"Yes," she said, swallowing hard past the lump that had formed in her throat.

"We have each other now." Blake kissed her head and added, "That's gotta count for something."

"Maybe, but I'm terrified to let myself feel anything too deep. To get too close."

"Me too. But you can't be brave if you aren't scared first."

Alex loved this. "It's true, I guess. Is that a motivational quote bandied about in the locker room?"

"No," Blake laughed. "That's all mine. Mostly what I hear in the locker room is stuff I wouldn't want to repeat around a nice, respectable lady such as yourself."

Alex laughed. Then she grew sober again.

"I've been intimate with guys over the years, I've had a few boyfriends or whatever, but I always felt paralyzed by the pain of my past. I've held back some important part of myself in every relationship because of what happened to me. I don't want to feel like that anymore, Blake. I want ownership over not just the process of being intimate, but the true pleasure of it."

"It takes a lot to admit that," Blake said softly. "When the time is right, it will happen. I'm sure of it."

"I hope so." She nuzzled into him.

"I hope so too, for both of us."

They held each other until the fire died down to embers. Finally, they walked upstairs to go to sleep. When they passed Alex's bedroom, she said, "Would you like to stay with me tonight? I don't want to let you go."

"I'd like that," Blake replied. "Thank you." Their fingers threaded together once more, and Alex led him into her bedroom. Their bodies collapsed, exhausted by the strange day, and they fell into the kind of sleep marathon runners have the night after a race.

EIGHT

Alex awoke first again, once more stealing the opportunity to study Blake. In a state of drowsy awe, she admired the contours of his face as he slept. His nose was straight. His cheekbones were high and pronounced. His jaw was strong, but not in a macho way. An attractive combination.

A growl emanated from Alex's stomach. She was famished. Quietly, she headed downstairs to start making breakfast. She longed for something sweet to eat, so she whipped up some cinnamon chocolate chip muffin batter. The muffins baked while she fried up some ham and cheese omelets. It was rare for her to bake, because two dozen muffins is one-and-three-quarters dozen too many for a single woman. *Maybe Blake would eat twelve.*

When he finally came downstairs, he smiled at her as she handed him a cup of coffee with milk.

With his free arm, he took her around the waist. "Angel." He kissed her and then sat down to drink his coffee. "I'd offer to help but looks like you've got things well in hand."

"Thanks, I do. I woke up early and made muffins. I hope you're hungry."

The timer dinged.

"Hungry is an understatement."

"Good." She took the muffins out of the oven and set them on a rack to cool.

Then she handed him a plate with an omelet and toast. A moment later, she brought over a few hot muffins and butter and joined him at the breakfast bar to eat.

"This is awesome. Thank you. The muffins smell delicious." Blake smiled as he ate his breakfast.

Although he didn't eat twelve muffins, he did eat quite a few. They were some of her finest, and he consumed one after another, deeply pleasing Alex.

After breakfast, they showered, and by mutual agreement, returned to work on the cabin. Alex was itching to finish sanding the stairs and stain the porch before the black flies arrived in full force, and the weather that day was supposed to be warm and sunny.

They pulled up to the cabin in Alex's truck and headed inside.

She stopped short. "You must be so curious."

"About what?"

"About what's inside that money box."

"Wow," Blake said, eyebrows raised. "I'd actually forgotten about it."

Together, they walked into the cabin. In the kitchen, Blake disinterred the box from its tomb under the sink and set it on the kitchen table. After hesitating, they sat down to look inside.

———

The rusty box opened on creaky hinges. Inside, lay stacks and stacks of cash, all hundreds, all bound neatly in wrappers, as though they had come directly from a bank. Looking up at Alex, whose eyes were wide with surprise, Blake held up one of the bundles.

"This single bundle is ten thousand dollars."

"Reparations." Alex shook her head in disbelief.

"I guess so." It felt dirty, but he took out the bundles and counted them. There were twenty. "That's two hundred thousand." He sat back, mystified. "Why would Dwight save all this cash?"

"I don't know," Alex replied, looking astounded. "What did he do for a living?"

"He didn't do much that I knew about. He had a military disability pension, and he lived off that. And as far as I know, they don't send you your pay in bundles of hundreds, though. You usually get a check."

"Did your mom have a life insurance policy?"

"I have no clue. I doubt it." Blake stared down at the money. "What am I supposed to do?"

"About what?"

"About the cash. What am I supposed to do with it?"

"Put it in a duffel bag and stuff it in the trunk of your car, gangster style." Alex answered, brightly.

Blake rolled his eyes. "Seriously, Alex. I have never seen this much money in my life."

"How should I know? It's yours, Blake. You deserve it. Spend it, save it, set it on fire if you want to."

"Hm. I hadn't thought about a fire."

Alex shook her head at him and smiled. "That's some crazy shit to find under a sink."

"Yeah, it sure is."

"What else is in the box?" She pointed at a folded manila envelope, flattened into the bottom of the box.

Blake pulled it out. It was unmarked. He unfolded it and unwound the faded red string holding the envelope closed. Unsure, he glanced up to meet Alex's gaze. His nervousness was palpable in the air between them, so Alex stretched out her hand and lay it on his arm.

"You okay?"

"Dwight didn't save anything. All I found in his room were clothes and hunting magazines. What could be so important that he hid it in a money box under the sink?"

"I don't know. It's okay, Blake. Open it."

With trepidation, he opened the envelope and drew some papers out. The first thing they examined was a wedding snapshot. A rakishly handsome Dwight stood there, looking surly, with a hard, cruel edge to his eyes, and a tie loose around his neck. His arm was draped around his bride's shoulders, but Caroline's face had been burned out with a cigarette.

Blake's heart wrenched. He turned over the photo and in Dwight's angry hand was written, *Bitch*.

He handed the photo to Alex, and as she examined it, her expression changed to deep sadness.

She shook her head. "My, God. Your poor mother."

Blake examined the next item, which was a marriage certificate. Next, he found his mother's death certificate. It was a real challenge to read it aloud, but he forced himself.

"*Caroline Anderson, nee Levesque. Born May 26, 1969. Cause of Death: Head injury.* I didn't know." Blake swallowed hard. "No one ever told me how she died."

"Oh, Blake," Alex reached out her hand.

He took it and squeezed, then handed the paper to her. She read it over twice.

"Blake, don't you think it's weird that there's no more

135

information? I mean, how did she get a head injury, let alone one that killed her?"

"I don't know. I've never seen a death certificate before. Is it supposed to have detailed information on it?"

"I have no idea. The first responders would've filed some kind of a report, I think. We could ask the police. That is, if you want to know."

He thought about it for a while. "Maybe," he said, softly. Then he picked up the wedding photo again, re-reading Dwight's writing on the back.

"Isn't it weird that she would suddenly die, right as she was planning on running away? Like it's not just a coincidence? She was really scared of him in the letter. She said it had gotten worse." He took his mom's letter out of his pocket and re-read it. *"I am leaving you this letter, though, because I am even more afraid than usual. I need you to know that if anything should happen to me, there's a man you must see."*

"It's like she knew," Alex said. "He must have put the fear of God in her. I can't imagine living in terror of the person who's supposed to love and take care of you. It must have been utterly horrible for you guys. What a fucking bastard."

"He really was. There was nothing good in him."

"Blake, do you think…I mean, is it possible that he…" Her face said it all.

"That he killed her?" Blake swallowed and thought about it for a moment. "When he was in a rage, he was exceedingly violent. He didn't hold back. I don't know, but it's entirely possible."

Alex leaned in a little and put her hand on Blake's knee. "When you first told me about him, you said he had killed her. What made you say that?"

"Dwight was so explosive, usually starting out

verbally and emotionally abusive, and often escalating into violence. He was impossible to live with." Blake hated thinking about this, but Alex was asking for a reason. "I thought maybe it contributed to her death, having to live with him and all that stress and pain. But honestly? I believe Dwight was capable of killing."

Alex suppressed a shiver and ran her hands up and down her arms. "Is there anything else in the envelope?"

Blake took out another piece of paper, this one a news clipping. Unfolding it revealed his mother's obituary. Underlined were the words *natural causes,* describing how she had died.

"Why did he underline that?" Alex asked. "Was it his own private joke?"

Blake was still reading the obituary. He had never seen this either. Tears brimmed, but he blinked them away.

Alex shot him a look and said, "This has been a lot. What do you need from me?" She took the papers, folded them back up, and put them in the envelope.

"I don't know," Blake said, mastering himself a little. "It's weird to read all this. It makes the loss feel like yesterday. You know, I never let myself think about her. I never let myself miss her. I can't believe I'm actually saying this, but part of me has always blamed her for staying with him for so long, and part of me hated her for leaving me when she died. But all that feeling was misplaced. It was him all along. She didn't deserve my anger or my blame, Alex."

"She loved you, Blake, unconditionally. Don't be angry at yourself. This was all his doing."

Blake nodded and stood up. Alex followed him out onto the front porch where he stood looking out at the lake.

"It was raining like crazy the night she died. One of

those storms that scared the daylights out of me, rolling over the water like God's fury, all lightening and wind and branches down. I was scared, so she stayed with me a little longer than usual. Then, she kissed me goodnight and went downstairs. I heard them yelling, but that wasn't unusual. I fell asleep and the next morning, she was gone. I'd slept through the whole thing. One minute she was there. The next, I was all alone. God, I loved her." He bent forward in agony.

The sadness of those memories threatened to rip him apart.

"She knows you love her, Blake. And she understands how angry you've been. You were an innocent little kid who got thrown into the most tragic and dangerous situation imaginable. Imagine the guilt *she* must have carried for not being able to help you?"

"I'd put her out of my heart, Alex. So far out that I thought I hated her. What kind of son does that?"

"A broken-hearted one."

They stared at the water for a few minutes more. Alex took Blake's hand and held it tight between her own. The buzz of insects was the only sound, and the day's warmth had finally crept up to meet them.

"Let's get some work done, okay?" Blake suggested.

"You sure?" she asked, eyeing him.

Blake nodded. "I want to be done with this place. With Dwight. I need to put this all in the past."

Alex's grip slackened on his hand, but Blake thought nothing of it. "Okay," she said, her voice soft, her face growing more resolute. She let go of his hand entirely, and told him what to do.

On their way home that afternoon, Blake was quiet. As Alex drove them through the woods, Blake watched as the trees sped by, their colors flickering between the darkness of the shadows and the brightness of the light filtering through the branches, in so many shades of green it was hard to believe.

The physical work had helped take his mind off his mom, off what they'd found in Dwight's money box. But without the distraction of work, he couldn't shake the image of his mom kissing him goodnight, on her last night with him. Had Dwight actually killed her? If he'd found out about Jacob Blackwell, he easily could have. How would he prove it, all these years later? Was it worth the trouble?

"Talk to me, Blake," Alex said after a while.

When he turned to look at her, Alex was tense and her expression serious.

"I have a sick feeling in the pit of my stomach, Alex," Blake began. "I can't stop picturing my mom that last night. It's like we opened up Pandora's box today and my mom's presence is stronger than ever. It started with the letter and now this, like she wants us to follow the trail she's left."

"What do you want to do next?" Alex asked.

Blake rubbed his face, trying to shake the nagging feeling that something was wrong. Something had always been wrong. "I don't know what to do," he finally said.

"Do you want to see what the police have to say?"

"At this point, how could it hurt?" Blake said, miserably.

Alex nodded her head and said firmly, "Maybe we can set the record straight and give you and your mom some peace."

Blake sat in silence for the rest of the drive to the police station. Picturing his mother's last moments at the hands of Dwight's insane violence, Blake fought back the years of stifled pain now threatening to overwhelm him. He'd fought so hard to survive his own experiences, he'd never had the bandwidth to visualize what his mom went through. Now, he had to face it head on, and the reality of Dwight's brutality was too gruesome to contemplate.

Maybe Alex was right, though. Maybe now, even though he could do nothing to change the past, Blake could finally set the record straight. He needed to find some peace for his mother and for himself. They both deserved that, at the very least.

Alex parked the truck in one of the two visitor parking spaces at the miniscule police station, got out, and took Blake by the hand. Together, they went inside. Of course, Alex knew the cop at the desk.

"Helena," she called.

A stunning young woman, with dark hair, dark brown eyes, and a warm, bronze complexion, looked up from the newspaper she was reading. She sat up taller in her chair, raised her eyebrows, and languidly replied, "Hi there, Alex. How've you been?"

"Good, you?"

"Good enough. What have we here? Did you catch me a perp?" Helena's dark eyes twinkled, and the corners of her full mouth lifted in a smile, as she eyed Blake up and down.

"That remains to be seen," Alex said, matching her smile. "This, however, is Blake Anderson. Blake, this is Detective Helena Montgomery. She's one of the best detectives in the area."

Helena folded her newspaper and rolled her eyes. "What Alex means to say is I'm the *only* detective in the area. What did you guys want to talk about? Make it quick. As you can see, I'm extremely busy." Helena leaned back, crossed her legs under the desk, and put her hands behind her head.

Blake looked perplexedly at Alex, and then around at the empty room, as if to ask, *Really?* There was one other desk and a door at the back of the room that probably led to a single cell. Alex smiled again, reading his mind.

"Thanks, Helena. We've been cleaning out the camp Blake grew up in and we found some things."

Helena gestured toward the two empty chairs before her desk. They sat down and Alex took the envelope from Blake. Wordlessly, she handed it to Helena, who peered into the envelope and took out the photo of Caroline and Dwight's wedding.

"Read the back," Alex said.

"I'm getting there. Burning out her face wasn't nice. Whoever did this didn't like that woman." Then she read the back. "I revise my statement. Whoever did this *hated* that woman." Next, she looked at the marriage certificate, the death certificate, and the obituary. "Let me guess. You want to know why the cause of death is listed as *natural causes* in the obit, when she died of a head injury?"

"For starters," Blake replied, speaking for the first time.

His deep voice may have caught Helena off guard, as her glance darted from Blake's intense face to a nervous Alex.

Helena shifted, her expression darkening. "Give me a second. I'll go pull the records." She went through the door at the back of the room.

"You didn't tell me you know the police," Blake said, once Detective Helena was out of earshot.

"I know everybody. I know I told you that." Alex winked at him.

When Helena returned, she was holding a manila folder and her face was grave. "Before we open this up, I want to know why we're looking at this little slice of ancient history."

"Caroline Anderson was my mother. Dwight Anderson was the man I grew up thinking was my father. I was ten when she died, and now that he's dead, too, I can start trying to figure out why things happened the way they did."

"That's fair. I only ask because the photos in here are graphic and disturbing. I don't want to upset you with them."

"Thank you for your consideration, Detective. I appreciate it. But I'd like to see them for myself," he replied, softly. "I owe that to my mom."

Helena nodded and opened the folder, confronting them with a grainy black and white photo of a woman on a coroner's table. The gash in her head looked like it had caved in part of her skull.

Blake gasped. He couldn't believe how much it hurt to see his mother again, especially like this. He teared up, his body tensed, and his heart ached.

Alex laid her hand on his. "I'm here."

Helena flipped over the photo to reveal another one, shot from a different angle. The third was the most graphic, with a close-up of the wound. The coroner's report was succinct. *Blunt force trauma to the left occipital was the cause of death. In addition, skull fragments found in skin and brain suggest an unusually strong force inflicted the wound.*

The police report was equally vague, with one exception. The second part had been written in the handwriting of a different person.

Blake read out the entry by the second hand. "*No weapon was found at the scene. The rainy weather conditions may have obscured evidence. Dwight Anderson, victim's husband, described a fall the victim sustained on the wet stairs. No blood was found on the stairs, however. By the time the detectives processed the scene, any evidence had been washed away in the heavy rains. Husband is the only witness. We have no evidence to contradict his statement. Note: The hypothesis of the fall does not match with the coroner's report of the injury. Sister of victim says multiple domestic abuse claims had been filed over ten years, but none can be found. Case will remain open, pending more evidence.* What does that mean?"

"It means the first person to write the report of the scene didn't satisfy the curiosity of the second. They didn't have enough evidence to arrest Dwight Anderson, but the second entry means he may have been suspected of involvement. That is a nasty injury, and I don't think it looks consistent with a fall, either, but I'm no coroner."

"Why didn't they pursue justice for my mother? Why wasn't this case investigated further? It sounds like there were questions." Blake's voice was low and had an edge to it.

"It does seem like there should be more in the file," Helena agreed. She sat on the edge of the desk and twisted to face Blake. "I'll try to dig a little if you want me to, but dead horses tend to stay dead around here. The investigating officer who wrote the second half of this report is retired and no longer lives around here. The responding officer, the one who didn't write much of anything, was Dan Arquette, who incidentally was also the Chief of Police at the time. It is a little weird that he would've responded to an emergency call himself. Usually, the chief doesn't go out on calls like this. He still lives nearby if you want me to talk to him. I'll tell you, though, he's got a rep for being a colossal asshole and horribly corrupt."

Blake hesitated as Alex looked at him with a searching expression.

Finally, he said, "I need answers. I think Dwight killed my mom and those photos seem to back up this idea." Blake breathed in, steadied himself, and said, "Please talk to him. I also want to talk to the coroner who did this exam."

"Sorry," Helena said, "That might be a tougher order."

"Why is that?" Blake asked.

"He died not long after this incident. Back in the early 2000s. He was pretty old."

"Who is the current coroner, then? Call him in."

"*She*," Helena corrected, pointedly, "Is Dr. Antonia Palermo, and she's down at the county hospital in Pleasant Lake. It's about an hour from here, so she probably won't come to you. But I can make copies of all of this for her to look at. I'll email them down."

"Fine," Blake said, sounding deflated.

"If I may," Helena looked at the folder, "and forgive me, because I realize that none of this is my business, but with the perpetrator and the victim both deceased, what is it that you hope to accomplish here, Blake?" She met his gaze.

"I want the truth. The truth has been obscured, hidden from me and from my mom's sister for too long. I need to know what really happened. Who failed my mother? Who failed me? Why was a psychopath allowed to kill my mother and then torture me, right under everybody's noses? There's a missing piece of this puzzle, detective. I can feel it."

Helena hesitated. Her dark hair was pulled back tight. Her deep brown eyes were pensive, almost worried. Then, her expression cleared, and she said, "And here I thought it was going to be another quiet day. All right," she said, sounding official, "I'll do some digging and make some calls. Is there a number I can reach you at?"

Blake glanced sidelong at Alex, unsure if she wanted to broadcast their relationship by offering her own phone number.

She didn't hesitate. "You can call over to the house, Helena. You have my number. Thank you for all your help."

"Don't thank me yet. We'll see what happens. All I ask is that you don't get your hopes up. I'll go make some copies."

Blake and Alex walked out into the late day sunshine. It had been an eventful meeting; yet more questions had been raised than answered.

"What do you think?" Alex stretched out her back.

"I think we're going to have some work to do to get at the truth."

———

They drove the short distance to Alex's house and headed inside. She kicked off her work boots and Blake followed suit. In the kitchen, they washed their hands, and Blake got plates out. Alex didn't feel much like cooking, so they made sandwiches and ate them at the breakfast bar. Blake was reserved, pensive. So was she.

Earlier, when Blake had told her he wanted to leave the camp in the past, she had tried hard not to put herself in that category. He'd only been talking about Dwight and what had happened to Caroline, wasn't he? He wasn't talking about her. About them. But she couldn't help wondering what would happen after they finished their work.

Instead of focusing on that depressing topic, Alex tried

to turn her thoughts back to the things they'd learned at the police station. Now, her insatiably curious mind reeled. Trying to add up all the facts in her head was confusing, though. Putting it all out on paper would help. After finding a pencil and a piece of copy paper, she started drawing as she ate. Blake regarded her with bemused interest.

Finally, she held up the paper. "Okay. I've created a flow chart for us to keep track of things. As facts come in, we'll add them to the proper categories. We can speculate about theories down here in the notes area. Up here, we can connect any information that wasn't connected before. Today, we learned about the photograph, the discrepancies between the death certificate, the police report, and the obituary. These lines represent leads—the coroner and former Chief of Police Dan Arquette. I've put them in their own bubbles. I also think we should interview anyone that knew your father—I mean Dwight—well. Did he hang out with anyone regularly?"

"You have an organized mind. This is what I was spinning around in my head, and I couldn't keep it all straight. Putting it out like this helps. As for friends, not that I knew. But he talked about Army buddies, sometimes. He played cards with them a couple times a month at the VA."

"Okay. We'll follow that lead." She drew another connected line by Leads and a bubble that said Army Buddies.

"Thanks, Alex. Thank you for helping me figure this all out. I wouldn't have known what to do with that box— if I'd ever even found it, that is—if it hadn't been for you. Angel."

He took her hand in his and squeezed. She absorbed his energy and internalized his impassioned remarks. As he gazed at her, his expression transmuted into one of transcendent understanding.

"Angel. Do you realize I've called you that since the day after we met? You brought me coffee, and I called you angel."

"I remember." She smiled at him affectionately.

Blake grew more animated by the second. He stood up and pulled his mother's letter out of his pocket and read, *"Someday, the angels will bring us back together."* He looked at Alex with an awed expression and said, in a soft voice, "It's you. You brought my mother and my real father back to me after all this time."

Alex regarded Blake's animated face with surprise. "I'm hardly an angel," she said.

Blake came over to her and took her hands in his. "You are, though. From the moment you came to my door with coffee. From the moment I saw you up there on the roof, curls bouncing in the sunlight. From the beginning, you've been my angel."

He cupped her face in his hands and searched her eyes. Her insides melted at the intensity of his gaze. She leaned in towards him, just a tiny bit, and he kissed her. Then, he kissed her again with such passion she thought her heart would combust.

When their lips parted, Alex said breathlessly, "I haven't done anything, Blake. I'm flying by the seat of my pants. I called Jacob because I thought I should. I noticed the letter because I'm observant. And I'm not sure you'd think my thoughts right now very angelic." She blushed.

"Mmm," Blake growled, fixing her with a carnal expression. "Then you're the perfect angel for me. You're gritty and strong, feisty and smart, and unstoppably sexy. I wouldn't have it any other way."

Alex looked into his earnest blue eyes and ached in her

deepest places for him. She wanted him. Whether or not she was the angel his mother had meant, she was here now and Blake wanted her, too, she could feel it. She slid her hand from his waist to his lower back and pressed her hand against his warm skin, above his tailbone. Blake's body came alive against her, willing them together.

Alex fought her negative thoughts, fought to stay in the moment, as all her therapy had trained her. It was usually a fierce struggle in moments like this, but Blake was making it a little easier. He kissed her deeply, frantically searching her with his hands, his tongue. She pushed him away for a moment, smiling at his quizzical expression, and lifted his shirt over his head. A seductive smile spread across his features as he moved close to her again.

Without breaking from him, she walked him backwards out of the kitchen towards the couch in the living room. She kissed his chest, his neck, his mouth. His hands were on her hips, sliding down over her rear.

Alex undid his belt and slid it out, savoring his wide-eyed expression. He kissed her once more. Her fingers roved along his shoulders, then over his back, its uneven surface a topographical map of his history, beneath her fingers. She read the story of his pain with her hands, and it mirrored her own pain. These old scars were the record of a past neither of them had chosen. Blake didn't try to stop her, but his eyes were squeezed tightly closed, his breathing heavy.

She pulled away and asked, "Is it too much? Do you want me to stop?"

Blake opened his eyes, and in them, she saw the full galaxy of his experiences. Softly, Blake whispered, "Never. I never want you to stop, Alex."

She kissed him again and lowered them to the couch. Blake followed her lead. Sitting back a little, she slowly lifted her shirt up over her head, and Blake smiled at the sight of her. Leaning over, he kissed the place on her chest just over her heart. Then he worked his way down to her abdomen, where her muscles tightened in anticipation and relaxed in pleasure. Arching her back, she giggled at the sensation of his stubbly chin against her soft skin. Blake sat back and smiled as he greedily took her in. Alex obliged the view, leaning back against the pillowy arm of the couch like a painter's model.

"You are so strong," he said, in awe. "Look at your muscles. I've never seen a girl with such incredible tone. Your arms are totally cut. You're so beautiful."

Alex laughed. "I work hard and use my body all day, every day."

"I studied anatomy to become a physical therapist, but the definition in your abdominal muscles is extraordinary. You're a specimen of perfect physical form."

"Well, to be fair, so are you." Alex was still smiling. "Now, where were we?"

"I believe I was kissing every inch of your lovely body."

NINE

Blake and Alex woke up in each other's embrace. The mid-afternoon sunlight streamed through the windows of her bedroom, warming them, and lighting them with its golden glow. She shifted under the weight of Blake's arm, and they gazed at each other in silence, reluctant to ruin a perfect moment. How well they fit together.

She hadn't been this at ease in her other relationships. She'd been unable to let her defenses down fully, for fear of being hurt again. It was no way to live, but she had protected her heart anyway, at the cost of learning to love another. Blake, however, had reduced her fortifications to mere rubble. He understood her like no other, and she understood him. Part of her deep attraction to him was based on this understanding. Part of it, she admitted, was based on his extremely alluring qualities, physical and intellectual. She was falling for him. Hard.

Blake took in Alex as she gazed at him. She was like a Victorian cherub in a painting. Her hair had this sublime way of framing her face and making her look sweet and innocent. Of course, she was those things, but she was also strong, kind, and genuine. Her clear blue eyes bore neither guile nor malice. She had gotten under his skin, and he was only too happy to have her there.

The honesty of this sentiment surprised him. He wanted to be with her, and she clearly wanted to be with him. As he smiled at her, his eyes, hardened by so many years of holding back all the pain and fear of his childhood, softened. She smiled back, vivacity bubbling out of her very soul.

Since they'd gotten so little done at the camp, the day before, they got up, grabbed breakfast at the bakery, and ate in the car on the way. The coffee was just what he needed, as they headed back up the mountain road to the cabin.

They sheetrocked together, which, as Alex stated, is a job no one in their right mind enjoys. Yet somehow, together it bordered on fun. They brought a speaker from her house and listened to music from Alex's phone, which made the day go by faster. They finished putting up all the sheetrock in the dining room, then they taped and mudded.

When the day's work was done, Blake stood back and surveyed the room. "It's weird that I hardly recognize the place anymore. I think after we get the sheetrock sanded and painted, I'll call a realtor. Do you know anyone good?"

"Sure. I'll hook you up," said Alex. "There's a gal in Moose Creek who's done a lot of sales around here. She'll be honest with you about the pricing and get you the money you deserve."

"I also need to go to City Hall and pay all the back taxes."

"Well, I don't know where you'll come up with the cash for that," Alex said, in jest.

"You had enough of this for today?"

"Yep. Needs to dry before we can sand anyway. Let's go."

In the morning, they stormed City Hall. They didn't have to wait in line, as they were the only people there. Blake paid the back taxes with the cash from Dwight's money box. Naturally, the clerk didn't bat an eyelash. It seemed cash transactions were alive and well in the Adirondacks. Anywhere else, the bank would have called the police on him. Although if they had, Helena would've showed up, with her dark hair and laughing expression, assuring the clerk everything was fine.

Afterwards, at the hardware store, Blake chose some paint for the dining room. The absurdity of the paint names had both of them doubled over in a fit of giggles. Things got out of hand when they started making up their own.

"Everyone's Ecru?" Alex's cheeks were rosy with glee.

"Boisterous Bananas?" Blake tried to suppress his giggles.

"Indubitable Indigo?"

Blake suggested, "Conflagration Crimson?"

"The perfect complement to Glowworm Green?" She was laughing so hard tears peeked out.

"I bet that's a real one," Blake said, laughing along with her. His smile was so wide it hurt his cheeks. "Do we need anything else while we're here?"

"I've got everything else we need," Alex said, still beaming.

They finally made it to the checkout counter, barely able to keep a straight face.

"You don't have one of these, I'll bet." He showed her a novelty mug that said *Wishin' I Was Fishin'*, with a picture of a downtrodden man in a tackle vest, sitting by a window, watching the rain.

She burst into laughter again. "Now you know what to get me for Christmas." Her eyes sparkled.

The elderly salesperson at the checkout counter simply shook his head at their shenanigans. After they paid, Alex and Blake left as fast as they could, arm in arm and giggling like goofy teens.

They worked straight through the day, sanding, priming, and painting the dining room, happy to knock it off their to-do list. They agreed that the living room and bedrooms needed little attention, for their knotty pine paneling was part of the historic value of the place. The kitchen cabinets looked shabbier now, in contrast to the glittering dining room and sanded floors, but they would have to do.

"Man, refrigerators are heavy. Good thing I've got you." She winked at him, and he shook his head, smiling. "Did you ever order new appliances?" she asked, as she wiped the sweat from her forehead.

"Shit, I didn't," he admitted.

"No worries. We can do it from my house later."

"What's our plan for tomorrow?" he asked her, as they cracked open the last of the beers they'd excavated from the fridge and sat on the porch together.

"The weather looks clear, so let's finish staining the railings, work on the porch skirting, and scrape and touch up the paint around the windows. That'll take a few days and keep us busy. Then we tackle the roof."

"This is kind of fun, you know. I like physical labor. It

makes the time go by fast, and you've got so much to show for it in the end."

"I agree," Alex said. "The transformation is satisfying."

Picturesque ruby clouds glowed overhead and were mirrored in the glassy lake. The view was magnificent.

Alex stared out at it with a bleak expression on her face, despite the beauty before her. "Blake," she finally said. "Did you want to ask around about Dwight's Army buddies tonight at the bar? Maybe someone will know who they are."

Blake nodded, "Yeah. I guess we could. Thanks for suggesting it, although it's not exactly the kind of date I'd prefer to take you on." He paused for a moment, thinking. "I also need to call Aunt Sal. I still owe her an apology."

"Would you like to invite her to my house for dinner? Maybe neutral territory will help you guys start over."

"I don't want you to have to do that. Thank you, though."

"Listen, Blake," Alex pressed. "I wouldn't offer if I didn't want to. We can cook together. It'll be fun."

He regarded her heart-shaped face, so full of kindness, and once more, he couldn't say no to her.

"Okay, Alex. I think that would be nice. Thank you."

Alex stared at him with a smug smile. "Boy, that was hard for you, wasn't it."

"What?" Blake asked, incredulously.

"Saying yes to my offer."

He laughed a short, mirthless laugh. "Well, I've always been self-reliant. It's hard to shift after a lifetime of one kind of behavior, but I'm trying."

"I'm glad you're trying. I'm trying, too," she admitted, shyly.

"I know," Blake replied, softly. "I'm thankful for it."

They kissed each other as Venus glimmered into the changing sky.

"It's scary, though," she said.

"I know. But we're brave, Alex."

She nodded. "We are. Like you said, you can't be brave if you aren't scared first."

When they got back to Alex's house, she got online and ordered a fridge and stove of the proper dimensions. They were to be delivered the following week. While Alex took care of that, Blake called Sal, apologized for his outburst, and invited her to Alex's house for dinner Saturday. Sal, as always, was gracious and accepted both his apology and the invitation. The urge to start fresh appealed to Blake, and he was thankful to have a place that didn't reference their turbulent history in which to do it. Alex was thrilled.

"We can look through cookbooks for a nice recipe or two," she said, excitedly.

"Nothing too fancy, Alex," Blake warned. "They've got pretty simple taste."

"We'll find something perfect. Let's go to Ricky's now."

"I wonder if Darla will be there," Blake quipped.

"It's a fifty-fifty shot. There's only two bars, after all. Besides, she won't remember you at all, so don't flatter yourself."

Blake and Alex walked down to the bar behind the pizza shop and ordered beers. They chatted with the bartender, whose name was Roger, and he said they should check the VA in Moose Creek, a few miles away. It would be a good place to scout, but Alex was disappointed that Roger didn't know Dwight Anderson.

"I've only been here a few years, Alex. You know that. Ask some of the other guys,"

"Thanks anyway," Alex said, as they headed toward the pool tables. "Maybe Stan will know something."

They walked over to the same bearded elderly man who had asked about Blake's intentions the other night. If he only knew. Blake blushed as he pictured kissing Alex. Alex didn't notice his embarrassment, instead plowing ahead.

"Hey, Stan," she said cheerfully, as she approached the high table where the man sat with his buddies.

"Alex," he said, his voice low and gravelly. "I see you're still consorting with this fellow."

"Yeah, he's not so bad. Say, I was wondering if you knew Dwight Anderson?"

"I did." Stan's expression darkened, and he stared at Blake suspiciously. "Why do you ask?"

"Can you tell us who his cronies were? He's dead, you know. This here is his son, Blake."

The man studied him. "I had a feeling the other night. I heard about your daddy passing on and that you were back working on his place."

"It's true. Alex here is a marvel. It's unrecognizable," Blake said, putting his arm around Alex. She blushed visibly.

Stan looked pensive for a moment and said, "I remember you from when you were a boy. Your mama too. You've been away a while. Looks like you grew up strong."

"Thank you, sir," Blake replied, staying guarded, unsure whether Stan was going to be helpful at all.

"Yes, you got away. I was always glad for that."

Blake swallowed uncomfortably. "Why?"

"You know why. Your daddy was a right bastard if ever there was one, and we all felt bad for you after your mama died. Like I said, I'm glad you got away."

Blake's heart squeezed. It was strange to think of people he'd never met rooting for him when he was a kid, even if they hadn't been able to help him. "Me, too," Blake said. "And you're right, he was a pretty awful son of a bitch. We need to know who he hung out with, though. He never came around here, did he?"

"No. Knew we didn't approve of how he treated that poor wife and kid of his. He always went up to the VA in Moose Creek. Maybe they reminisced about the war. Freddie might know more. He's a vet."

"Thanks, Stan." Alex shook the old man's hand.

His skin looked thin as paper and his veins stood bolt upright, as though they were attempting to levitate from his body.

Blake and Alex walked over to another table, where a few other men were gathered.

She approached one of them. "Freddie? Would you mind if we bothered you for a second? We need to know if you knew Dwight Anderson?"

Freddie's eyes darted to the side, then back to Alex. "I served in the war with him." The color drained from his face.

"Can you tell us anything about him?" Alex pressed.

"Not much. Been a while since I saw him. Sorry." And with that, Freddie turned back to his friends at the table, picked up his drink and avoided eye contact with Alex.

"Okay, if you think of anything important about Dwight, let us know."

Blake and Alex lingered for a few moments to finish their beers and then headed out into the brisk night air. Out on the sidewalk, a man's voice stopped them.

"Alex," he called.

Alex and Blake turned to find that Freddie had followed them outside.

"Blake, I didn't introduce you properly inside. This is Freddie Cormack. Freddie, Blake. You got something to tell us?"

"Yeah. I didn't want to talk in front of the guys. Dwight is dead, so it can't do any harm, I guess." His body language shifted, as though he wasn't sure that was true.

"We're listening, Freddie," Alex said, trying to placate the man.

His rheumy eyes and weathered skin looked ghoulish in the neon light of Ricky's Pizza. His expression now betrayed his abject fear.

"You didn't hear any of this from me, you understand?" He looked around to make sure they were alone. "I gotta live here with these people, and so do you, honey. I wanted to tell you to think twice about digging. You may not like what you find."

"Freddie." Blake dove into the conversation with earnest vehemence. "Please tell us everything you know. I'm trying to figure out how my mother died. I know it was ages ago, but I need to know. Please."

"The truth doesn't always set you free, like they say. Sometimes it's a weight that pulls you under the surface and never lets you go. I served in Vietnam with Dwight Anderson and some of the other guys."

"Which guys?" Blake and Alex asked, in unison.

"Since that's a matter of public record, I'll tell you, but I'm warning you again. You're about to exhume some nasty ghosts. Dan Arquette, Vinny Frazier, Peter Dickenson, your daddy, and I all served together in some awful times. We saw things no one should ever have to see and did things no one should ever have to do. Peter, he's dead now. But he and I saw eye to eye on it, even then. We knew it was awful shit, and that we were only doing a job for our country. The other guys, though, they were different."

He stopped talking, as though he'd been thrown back into the war of the sixties and seventies that had wrecked so many lives. His had clearly been one of them.

"Dan Arquette?" Blake said. "The former Chief of Police?"

"The same." Freddie's expression was full of disgust.

"Freddie, do you want to come to the house and talk somewhere more comfortable?" Alex said. "I'll make you a nice whisky and soda, the way you like."

But her charming manner wasn't getting through to the old vet.

"No, honey. I'm going home. I hate thinking about all that old shit. It was the worst time of my life. Just be careful, whatever you do."

"Can you tell me anything else?" Alex asked, trying to delay him.

"No, I can't, Alex. I can't." Freddie's tone was defeated and lost.

He turned around and walked away, leaving Alex and Blake bewildered on the sidewalk.

A weight of despondence settled over Blake as Freddie left. Then, turning back toward Ricky's, through the windows he saw a large man whose eyes were fixed on the spot where old Freddie had been. They bore an expression of sheer malice and cruelty. They reminded him of Dwight's eyes. The man's gaze then shifted to Blake. They stared each other down for a moment through the glass and Blake could feel the burn.

"Fuck. Alex, let's go home. Right now. We need to talk."

Taking her arm and forging the way, he briskly led her down the street, not speaking until they got to her door.

He scanned the street for signs that they'd been followed, but no one was there. What did it matter? Everyone in town knew exactly where Alex lived. When they were inside, he locked the door himself and leaned against it for a moment.

"What's up, Blake?" Alex asked, out of breath, her eyes gigantic. "Why the sudden rush?"

He grabbed her firmly by the shoulders. "Alex, right after Freddie left, I looked into Ricky's and caught the angry glance of a man at the bar. He had dark hair and dark eyes. He was pretty big around and had a tattoo on his forearm. Who was that?"

Alex swallowed hard. "Shit. That's Vinny."

"As in Vinny Frazier?"

"Yes. I wish he hadn't seen us talking to Freddie." They walked into the living room as Alex asked, "What have we stumbled into?"

"I don't know, but I got the distinct feeling that good ole Vinny wants us to stumble back out and forget we were ever here."

Alex turned to face him, her face full of determination. "Doesn't that mean we're onto something?" she asked, excitedly.

"Alex, he's menacing." Blake was genuinely freaked out. "I know that look. I saw it every day of my life, for eighteen years."

"So? If anybody's curious, we're asking after your dead father. That's all. What's the problem? They don't have to know we think he killed your mom. They don't need to know anything."

"Alex, I think I've gotten you into something danger- ous. We need to stop now. Let's leave it alone. Freddie's right, I don't need to know what really happened. The past is dead."

"No, Blake. The past is right here with us, right now. It lives and breathes as we do. It's a part of us and we're not going to abandon our search for the truth because Vinny and Dan might get flustered. Screw them. You deserve to know the truth and we're not going to rest until we figure it out."

Blake looked at Alex's animated eyes, her feisty little body, and her pugilist's stance. She wasn't about to cower and give up.

"Oh, Alex," he said, softly, pulling her to him.

They held their embrace for a moment.

"Remember, we need to be brave," she said. "Let's be brave together."

"I don't want you to get hurt, Alex. I couldn't bear it." He kissed her on the head.

"Then we need to be smarter about our investigation. I'm calling Helena."

He made a fire for them, while Alex called the detective and put her on speakerphone.

"Don't you know I'm not working?" Helena answered, her tone surly. "I'm in sweats, watching the game,"

"What game?"

"Whatever game. Who even cares. Point is, I'm not working."

"Please, Helena. This is important. Can you come over?"

"No," Helena answered, exasperated. "Come by the station tomorrow."

"We can't." Alex shot Blake a look and continued, her voice finally betraying how nervous she was. "I think we've stumbled onto something serious, and we don't want to be seen going to the police station."

"But it's okay for me to come to your house?" Helena sounded ten steps past annoyed.

"We checked the street," Alex assured her. "No one's out."

"You suck. I'll be right over, but I'm not changing out of my sweats."

"Thank you, Helena. See you in ten."

The fire wasn't exactly flourishing under Blake's care. In fact, it had barely caught at all.

"Allow me," Alex said, gallantly, failing to hide her smile.

She stirred it around and added some kindling to the hardwood. Immediately responding to her ministrations, the fire sprang up, alive and blazing.

"There," she said. "All better."

"Great." Blake smiled.

He was amused rather than emasculated by not being as handy as Alex.

She headed to the kitchen, returning a moment later with three beers. She set them down on the coffee table and went back to the kitchen. She returned once more with a tray of crackers and cheese and orange segments.

"They are better than flowers." She popped one into her mouth, with a smile. "They taste better, too."

When she returned from a third trip to the kitchen, Alex held the paper with her flow chart drawn on it, and a pen. Sitting down on the sofa next to Blake, she added Vinny and the other vets' names to her chart. Then she grabbed her laptop and Googled them all together. She and Blake searched through the results until they found something on a history site about the Vietnam War. It had pictures of some of the campaigns that certain battalions had run. It also had a picture of one battalion, and in it, Blake recognized Dwight.

"There he is. Look at his face. He was a bastard even then."

A young Dwight glared out from the past, with the same malice and evil intent Blake knew so well. The other men in the picture were harder to recognize. One man had Vinny's chin, and another had Freddie's nose and mouth. They saved the photo to Alex's desktop and kept searching until they heard a knock at the door. They both started in surprise, having forgotten they'd summoned Detective Helena.

Alex went to the door and escorted the sweatpants-wearing Helena into the living room. She looked nonplussed. Alex handed her a beer and an orange slice as a peace offering.

"To what do I owe the pleasure of your company this evening?" She sprawled out in the club chair across from Blake and Alex.

They gave her an abridged version of the evening's events, showing her the flow chart and the picture they'd found of the soldiers.

"So?" Helena clearly didn't find any of this interesting.

"Freddie was obviously nervous about talking to us, and Vinny looked at Blake like he wanted to kill him. They're clearly hiding something. I think it's all connected somehow."

"Connected to what? Caroline Anderson?"

"Yes. To my mom." Blake was trying to stay patient, but it wasn't an easy task.

Helena sat back in the chair and slumped down, looking defeated. "Well, I did a little digging of my own and got a door slammed in my face. Literally. Dan Arquette wasn't exactly friendly when I brought this folder to his house. In fact, his behavior bordered on harassment. I should've written the fucker up, ex-cop or not. He was a real asshole. If he and your dad were friends, they were meant for each other. Two peas in a pod."

"What do we do now?" Blake asked.

"Well, it depends. How far do you want to go?"

"I want the truth, Detective. I need to know if Dwight killed my mom."

"That's what I thought you'd say. We have a choice, but I don't recommend it."

"What is it?" Alex said.

"You can sue the police department for negligence and bring Dan Arquette out of retirement and onto the witness stand. Get the DA involved. As I said, it's not a great choice. It'll be expensive. Lawyers always are."

Blake and Alex glanced at each other, thinking the same thing. Jacob Blackwell.

"Do you think he'd do it?" Alex asked him.

"I don't know. I only recently met him."

"Who?" Helena asked, looking confused.

"We're not quite ready to say, but we've got a lawyer. Maybe." Alex looked pensive.

Helena sat forward, anchoring her elbows on her knees, and fixed the couple with a serious expression.

"I want you to know that this is dangerous. Part of me kind of hoped you'd just let it go, but I can tell you won't. Dan Arquette still has a lot of connections around here. He's a tough bird to tango with. And if Vinny's involved? Don't get me started. Vinny should have a record a mile long. Harassment. Assault. DUI. Drugs. Domestic abuse. You fucking name it, he's done it, but somehow the charges never stick."

Blake shook his head. "What the actual fuck. Who do these guys think they are?"

"I don't know, but I took the liberty of pulling every police file associated with Dwight Anderson for you. Get this, your mom filed *numerous* complaints against him and *none* of them were followed up on. Not one. Every single one was signed off on by Dan Arquette and filed away. See what I'm talking about? There was a systematic blind eye being turned. Dwight was a terror, but he never got arrested for anything, just like Vinny. I copied Dwight's file for you and put the originals under lock and key at the station, in case anyone goes looking. I will dig out Dan and Vinny's tomorrow, too. You have a safe place to hold onto these?"

Alex got up and took the folder of copied police reports from Helena. Then, she took it into the kitchen and put it in the freezer.

"Good enough for now," she said, and returned to the sofa.

"What next?" Blake asked.

"Meet with your lawyer friend. I'll call Dr. Palermo and see what she says about the coroner's report. Seriously guys. Keep this on the DL, and for fuck's sake, don't go asking any more questions down at the bar."

"We were going to go to the VA tomorrow to ask about Dwight. Do you think we should wait?" Blake asked, to be sure.

"Hellz yes, you should wait. Why go waltzing into the snake pit?" Helena shook her head. "You guys don't know jack shit about investigations. Be subtle. Prepare. Collect information. Don't dance down Main Street, announcing that you're investigating something fishy. Fish fucking hate that." She downed her beer, then stood up and headed for the door. "I'll be in touch. Don't do anything stupid. Please."

"Thank you so much for all the advice and information." Alex walked Helena to the door. "Talk to you soon." She closed it behind her.

Blake was dazed. "You honestly think we've hit on some conspiracy? In the middle of the fucking Adirondacks? How could that even be?"

"I don't know. It seems so unlikely." Alex sat next to him again and asked, "Why would all these guys protect Dwight? He was an asshole."

"It doesn't make any sense. Unless..." Blake's face grew pensive.

"Unless what?" Alex leaned in, expectantly.

"Unless they were protecting him for a good reason."

"What," she asked, "like he saved Dan Arquette's life in the war and Dan owed him one?"

Blake nodded. "Something like that, yes."

Alex raised her eyebrows and looked impressed. "Geez, that's actually a good theory."

"Don't look so surprised." Blake feigned a bruised ego, and then his serious expression returned. "We need to know more. I hope Helena can get us some answers. Otherwise, I'll have to head to the VA."

"She said not to, Blake. Be patient. In the meantime, let's keep looking on the Internet, too."

They spent another hour looking through the hits and found some references to campaigns fought by Dwight's division. The pictures attached to each of the hits were disturbing, at best.

Eventually, Blake said, "Enough for one night. Sorry to put you through that."

"War is ugly, Blake. That's the long and short of it. People do this shit to each other. Innocent people die. All for power or ideology or revenge. I've never understood it."

"Me neither, angel. Even good people do horrible things in a war."

"I can't stomach any more," Alex said. "You're right, let's stop. It's time for bed."

Soberly, they closed up the laptop and turned out the lights. When Alex wasn't looking, Blake double-checked that the doors were locked. The image of Vinny's malicious glare haunted him, and he wasn't about to take any risks with Alex. He'd never tried to protect anyone before, other than himself, and he'd done an abysmal job of that. *You were only a child*, he reminded himself bitterly.

After vowing to do a better job this time around, he headed up the darkened stairs.

TEN

On Saturday, Blake was clearly nervous about the impending dinner with his aunt and uncle. He was edgy and distracted all morning, leading to several paint spills and snarky comments. Alex was fed up with his shit by noon.

"Listen," she demanded, "do you want to cancel the dinner?"

Covered in brown paint and looking surly, Blake was in the middle of painting his second coat on the porch skirt. Alex, who had done as much of the work, if not more, didn't have a speck of paint on her.

Blake glared at her. "What would make you think that?"

"Your shitty attitude, that's what. You've been stomping around and muttering all morning. I know you're nervous about the dinner. I don't mind calling it off if you're not ready."

"I'm fine," he snapped. "Don't assume you understand how I feel right now. You don't."

Alex took a steadying breath and mustered her deepest reserves of patience.

When she could speak without eviscerating him, she said, "You are a kind and gentle man. I like being with you. I do not, however, deserve to be spoken to with that tone. I know you know that. Shall we try again?"

Blake stewed for a moment. "I hate how I act when I'm nervous or stressed. It's not fair to you and it's not fair to Aunt Sal. I'm sorry. You're right, I'm nervous about dinner."

"Thank you. I'm not going to pretend to understand how you feel, but I am going to offer what support I can. Shall we stay the course or bail?"

"I don't want to bail. Sal deserves to hear my apology, and I'd like to do it tonight."

"Okay, then. Let's call it quits here. We're almost done with the porch anyway. Looks good, doesn't it."

Standing back, they surveyed the camp. It was unrecognizable. The new porch alone had given it a cared-for, attractive air. It still needed roof work and a full paint job, and the floors inside needed poly, but it was getting there.

When they got back to Alex's house, the scent of cooking meat was mouthwatering. They had put a pork shoulder in the slow cooker and were going to have *carnitas* tacos, a dish that Blake assured her he'd perfected in Chicago.

"You're a great cook, aren't you?" Alex pressed.

"The bachelor life can go either way, nutritionally. Either you succumb to the frozen pizza lifestyle, or you learn to cook. I opted for learning to cook."

"Amen to that."

They made salsa and roasted corn, guacamole and beans, and a couple pitchers of homemade margaritas for good measure.

Alex tasted the pork as they worked on shredding it. "Holy shit, that's good." She licked her lips.

"The secret is the can of Coke I put in."

"I wondered about that. It looked like a weird addition."

"Yeah, it is, but for some reason it breaks down the meat."

By six o'clock, everything but dessert was ready to go. Blake paced the kitchen while Alex put a cinnamon and chili-powder-laced chocolate cake in the oven, in keeping with their Mexican theme. Blake was insanely nervous, but Alex didn't dare comment. Instead, she took his margarita out of his hands and placed it on the counter.

Seductively, she slipped her hand around his waist, reached down his backside and squeezed. "I'd like to kiss the chef."

It seemed to be all the distraction he needed. Pressing her up against the refrigerator, he kissed her passionately, thrilling their bodies to life. Alex wanted him, then and there, right in the middle of the kitchen, but the doorbell startled them back into reality. *Maybe later.* Alex straightened herself out and smiled sheepishly. Hand in hand, they answered the door.

Just before Alex opened it, Blake whispered, "Thank you for doing this."

She turned to look at him and smiled so sweetly and affectionately that Blake smiled back, right as Alex swung the door open wide. When Sal saw Blake's unguarded smile, the look of shock and love on her face melted Alex's heart.

"Blake, that is the first time I've ever seen you smile," Sal said, in a shaky voice. "I mean, really smile." She burst forth and hugged him.

Awkwardly, he patted her on the back. Eventually,

though, he let himself hug his aunt. Little by little, it seemed to break down the invisible wall he had put up an age ago, as he beheld this woman, his mother's twin sister, in all her true and deep love for him.

"I'm so sorry, Aunt Sal. I have been awful to you. I know you guys tried to help me. I'm sorry I've been so angry." Blake spoke through his tears, for they had flooded out in this moment of raw emotion.

"It must have been impossibly hard for you to look at me and only see her. I have that experience every day of my life when I look in the mirror, Blake. I miss her so much and I know you do, too. She was stolen from us too soon. I'm sorry I couldn't do more."

"Don't be sorry. It was not your fault. I was in so much pain I couldn't let myself love you or I would've fallen apart. But Aunt Sal, I do love you. I always have."

"I love you, too, sweetheart. You're my blood, Blake. And you should have been my adopted son." Sal wept as she said these words.

Blake held her even tighter, his eyes still closed.

Alex cried, too, as Blake came to terms with this woman who clearly loved him. She was his mother's twin, and so it was impossible to think about the one without the other. How hard it must have been for Blake, especially as a child, to see his dead mother's face every time he looked at Sal. Even now, Alex could feel how painful it was.

"I'm ready to talk about all of it, Sal," Blake said. "If you are."

He released her from his hold, and she looked up at him, unsure. Gently, she reached up and wiped a tear from his cheek. She seemed to read his expression, judging his strength and resolve.

"Okay, Blake. But first, introduce me to your friend, this incredible woman who has made you smile."

"Sorry. Aunt Sal, Sam, this is Alex Taylor. She's my, um…" he hesitated for a split second, looking at Alex in all her discomfort, "my angel."

Alex, who had been holding her breath, said, "I thought you were going to say contractor."

All four of them, still in the entryway, burst into laughter. Blake pulled Alex close and kissed her on the head. Then, Alex reached out her hand to Aunt Sal first and then to Sam, earnestly greeting them and welcoming them into her home.

"What a great house," Sam said.

"Thanks. Let me get you guys some drinks, and later we can do the tour if you want."

"A drink sounds great," Sal said. "Thank you, Alex. Can I help you?"

"Nope, make yourselves comfortable. I'll be right back."

Alex scurried away to the kitchen, where she poured four margaritas and carried them out to the living room on a silver tray she'd found at a yard sale. Then, she bolstered the fire a bit as everyone sat down. Blake smiled at Alex and lifted his glass to her. She smiled and blushed and nodded to him.

"Why did you say you thought Blake would introduce you as his contractor?" Sam asked.

"Because I am." Alex smiled. "I have my own architectural restoration company and Blake hired me to work on the camp. It needed a real overhaul."

"Oh. You guys are working together?"

"Yes, and together-together, if that's what you're wondering. Not the most professional thing I've ever done, but I guess these things happen sometimes."

Sal almost spit out her drink. Sam's eyes grew huge, and he looked away toward the ceiling.

"Thank you for your honesty, Alex," Sal said, once she recovered from her coughing fit.

"Alex and I have experienced a lot together in a short amount of time," Blake said. "And I'm thankful for all of it."

"It's been a little crazy, I guess," Alex said. "But we're making progress on many fronts."

"We are indeed," Blake concurred.

"Are you still going to sell your dad's camp?" Sam asked, tentatively.

"Yep. We're fixing it up, and then I'll flip it. It's a nice piece of lakefront, I guess, but I don't want it."

"No one could blame you for that," Sam said. "If you need a hand with anything, let me know."

"Thanks, Sam. I appreciate it."

"The food smells so good. What did you make us, Alex?" Sal asked.

Alex looked at Blake and smiled to herself, at their assumption that she had cooked the meal.

"Actually, Blake cooked today. I made dessert."

"Well, I'm learning a lot about you tonight, my dear," Aunt Sal said, looking wistful. "Tell me more."

"Like what?" Blake asked.

"Well, let's start with the easy stuff. Where did you learn to cook?"

"I taught myself after college," Blake answered. "It was either that or starve."

"Do you have a specialty?"

"Not really. I like everything. I try to make healthy food most of the time, and I like Mexican a lot. I also like a good soup."

"There must be a lot of great restaurants in Chicago, too," Sam added.

"Yeah, but I'm on the road with the team a lot, so I have to eat out quite a bit. It's not the best for me. I try to make up for it by cooking when I'm home."

"That's smart. It must be a lot of fun to work with the Bears, buddy. I'm real proud of you." Sam was a mega fan of all things football.

"Thanks, Sam. I do like it a lot. Plus, like I said last time I saw you, I get to watch every game from the sidelines. Can't get better than that if you like football."

"That's the truth." Sam finished his margarita and looked lost for a moment.

"Do you need another one, Sam?" Alex readied herself to get up.

"No, but I'd take a beer, if you have one."

"Sure. Be right back."

While Alex was out of the room, Sal shifted in her chair before asking the inevitable questions. "When did you guys meet?"

"A few weeks ago. Right when I got to town. I called her to come and work on the place, and we sort of hit it off."

"She seems sweet," Sal said. "Is she a good carpenter?"

"Yes, she's sweet and a very good carpenter. She's incredibly knowledgeable and much stronger than she looks."

"Why would you start a relationship with someone when you don't even live here, Blake?"

Blake inhaled deeply, as though to buy himself a moment before answering. "We're both adults, Sal. We know what we're getting ourselves into."

"Maybe *you* do, but does she? She looks really young."

"She's twenty-six, Sal. And I won't hurt her, if that's

what you're hinting at. We're both being open and honest with each other."

Alex heard the entire conversation and now hesitated at the doorway between the living room and the kitchen. Holding Sam's beer in one hand and a platter of crackers and cheese in the other, she deliberated on whether she should rush in and save Blake or wait and listen to what he said. She desperately wanted to hear Blake's opinions on the topic, but she didn't want him to get grilled even worse by Sal. Alex opted for the less selfish route and plunged into the fray.

"Here you go, Sam. I brought out some crackers and cheese, too." She smiled at Blake and gave him a surreptitious wink.

He exhaled a deep breath. "Thanks, Alex."

This time, she sat right next to Blake, with their legs touching to let Sal know that she was in control.

Alex smiled at everyone. "Sal, what do you do?"

Sal looked away from Blake and returned Alex's smile. "I'm in customer service with the gas company. It's not glamorous, but it pays the bills."

"How about you, Sam?"

Sam shifted on his chair. "I've done a lot of different things, but these days I work for the county, on the road crew." He held up his hands, which had a tarred patina. "Also, not glamorous work, as my lovely wife put it. I don't mind it, though. It keeps life interesting."

Blake reached forward, picked up the platter with the crackers and cheese, and offered it first to Sal, who helped herself, and then to Sam.

"That's good cheese," Sam said, through a mouthful of crackers. "What is it?"

"It's goat cheese," Blake replied.

"Goat?" Sam choked and took a swig of his beer. "Never had that before. It's not bad."

"For a goat," Alex giggled.

"Shall we eat?" Blake asked the room at large, in an obvious attempt to move the festivities along at a brisker pace.

"Sure," Sam replied. "I'm starved."

They all moved into the dining room, where Alex and Blake brought out dishes of food. They enjoyed the feast, eating most of a pork shoulder between them.

"I'm glad you guys like the food," Blake said, looking relieved. "I didn't know what to make."

"Well," Sal said, "it was unbelievably delicious. You sure that was your handiwork, Blake?"

He laughed and nodded.

"Why don't you two go talk while Sam and I clear the plates," Alex said. "Sam, do you mind?" She looked at him with her most winning smile.

He stood up from his place. "It would be my pleasure, Alex."

"It certainly isn't your pleasure at home," Sal quipped. "I hope you teach him a couple tricks, Alex."

———

Blake escorted his aunt to the living room, where they sat in the armchairs closest to the fireplace. Pensively, he stoked the fire back up and stared into the flames.

"You asked me a question the other evening," Sal said, her voice earnest and strong, "and I owe you a proper answer."

If Sal had one defining quality, it was that she never beat around the bush. Blake could see that she'd been steeling herself for this moment, and he realized, so had he. With a deep breath, he waited, his heart racing.

"Caroline was always a bit of a rebel growing up. You never knew them, but our parents were very religious and strict. They forbade us to go over to friends' houses. We didn't get to play sports, and every Sunday we spent all day at the church. It was fine for a while, but when we got to middle school, Caroline started to resent it. She fought with them, terribly. I was always on the shy side, whereas she was the outgoing one, so all our family restrictions didn't have the same impact on me. But for her, it was like caging a bald eagle. Her spirit couldn't take it.

"She started sneaking out, hanging out with the wrong crowd, and got defensive when I asked her about any of it. She hated that I wasn't furious with our parents. We grew apart as she started talking to me less and less. And by the time we graduated, she had slipped away altogether. I felt alone and abandoned, but also terrified, because I saw the trajectory her life was headed down.

"She met Dwight not too long after we graduated. He was much older than her, like twenty years older, a war vet, and pretty intense. He must have appealed to her danger-seeking side, but all I saw in him was anger and the desire to dominate. She was taken in by the strong tough-guy image he projected, and they dated for a while. Then she snuck off and married him."

Sal took a sip of her drink, starting to tear up. Blake stared at the fire, trying not to lose control.

With a quavering voice, Sal continued. "It didn't take her long to realize what a maniac he was. A few months later, she showed up at the apartment I'd rented with my best friend. She'd walked all night through the mountain roads to get to me. Caroline was covered in bruises. Never on her face, mind you, but the rest of her body was a disaster. She cried and cried, begging me to help her. I told her to stay with me, that in the morning we would go to the police and file a report. We did. Blake, I tell you, we did. We filed report after report, and nothing was ever done."

"Dan Arquette," Blake muttered.

"How did you know that?" Sal turned white. "Blake, how did you know that?"

"We've been doing a little investigation of our own."

Sal shook her head. "I never understood it. Every time, Dwight would show up to claim her and she would be dragged back into that nightmare. Eventually, she gave up. I saw her less and less. I drove out to Dwight's cabin once and he confronted me with a loaded shotgun and told me he would kill me if I ever set foot on his property again. I knew he meant it. I went to a lawyer. He said he'd see us. I pretended like I had some business with him, but I wanted Caroline to know that there might be another way out. The lawyer met with us, and then a few weeks later Caroline all but disappeared. Dwight kept her locked up in the cabin. I saw little of her after that. Then she had you. We'd see you now and then when he would leave town for a few days and she could get away from him, but by that time she was broken. She was totally broken. The lawyer came back to ask me what had happened, and I assured him I didn't know. I still don't."

"She had an affair with him."

"With whom?"

"The lawyer. Jacob Blackwell. She got pregnant with me."

Sal looked like she was going to fall off her seat. "Holy shit, Blake." She paused for a moment as the gravity of this confession sank in. "So, Dwight wasn't your real father?"

"No. My guess is that once Dwight knew Mom was pregnant, he wouldn't let her out of his sight. Jacob wanted to run away with her, but he never saw her again. Dwight literally kept her under lock and key for years."

"This is completely insane. This can't be true. How do you know this?" Sal was in disbelief.

Blake removed his mother's letter from his pocket and handed it over to his aunt. She read it, finally letting go of all the emotion she'd held back during the conversation. Her whole body was racked with sobs. Blake went over to her, sat on the arm of the chair, and held her as she wept.

"My poor sister," she sobbed. "My poor sister. That fucking bastard. How could he do this to her?"

"Listen closely, Sal," Blake said, in a low, serious voice. He knelt beside her chair and took her hands in his. Looking into his aunt's eyes, his mother's eyes, he said, "You need to know the rest. I have reason to believe that Dwight killed her. He murdered my mother in cold blood. Somehow, he must have found out I wasn't his son, and he murdered her. Dan Arquette has covered for him all this time and I'm going to find out why. But please don't tell anyone, even Sam. For now. I think we may have uncovered a small-town conspiracy, and until we figure it out, I don't want to put you in danger. I'm going to get justice for her, Sal. I promise. I'm going to get justice for my mother."

Sal's shock was evident on her face. She slowly shook her head, her eyes wide. "I'd like to say I can't believe it, but I can," she said. "Dwight hated her. He hated everyone. Cruelty ran through his veins like blood. Alex is helping you with this?"

"Yes."

"Keep her safe, Blake," Sal pleaded earnestly, gripping his hands tightly. "Please don't let her get hurt and don't you get hurt. If it's one thing we've learned, people are crazy."

"That's the truth. We're being careful and the police are involved. Thank you, Sal. I know talking about Mom isn't easy. Maybe once we get some truth about what really happened, we can move on."

"Closure would be nice, Blake. I love you, you know. Always have. If I could've saved her—or you, for that matter—I would have. I really tried."

"I know you tried, Sal. Thank you for that. I...I love you, too."

They held each other for a moment.

Then Sal said, "Should we go rescue Alex from Sam?"

"I think she's probably fine, but let's go see."

They stood, hugged each other for another moment, then went to the kitchen, where they found Sam and Alex looking through cookbooks. They had four or five of them open on the breakfast bar and were cross-referencing some recipes.

Sam looked up. "Sal, I'm going to learn to cook."

Sal's eyebrows raised and she said, "I hope you're going to learn to clean, too, because I'm not mopping up after you."

Alex met Blake's gaze with a question, and he nodded and smiled to let her know everything was okay.

"Sam helped me frost the cake," Alex said. "Shall we sample his hard work?"

"Sounds good," Blake agreed.

They ate dessert, and Sam and Sal left not long after.

"Remember, Sal. Not a word," Blake softly reminded her, as she left.

"I promise. Thank you for this evening, you guys. It was exactly what we needed." She hugged Alex and whispered in her ear, "You really are his angel. Thank you."

———

Alex's heart clenched as she looked into Sal's blue eyes. Wishing Caroline had had a better life was useless. Time couldn't go backwards, nor could fate unravel.

Alex forced a smile and whispered, "He's a wonderful man."

Sal nodded and hugged Blake once more. When they were gone, Alex and Blake cleaned up the dessert dishes and put the scant leftovers in the fridge. Then they lounged in front of the fire, wiped out from the long day's work and from the deep emotional exertions of the evening. Blake sat on the floor with his back against the armchair, and Alex lay in front of him with her head resting on his thigh. She didn't want to ask how the conversation with Sal had been, knowing that when Blake was ready, he would tell her everything.

Eventually her patience was rewarded, as Blake recounted his aunt's stories of her early life with Caroline and what had happened when she married Dwight.

"I told her about our investigation," he said, after the story had unfurled. "She wasn't surprised. Dan Arquette had always been a dead end for her and my mom. They filed so many complaints, and nothing was ever done to help. Dan Arquette is at the heart of all this. We need to know what he's hiding."

"Give Helena a little more time to dig, and then we'll hit it full force. I'm with you, Blake. We need the truth."

"Alex," he said, in a serious, unfamiliar tone.

She sat up and took his hand. "Yes?"

"Thank you. Thank you for everything. Without you, none of this would be happening. I'd be trapped at that camp, hating my past, sleeping on the floor, and ready to get the fuck out of dodge. I probably wouldn't have lasted this long. I would've left it all in some realtor's hands and been back in Chicago by now."

"Wouldn't that have been better?" Alex asked, miserably.

"No. The truth is always preferable, remember? You're the catalyst for all this. You brought me and my mom back together, me and my real father together, me and Sal back together. And now we're going to find out the truth about what happened to my mother. It's all because of you. I…" He swallowed. "I love you, Alex. I don't expect you to feel the same so soon, but I needed you to know. I love you, angel."

Alex's heart was ready to burst. No man, aside from her father, had ever said those words to her. She had never let anyone close enough before. She certainly hadn't loved any of them. Blake, however, was different. He had been from the start.

Trying to hold back her tears, she took his hands in hers. "I love you too, Blake. I do."

His relief at hearing her say those words was evident on his face. He held her tight to him and Alex savored the mingled warmth of their bodies. Blake shifted back a moment to look into her honest, glittering eyes, and then kissed her. He kissed her deeply and a flood of mutual love surged like electricity between them, resulting in an inexorable attraction.

If Alex was being honest with herself, she had been contemplating sex with Blake since they'd met. He was attractive and strong, after all, and ripe for a fantasy. But since they'd been dating, she'd put it off, and he had never once pressured her. He was leaving after the camp was done. There was no way they would stay together, so how could she let herself get attached to him in that way?

It was too much trust to put in their bond, only for him to leave.

But as his words spun in her head and onto her tongue, Alex didn't care about her reasons for holding back anymore. She didn't want to wait. The longer she waited, the less time they'd have together, when all was said and done. It was already in the two-week countdown until he was supposed to leave. She could either savor those two weeks, wringing every drop of pleasure from them, or she could let them slip by with her guard up. Regret was sure to follow him when he left if she didn't enjoy this moment. There is no such thing as forever, anyway. There is only now.

"Blake," she breathed, as their lips parted for air.

"Yes, beautiful?" he asked, stroking her outer thigh with his hand and nipping at her earlobe.

"I think we should…" Alex realized she'd never said these words to a man. She'd gone with the flow, letting passion take its course, as bumpy as it usually was for her emotionally. But never had she told a man she wanted him. How did one even say it?

Blake pulled back and fixed her with a remorseful look. "I'm sorry baby. I hope I'm not being too—"

Alex cut him off, "No, no, that's not what I'm trying to say. In fact, I'm trying to say the opposite. I want you, Blake. I want to be together."

His eyes went wide, and he asked, "Are you sure? I would never want to pressure you."

"You're not, Blake. I promise. I've wanted this for a while."

"Promise you'll communicate," Blake said, earnestly. "Tell me what you want and need and if you want me to stop at any point."

Loving him even more for this sentiment, Alex said,

"I'll need to go slow. My mind has a way of getting in the way."

"I'm yours, Alex. However, you want me and however you need this to be."

"Okay. Thank you, Blake." She leaned in and kissed him again, gently at first, then passionately. She lifted off his shirt and he took off hers. "I really hope you have a condom," she said, in a low, carnally charged voice.

"I do," he said.

Bending in close, he kissed her, relishing her soft flesh. He went slowly, monitoring her closely for signs of hesitation. She leaned her head back and closed her eyes, a smile glimmering at the corners of her mouth. He licked the space on her chest between her breasts and worked his way back up the other side, then up her neck.

"You taste so good." He unfastened her jeans and slid them down, ever so slightly, over her hips.

Alex's body froze, a reflex, a spotlight on her deepest fears, her hidden scars. Blake paused and stroked her hair. He held her gaze until the fear passed, and she smiled, sadly.

"Are you okay?" He leaned forward and kissed her cheek.

"I am."

"What do you need?"

She looked at him, directly and said, "You're doing everything right." She kissed him, lightly, then more urgently.

Blake responded to her wishes, taking everything slow, while somehow maintaining the passion he felt for her. With a naughty smile, his gorgeous face, even more handsome from this new glimmer of adoration, he kissed down her throat and kept heading south. Their feelings for each other had intensified exponentially now that their guards were down, and his focus on her gratification was evident.

The guys she'd been this intimate with before had never sensed her hesitation. When Alex would stop them, it made her feel in control, more powerful, but at the cost of the moment. When she didn't stop them, it felt uncomfortable, never quite right. But Blake was putting her in charge. Rather than stopping him to maintain control, Alex wanted the opposite. She wanted control of her own pleasure. It was a revelation.

She breathed through her anxiety, pushing the pain of the past away, and focusing on Blake. Only Blake. He wanted her, she wanted him, and it was her decision to make. It was all that mattered in this moment.

Taming her negative thoughts wasn't an easy task, but she concentrated on Blake's attentions and relaxed into the moment. He possessed an inherent ability to sense her desires, respect her limitations. Together, they would push through the fear.

Afterwards, Blake asked a spent Alex, "You okay?"

She assessed herself, her thoughts, her feelings, and decided she was more than okay. She nodded and said, "Yes. I feel like I've reclaimed my body. It was long overdue."

Blake held her tighter, as the wetness of her tears spilled out against his chest.

"Why are you crying? Did I hurt you?" Blake asked, desperately.

"No, the opposite. I mean, that was crazy wonderful," Alex breathed, when she finally could breathe. "I'm so glad I finally know what it's supposed to be like."

"Alex," Blake whispered. "You deserve the world's most exquisite pleasures and joys."

"Tell me again," she whispered into his chest.

Blake somehow knew what she wanted to hear. "I love you, Alex. A thousand times, I love you."

Stifling a sob, Alex murmured, "Thank you."

"For what, angel?" He stroked her hair.

"For loving me. No one's ever loved me before. I've never let anyone this close. It's overwhelming."

"I understand. It's okay. I've never let anyone this close either. It's honestly terrifying."

He comforted her, enfolding her body against himself as she sobbed out a lifetime of pain.

He was her life raft, and she was his.

"It's okay, baby. It's okay. I love you."

ELEVEN

They fell asleep in each other's embrace before the dying fire. A few hours later, driven by the chill of the night air, they blearily crashed into Alex's bed, only awakening to the chirping of the chickadees outside her window.

Morning had a tough time finding them through the blackout shades. Normally, Alex awoke at the same time every day, but Blake was throwing off her body clock. Now, she was shocked to see it was after eight. She was more shocked to find Blake's sleeping form beside her. He looked gigantic in her full-sized antique bed. Rationally, she knew he was a big guy, but here he looked mountainous.

The sun was shining. It was Sunday, and as Blake awoke, Alex remembered the most important thing in the world.

"You love me," Alex whispered.

"You love me, too," Blake returned.

They looked into each other's gaze and found that they'd never been so happy before. Their still-naked bodies had been pressed together all night, and now it was as though they had never been separate creatures. The notion warmed them utterly.

Languidly, Alex asked, "What do you want to do today? Before I met you, I usually took Sundays off."

Blake laughed and said, "Sorry we've been working so hard. It has been non-stop, hasn't it." He considered the idea for a moment. "I'm open to suggestions."

"How about we drive down to Saratoga? It's a couple of hours, but it's a pretty drive."

"Yeah, that sounds great," Blake said. "We deserve a little fun, don't you think?"

"Well, to be fair, last night was pretty fun," Alex said, blushing. Blake ran his hand along her thigh.

"Absolutely," he agreed, fixing her with his most carnal gaze. "The most fun." Gently, he teased her to life and before Alex knew it, they were unraveling in each other's embrace again.

Eventually, they showered, dressed, grabbed some donuts and coffee from the bakery, and headed out of town. The lakes glittered in the morning sunshine. Alex drove carefully, but faster than usual, propelled by excitement about the day ahead. The radio was spotty, so they sat in companionable silence as the trees whispered past. The little towns whizzed by, quick as a blink.

The sign *Entering Moose Creek* appeared ahead.

"Hey, isn't Moose Creek where the VA is?" Blake asked.

Alex, as though shaken from a dream, said, "Yeah, it is. It's right on the main road actually."

A few trucks were parked outside the unassuming brick building. A group of men were talking animatedly outside. One had a baseball cap on.

"Holy shit, Alex." Blake sat up straighter.

"What?" she asked. With her eyes fixed on the road ahead, she hadn't noticed anything special about the group of men.

"They're all there. Vinny's talking to someone—probably Dan Arquette—and another guy who looked like Freddie. What are they doing?"

"It's the VA, Blake," Alex answered, suddenly nervous. "Maybe they meetup all the time. Maybe they're not *doing* anything." With the VA in their rear-view mirror, Blake turned around in the seat and stared back until the group of men was out of sight.

Then, Blake turned back to her, his energy almost manic. "I think we should go back, Alex. I want to follow them."

"Follow them?" Alex was terrified at the idea. "No. Helena said to wait. She said not to go waltzing into their lives, asking questions. I'd bet she'd say not to follow them either."

Blake slumped down in the seat and agreed. "No, you're right. We can't follow them. Can you circle back, though, so we can watch them from far away?"

Alex nodded. "I'll turn around and park close by, and we can save Saratoga for another day. It's not going anywhere."

"Do you mind?" Blake asked miserably.

"Of course I don't," Alex assured him. Her heart was racing and part of her really wanted to know what the men were up to as well. "I'm not even a little disappointed. If you want to be here, we'll stay here."

"Thanks, angel."

"You don't have to thank me."

They parked in a church parking lot up the road from the VA and watched the three men interact. The tall one with the hat might've been Dan Arquette, but they'd never met him. The big one was definitely Vinny, and she was sure that the frail, cowering, white-haired, white-bearded man was Freddie.

Her heart twisted as she analyzed his body language. "Freddie looks scared," Alex said.

The tall man was accusatorially waving his finger at Freddie. He was definitely yelling, and his manner was threatening.

In a few moments, the group broke up. Vinny shoved Freddie back a few steps, then he and the man who was most likely Dan Arquette got into a shiny black pickup truck and drove away in the opposite direction, back toward Edison. Freddie stood there, looking desperate and upset.

"Now's our chance," Alex said. "We're going to go talk to him."

And before Blake could stop her, she was out of the truck and loping across the road. He followed her and caught up in a few paces. Freddie caught sight of them and looked like he'd been kicked in the guts. His face went as white as his beard.

"Was that Dan Arquette?" Alex asked, brazenly. "Was he threatening you?"

"Alex, Jesus, what're you doing here? Don't you know you could get us all killed?"

"Killed? Freddie, you need to tell me what the fuck is going on here," Alex said, fiercely.

"Not for anything, girl. Leave it alone. Get out of here before someone sees you. Before someone sees me." He was looking around wildly as though they were being closely observed.

"Come with us," Alex said. "We need to talk, Freddie." Her tone was no nonsense and firm. "The truck is right there. We'll keep you safe."

"Safe? You think anyone is safe? Think again, Alex. Think again. Not with people like Vinny and Dan out there, we ain't. Go home, child. Go home now."

"No." Alex folded her hands across her chest.

Her eyes blazed with such intensity that even Blake took a step back at her vehemence.

"Jesus," Freddie acquiesced. "Fine."

And to Alex's astonishment, Freddie blustered off toward the church parking lot across the street, all the while looking around like a terrified animal.

Once they were all in the truck, Freddie said, "Drive, Alex. Drive the opposite direction. Get us out of here."

She didn't hesitate. She threw the truck into gear and squealed out of the gravel lot. Freddie was shaking. His body, mostly bones under his overcoat, trembled like that of a frightened child. His lined face was contorted in fear and worry. Alex's heart rate sped up in anticipation.

When Freddie had sufficiently recovered his wits, he spat, "Why you two gotta come around and open that particular can of vipers? You sent the police girl to talk to Dan? At his house?" He put his hands on his head and squeezed his eyes closed. "Do you have any clue what you've done? I thought all that past shit was good and dead and buried with Dwight, but here you are diggin' up the fucking ghosts. Goddammit."

Alex had never seen Freddie be anything but a docile old man. This new side of him had her downright alarmed. She shot Blake a look across the front seat and Blake's eyes were wide and concerned.

In a soothing tone, Alex said, "Freddie, we're so sorry if we made things more difficult for you by asking questions. Blake is trying to figure out some stuff from his childhood, is all. Dwight was a monster, you know, and no one stopped him. No one ever even tried. We want to understand why."

"I know he was a monster. I saw what that man did to everyone in his path. I served in the worst of the worst campaigns with that fucker. I saw what he did. And that was the problem. I saw what they all did."

Blake shuddered. "What do you mean? In the war?"

Freddie went silent. He clamped his jaw shut as though he was reliving those moments of his life, in all their gore and horror.

"There will never be peace," he said, through gritted teeth. "Not for me."

Alex shuddered. What had they gotten themselves into?

They drove for another ten minutes before they hit the next little town. Alex pulled over and parked at a lakeside playground. It was abandoned, but for the wind swirling last autumn's dead leaves in tiny cyclones around the rusty antique equipment.

"Come on," she said. "We could all use some air."

They got out of the truck and walked along the empty sidewalk leading over to the desolate playscape. She wished there was something to do with her hands. *Maybe that's why people smoke. Moments like this. Take one out, light it up, blow that puff of smoke out into the cold spring air to dissipate, like souls after death. What a morbid image.*

Freddie's weeping brought Alex back down to earth. He had sat on a picnic bench in the thin, dappled sunlight. Bitter, angry tears, the tears of a tortured soldier carrying around decades of guilt and tattered pride, streamed down the man's withered face. Her heart ached for him. It wasn't his fault he'd been conscripted. It wasn't his fault he had to serve in Vietnam, that war of dubious moral ground. She'd seen the documentaries. She knew the worst of it. At least she thought she did.

Blake took out his phone and set it to record. "I'm going to record you, with your permission, Freddie. Is that okay?"

"I'm past caring, son. I owe you this much. I owe you the truth. But I want you to know Dan will have me killed for this if it gets into the wrong hands."

"Dan Arquette?" Blake said.

"Dan fucking Arquette. He and Dwight and Vinny had what you might call a black-market crime ring going, back in the war. I found out the hard way. Dwight was my commanding officer, and I had to follow his orders. For a while, they satisfied themselves running heroin and opium and black-market liquor through an abandoned warehouse close by where we were stationed. They paid me off so I didn't tattle on them, and I didn't really care one bit. Then we received orders to move a bunch of POWs from one camp to another. Dwight saw it as an opportunity to start trafficking girls. He culled a whole bunch of girls from the POW bunch and sold them into slavery. Do you know what I mean by that?"

Alex and Blake nodded.

Blake said, quietly, "I think we do. Sex trafficking."

"Yeah. Well, imagine these poor war-ravaged folks, all huddled together, their villages destroyed, their parents murdered, and we rope 'em up and drag 'em into his warehouse. The drugs and contraband I could've lived with. Trafficking? No. I had a hard time with that one. Then Dan takes a fancy to one and Vin to another. Do you see what I'm saying? Those men, those soldiers in their fucking uniforms, tortured those girls. Jesus, the screams. I can still hear their fucking screams." He sobbed as he relived watching that horror. Freddie was a broken man.

"I never stepped in to save them. Not once. I never said, listen guys, this is horrible. This is wrong. These girls are humans. They're people. They're not things. They treated them worse than animals."

Alex couldn't keep the tears from streaming down her face, as she all too personally understood what had been done to those defenseless girls. It turned her stomach to battery acid. She looked out at the playground, a place of joy where so many kids had capered and yelled through their childhoods, contrasted with the stolen lives of all the children of war. She hated it. She hated it with her very being. It was gut-wrenching and painful, but she mustered her courage and brought her emotions under control. She could grieve for those girls later. Now was the time to press for the truth.

"Go on, Freddie. Please." She placed her tiny hand over his weathered one.

He looked up at her tearstained face and shook his head. "That's most of it. I been carrying that nightmare around in my head all these years, trying to subdue the angry voices telling me to stop them, to tell a superior. It was the fucking wild west, though. Dwight banked the cash from trading in human suffering. The guys got their pick of the group to have their awful way with, and I stood there watching it happen. They threatened me within an inch of my life not to tell, and I haven't. Not until now. All I have to prove it is some snapshots they don't know I still got." He reached into his pocket and drew out a tattered envelope full of pictures. "Here. These will help you guys bring them down. Just do it fast. I can't live with it anymore. The second they know I gave 'em up, my life ain't worth shit. Not that it's worth much anyway." He handed Blake the envelope.

Blake didn't have the heart to open it.

He put it in his jacket pocket. "Thank you. This will help."

"It's way too little, way too late. I couldn't save any of those kids, but I could've tried harder to save you. I knew what Dwight did to you and your mother. And I stayed silent. All those years, I stayed silent 'cause I was afraid they'd kill me. I drank and stuffed it all down and pretended not to see. Can you forgive me, Blake? I know it's too much to ask."

"Freddie, you are not the one who beat me or hurt those girls. There is nothing to forgive."

"Like hell there isn't. I have a battery of sins to work off in the next life, if I'm so lucky as to have another chance to make it all up. I hope so, because I surely failed in this one. I was a terrible coward. I should've spoken up. About all of it."

"If it means that much to you to hear it, I forgive you, Freddie." Blake's voice was thick with emotion as he patted Freddie on the back. "I forgive you. I wish you peace."

"Peace isn't likely for me, but maybe it is for you."

They drove back to Moose Creek in silence. A deep sense of foreboding that Alex couldn't explain had crept up on her.

When they got out of the truck at the church parking lot a little while later, she hugged Freddie. "Don't do anything stupid. We care about you, Freddie. The courage you displayed today was amazing. You did the right thing. Thank you. Please call us if you need anything. You know where we are."

He fixed her with his gaze. "Take care of yourselves. Make sure you go to the right person with all this information. Telling the wrong person will land you nowhere or worse, understand?"

"Yes. I understand," Blake assured him. "I'm going to bring it straight to the DA."

Freddie nodded his head. "That should be far enough."

"We'll need you to testify, Freddie. I mean it," Alex said, putting her hand on his arm. "Don't do anything stupid."

"I would've killed myself years ago, honey, if I was going to do that." He patted her on the arm, smiled sadly, and headed across the street, back to the VA, back to the weight of painful memories and crushing guilt. Maybe his pain would ease a bit now that he had finally confessed his sins, but she didn't hold out much hope.

"Holy shit," she said, when they eventually got back in her truck. "That explains so much."

"It explains how awful they all are, but it still doesn't explain whether Dwight killed my mother."

"No, I guess not, but we have a bigger lead than we had this morning, at least. I think Freddie's right about one thing."

"What's that?"

"That we need to be careful about who we share this information with. Let's go back to the house and Google the DA. If she has any connections to these guys, we need to keep looking. I'm afraid for Freddie. Do you think he'll be okay?"

"You heard him. If he was going to off himself," Blake said, "he would've done it years ago."

"Yeah, but I'm still uneasy. What if the guys find out he talked to us again?"

"I don't know, Alex. I don't know."

The drive back to her house was spent in oppressive silence. Alex couldn't get the images she'd conjured of what had happened to all those Vietnamese girls out of her mind. It was too awful to contemplate, but she couldn't help it. Their screams, their pain, her screams, her pain. It all came back to her with the force of a blow. Clenching her stomach, she bent forward as she drove.

"You all right?" Blake had been startled from his own reverie by her sudden intake of breath.

"Jesus. I'm having a hard time with this."

Blake rubbed her back gently and said, "It's fucking horrible. It is. War gives men an excuse to be utterly vile."

"Not only war," Alex whispered.

Anguish bloomed on Blake's face as he realized she was referring to her own experience. He held her hand as she drove. Alex didn't want to hurt him by revealing everything that had happened to her, but she felt like she'd burst if she didn't.

"The man's name was Foster. He was so good-looking. Tall, athletic, blonde hair and brown eyes. He had this sexy swagger. Every girl in school was drawn to him. We used to literally swoon when he walked by. He was a senior and I was a sophomore. When my friend Elizabeth told me he was into me, I couldn't believe it. Why? I wondered over and over. Why would he even notice me? It was like *Sixteen Candles*, which, in retrospect, is its own kind of awful. I was so fucking clueless. When he asked me out, I jumped at the chance. He picked me up in his car, took me out for burgers, and then drove me out to the trailhead down the street from my house and started making out with me. I wanted him to. I wanted to make out with him. I would've done that all day, every day, for the rest of my life. I felt so special. It was so exciting." Alex paused, feeling nauseous.

"Alex, you don't need to tell me," Blake said, his voice tortured.

"Yes, I do. I don't know why, but I do. Like I said, we

made-out for a while, but then he got aggressive, and I got scared. He ran his hand up my skirt and I told him to stop. He looked at me with this expression I can't describe. He *wanted* me to tell him to stop. It was a look of satisfaction. I still see that look on his face sometimes."

———

Alex's hand was trembling in Blake's. Her expression was bleak as she stared at the road before her. Blake didn't want to know how that man had violated her, fearing how much it would hurt to hear, but she needed to say it. It was a bloodletting, part of the healing process. He squeezed her hand for reassurance.

"When it was over, he drove me home. That was it. He stopped the car, and I opened the door and ran out. My parents made me file a report. I went to the hospital. I pressed charges. I thought my dad might actually kill him. Foster was a star player on all the high school sports teams and everyone other than my parents made *me* feel bad for dragging him through the mud. It was unbelievable. My poor parents. It aged them considerably. I can't imagine how much it hurt them to see me go through that."

"Did he serve time?"

"Of course not. He convinced the judge that he didn't understand what I wanted. They made him do community service."

"And you probably had to see him everywhere, all the time," Blake said, disgusted.

Alex nodded bleakly. "It was really hard."

"I can't believe that shit. Guys that think they own women. I fucking hate it. I'm so sorry this happened to you, Alex. You didn't deserve it."

"No, I didn't." She was quiet for a moment. Then with vehemence she said, "We will see justice this time. Justice for those girls and justice for you and your mom."

The intensity of Alex's vow deeply struck Blake.

He nodded. "Justice."

Later, when they pulled up to her house, they found Helena sitting in the sunlight on the front porch, looking at her phone. She hopped up the moment she spotted the truck pull up, her face a jumble of emotions. Blake and Alex looked at each other as Alex parked.

"Keep everything we learned today to ourselves?" Alex suggested, quietly.

Blake nodded in silent agreement. Helena had told them not to go to the VA, after all.

"Where the fuck have you guys been?" Helena accosted them as they got out of the car.

"Hi, Helena," Alex said, mustering her composure. "We were out for a drive. What's up?"

"I have an update. I did some more digging. I think you're going to want to see what I've found."

"Absolutely," Blake replied.

They escorted Helena into the house. Alex fetched a few seltzers, and they sat on the couch.

"Get this," Helena started, when they were settled. She leaned forward and spoke quietly despite the fact they were in the privacy of Alex's home. "Vinny and Dan had a business together. It was an imports and exports business by the name of Moose Trading Company. That's not strange in itself, but when you look at what they traded, or as the case may be, didn't trade, things get interesting. They never had a storefront, there were no products coming and going. They filed minimal taxes every year, but if you saw Dan's house, you'd know no one on a police salary could have afforded to build it. I couldn't understand where the money came from, so on a whim, I looked up *moose* in reference to the Vietnam War, and you won't believe what it means."

"God, what?" Alex sounded exasperated.

"A moose was Vietnamese slang for mistress. Like, a woman for an American soldier. Call me crazy, but I think that back in the seventies, maybe as late as the eighties, Dan and Vinny were trafficking women into the US as mail-order brides."

"Holy shit. Do you have any proof?" Blake whispered.

"Yeah, I'm still looking into it. There are some records of women immigrating here, all with Vietnamese names, all of whom listed a PO in box Moose Creek as their address. Guess who paid for that PO box?"

"My guess would be Vinny," Alex said miserably.

Helena nodded. "Then the women disappeared or were married off immediately. Isn't this bizarre?"

"It is. They had a fucking business," Blake said, putting it together with everything Freddie had told them. He swallowed hard.

Alex asked, "Was Dwight involved?"

"It's hard to tell. I never saw his name on anything, but I don't feel like I've gotten all the angles yet. Another thing. I heard back from the coroner. She said Caroline's wound looked suspicious, but that she can't confirm the cause of death because she wasn't the person examining the body. Sorry."

"Well, I'm sure that's reasonable," Alex said.

Helena stood to leave, and Blake said, "Thank you for all your work on this."

He put out his hand to shake Helena's. Then, he thought to ask, "Who's the DA for Hamilton County?"

"Her name is Jeanne Weathers. She's based in Lake Pleasant."

"That's a hike," Blake said. "Is she trustworthy?"

"I don't know," Helena admitted. "I've never heard anything to the contrary. We have little reason to deal with the DA usually."

Alex said, "I don't see we have much choice in the matter. It's time to act. Tomorrow, we're going to take everything we have to DA Weathers. Can you drive down with us, Helena?"

Helena thought for a moment. "Probably not. I'm on shift tomorrow. Plus, I don't know if it's a good idea. I think that you guys should take this all to her without me. Bring the lawyer you were talking about the other day. You have all the information you need to get the DA's attention focused on all this. If I go, alarm bells will sound, and the guys will go even further into coverup mode than they already are. I think they're spooked. Tomorrow should look like business as usual at the station. Do you agree?"

"Okay," Alex said, all business. "Tomorrow, we'll call our lawyer friend and hopefully get this investigation into the right hands. Can we call you on your cell or use you as a source if we need to? Or do you want us to keep you out of it?"

"Use me if you absolutely need to. I don't know if my boss is in Dan Arquette's pocket or not, and I'd hate to raise more suspicions."

"It's a plan. Thank you, Helena," Alex said. "Your work on this is amazing."

"It's my job. If you're concerned about trusting the DA, copy everything and mail it to the New York State Attorney General, too. He's notoriously hard on crimes like these. I can't believe this stuff goes on right under our noses."

"Believe it," Blake said. "We'll be in touch. Thanks again."

He shook Helena's hand again, and Alex hugged her before she left.

When they were alone again, Alex collapsed onto the sofa.

Blake sat in disbelief. These men had been running a human trafficking ring in the middle of nowhere, and no one had ever caught on, because Dan Arquette was in a role of power in the community. The Chief of Police. No one would've questioned him. He thought he was untouchable. Anger simmered in Blake's gut. Well, Dan was wrong. His time was up.

"What a crazy fucking day." Alex exhaled.

"Seriously. Are you all right?"

"No. It's insane. How could people be doing this stuff? Just think, this is one tiny place in the world. If this is going on everywhere, it's almost unimaginable the number of people who're being exploited. I can't wrap my head around it."

They sat in silence for a while. Alex shook her head and Blake regarded her, thoughtfully. Her confession on the way home had gotten way under his skin, and he didn't know how to handle it. No one had ever shared anything like that with him before. What was he supposed to say?

As a person who'd been hurt and victimized by a man in a position of power, Blake had a unique ability to empathize with Alex, but it still wasn't the same. He hesitated to bring it up with Alex, but there would always be things left unsaid if he didn't.

Mustering his bravery, Blake asked, "Can we talk about something, Alex?"

"Sure, Blake," she said, snapping out of whatever reverie she'd been in. "What's up?"

"Thank you for sharing your story with me today. It must have been hard. What happened to you was such a violation. It means your attacker felt entitled to your body. It means he thought of you as less important than himself."

Alex looked deeply uncomfortable and shifted on her chair. She folded her arms over her chest and quietly said, "I guess, but I don't even know if it's as self-aware as that."

"What do you mean?" Blake asked gently.

"I mean, I don't think he thought of me at all. He wanted something and he took it. And he derived pleasure in the taking."

"It's so sick," Blake said, feeling it in the pit of his stomach. "What leads to that kind of mindset?"

Alex breathed in and sighed. "I don't know. I've always wondered why he did it. I mean, if I was eating a sandwich, would Foster have come up and taken the sandwich out of my hands and walked away with it? Only a bully feels entitled to your stupid bologna and cheese. But Foster felt entitled to my vagina, like it was his to use. He got off on dominating me. I don't get it. I never have."

"Power dynamics combined with cruelty," Blake said. "It's the psychology of the bully to exert power over people who are smaller, weaker, or more vulnerable than them. No one else matters to them as much as they matter to themselves. That's exactly what Dwight did to me and Foster did to you. That's why the power dynamic worked in their favor. They were bigger and stronger and compelled to dominate. My question is, why?"

"I don't know," answered Alex. "And I don't know

how to change the way some men see women, other than to be the strongest woman I can be."

"You're by far the strongest woman I've ever known," Blake said.

"I don't feel particularly strong these days. I'm barely managing."

Blake thought about it. "I'm sorry about what happened upstairs at the cabin. I scared you back into your fear spiral."

"Don't be sorry. Maybe I needed to clean the wound out in order to help it heal. Maybe we both did."

"If this investigation is hitting too hard, too close to home for you, please tell me. I care too much about you to put you through something so painful."

Alex studied Blake's tortured expression. "I shouldn't have told you the details of what happened to me. I should have spared you that." Alex's face was full of remorse. "My memories were suddenly so close to the surface. I didn't mean to upset you."

"What? No, Alex," Blake said, leaning forward. He gazed at her intently. "It's not about how I feel. Not with this. Your story is a part of you, and you are a part of me. If you didn't feel comfortable telling me, that would be the travesty. Of course it's agonizing to think of what he did to you. It rips me apart inside. It's so much more personal than what I went through. But I am here for you no matter what and I want to spare you any more pain."

"A crime is a crime, Blake. What Dwight did to you is every bit as horrible as what Foster did to me. And I appreciate you wanting to spare me the details of what we're uncovering about Vinny and Dan's crimes. But I'm here for you, too. No matter what."

"Thank you, Alex." Blake kissed her.

"I'm spent, Blake. I need a nap. Or a beer," Alex said.

Then brightening, she added, "Or a swim. How about swim, Blake? What do you say?"

"I don't mean to be negative, but are you insane? The water's going to be freezing."

"The ice is gone. That's always been good enough for me. Besides, the water is cold even in the middle of July. The air temperature must be up near seventy today. Plus, it's warmer in the sun. Come on, let's do it."

Blake hesitated. His reasons for not swimming were carved into his skin. Now, he realized that he'd been missing out on yet another enjoyable experience because of Dwight's dominance over his life.

He'd trusted Alex with everything else. Why not this? "I don't know how to swim," he confessed.

She didn't laugh at him. She didn't exclaim her surprise that a sporty guy like him had never learned to swim. Instead, she met the comment with her typical compassion and understanding. He loved her even more for it. Alex looked him in the eyes and said, "You never learned because of your back, right?"

The familiar sensation of his heart tightening up in fear, in self-protection, gripped him before he could do anything about it. It was muscle memory, a reflex reaction to the pain, and he had to fight it hard.

He nodded. Then, he said, "Fuck it. Let's do it."

"You're a survivor, Blake. Your scars are just the proof."

Blake nodded again and kissed Alex on the lips.

Then, she said, "I'll teach you to swim today. No one'll be on the lake. We'll have it all to ourselves."

TWELVE

Hand in hand, they walked down Alex's street, across Main Street, and through the wide field that led to a public beach and boat access point. They carried towels, and Alex's resolve bound them to the moment. As she had anticipated, the place was deserted. They took off their clothes and stood, shivering in their underwear. She hadn't put on a swimsuit because she didn't want Blake to feel bad about not having one.

"Ready?" she asked.

"No. This is completely insane. I'm going to head back to the house and make a fire. Have fun."

He turned around and pretended to walk away, and as he did so, Alex caught sight of his back again. Although she had seen his scars during their private moments, somehow set against the fresh spring backdrop of budding trees and blue sky and the gentle sound of waves lapping against the tiny beach, the sight broke her heart all over again. The torn-up skin was its own topography, a physical record of abject human cruelty, an ever-present reminder of his past.

Alex grabbed his arm, gently spun him to face her, and threw her arms around him in a bear hug.

"You are so beautiful," she whispered into his chest, holding him close.

As she pulled away, he bent down to kiss her. Then, he smiled mischievously. "Ready or not, babe. Let's do it." Swooping her up in his arms, Blake cradled her against his chest as she kicked her legs and squirmed.

"Don't you dare drop me," Alex cried out as he ran towards the water.

"Never," he said, and she believed him.

Fearlessly, he splashed into the lake, Alex still in his arms. Goosebumps bloomed along her flesh as Blake dipped them into the frigid water, but where their bodies met, warmth remained. With her arms draped around his neck, Alex felt serene and secure and beautiful. She realized she was smiling like a lunatic.

She kissed Blake on the cheek and then wriggled free of his arms.

She dove under the water, emerging a few feet away, where she stood up. Through chattering teeth, in her most authoritative voice, Alex said, "Are you ready for your first swimming lesson?"

"Yes, Miss Taylor," Blake replied, with a mischievous grin.

"Okay. First, lean back into my arms and try to float. Let the water hold you up. You are made of water, so you should float naturally. Turn around."

Blake obeyed. He turned his back to her, held his breath, and leaned back into her arms. He howled as the cold water enveloped him. Alex laughed. It was a good thing she was strong, though, because even underwater Blake was heavy. She held his weight, admiring his trust in her, savoring the sensation of his skin against hers.

"Do you feel lighter?" she asked.

"No, but that's okay," he laughed. After a few moments of her holding him up, he stood again.

"Part of swimming is floating, but part of it is also understanding that forward momentum can propel you and keep you from going down. As long as you're moving forward, you won't sink."

"Sounds a lot like life, babe."

"I'd never thought about it, but you're right. It does. Except in life, you don't have to stand around windmilling your arms in the air." She demonstrated.

"You're cute," he said.

"Is that any way to talk to your teacher?" Alex scolded.

"No, ma'am."

"That's more like it. You try."

Once more, Blake obeyed without question, looking ridiculous.

"Okay." Alex tried hard not to laugh. "Now, if you can do that and kick at the same time, you can swim. It's shallow enough to stand here, so it's a good place to practice."

"Yes, Miss Taylor." Blake started trying to swim.

It was endearing to see him try so hard, but it was pretty dreadful.

After a while, Alex gave up. "Not bad for our first lesson," she said, trying to make him feel better.

Droplets of lake water glinted on Blake's chest like living crystals, and as he stood up rivulets streamed from the dips in his clavicles.

Beguiled, Alex swam to him, dove under the water, brushed by his legs like a fish and popped up a few feet away. She dove under again and swam as far as she could, eventually surfacing like a loon in an unexpected spot.

Blake seemed fascinated. "It looks like fun."

"You'll get the hang of it someday. Don't worry."

She dove again and swam straight for him, underwater the whole way.

When she surfaced this time, Blake said, "Alex, your lips are turning blue. You're cold. Let's get out."

"I'm not cold." She smiled through chattering teeth.

"Oh, okay," Blake mollified, leading her out of the lake by the hand, like a recalcitrant two-year-old. "I'm definitely cold. Come with me, angel."

She obeyed and wrapped herself in a towel. Shivering uncontrollably, it became clear she'd let herself get way colder than she should have. Maybe she hadn't eaten enough. She was feeling light-headed and almost tipsy. She was ready to get dressed and get warm. They walked home quietly, trying to absorb as much of the late afternoon sunshine as they could.

"Thanks for trying to teach me, Alex. Sorry I'm such a hopeless case."

"There's always hope," she returned, softly. "I'm sorry I'm not a better teacher."

For a few minutes, she walked in silence, staring down at the ground ahead of her. The emotions of the day had settled in again, and she was pensive, in addition to mildly hypothermic.

"Why so quiet?" Blake asked.

"I don't know. I'm just so sad. It's been a weird day. Blake, what's going to happen when you go back to Chicago?"

He hesitated, and Alex's heart stopped.

"With us, you mean?"

"Yeah, with us," she replied, quietly.

"I don't know. I've wondered, too. I guess I'm trying hard to be in the moment with you, Alex. But I know one thing." He stopped walking and pulled her in to face him.

Desperate longing strangled her.

"What?" she managed to squeak out.

"I know that I don't want to lose you. Whatever else happens, I don't want to lose you."

Bending down, he kissed her frozen lips. Unshed tears, barely held at bay, brimmed as she kissed him back, thankful his words could feed the unreasonable flame of hope that had kindled within her.

THIRTEEN

Back at Alex's house, they filled the tub with hot water. She undressed and slid into the tub after Blake. It was a tight fit.

"Can you move over at all?" she asked him.

"There's nowhere to go. Can you put your legs over here?"

Alex tried, then said, "I don't bend that way, unfortunately."

"This is uncomfortable," Blake said, twisting around.

Alex laughed and said, "They make it look easy in the movies."

"Here, let me perfume your hair with this scented oil," he said, in a deep, seductive voice.

"I'll rub you all over with my loofa, Blake," she returned, in her best movie star impression.

They laughed until it hurt, and once Alex warmed up sufficiently, they got out.

"That proves it once and for all," she said. "The stuff they make look sexy in the movies, actually isn't. It's awkward, if not impossible, to do it in a tub."

Blake shot her a seductive look. "Is that what you were thinking about?"

Alex's cheeks grew hot. "Maybe."

Blake chuckled. "Let's find a more suitable spot, shall we?" His gaze was full of carnal desire.

Despite the joking around, he stood ready for action. He was unstoppably sexy.

"You'll have to catch me first." Alex dropped her towel and sprinted, naked, into the hallway.

He chased her up the stairs and around the third floor until he finally caught her up in his arms like a doll, spun her around, and lay her down on the thick rug under the starry ceiling. Her cheeks were still flushed, and her wet, tangled hair stuck to her forehead, copper highlights glinting in the sunlight streaming through the windows.

He kissed her, beginning with her mouth, down over her chin, down the midline of her neck, between her breasts, and down her stomach. He stopped to stick his tongue in her belly button. Laughing, she screeched and wriggled beneath him. He continued his trajectory, holding her gaze.

"Yes?" he asked, making sure Alex was okay.

"Yes," she replied, breathing heavily.

Blake understood her body, down to her core. Ordinarily, her monkey-mind was preoccupied with a thousand little things, thoughts floating like bubbles blown into the breeze. But Blake's attention to her body grounded her in the moment, bringing her fully into their connection. The depth of her emotional investment was simultaneously terrifying and breathtaking.

Blake held her afterwards.

He rested his head on her chest and whispered, "I can't live without you anymore." He traced circles on her stomach as she stared up at the ceiling of stars. "I can't imagine going back to a time before we were together. I can't get enough of you."

"We'll figure it out. We can make it work. I know we can. I don't want to live without you anymore either, Blake. Besides, I could get used to that."

"Good," he breathed. "Me, too."

They lay together, as their heart rates settled, and their breathing calmed. Blake's eyes were closed, and in his peaceful expression Alex saw a glimmer of who Blake might have been, had Dwight not ruined everything. Had Blake ever gotten to show this vulnerable side of himself to anyone? What was he like with other people? Was he ever genuinely happy, or was the closed-off man she'd first met the one everyone had known all this time? She wanted to know everything about him.

"Tell me about your life in Chicago," she finally said, breaking the silence between them.

"What do you want to know?" Blake said, shifting onto his back and pulling her close.

"Tell me about where you live," she said.

"I live in Logan Square, which is a pretty cool spot, I guess. My place is one of those sleek, bleak new condo complexes. It's completely featureless. I guess that's what appealed to me when I bought it. I didn't want anything from the past. I was starting a new life, and that place was, and still is, a blank slate. I have very few possessions, so my décor is pretty stark. I've never wanted to feel tied to anything."

"Do you still feel that way?"

"Absolutely. I never want to be tied to my things."

"How about people?" Alex asked, unsteadily.

Hesitating, Blake replied, "I never wanted to be tied to anyone. Attachments meant the possibility of loss, which resulted in pain, and I couldn't handle any more pain. But now I feel differently. I want so much more. I want you. I want connection. I want family. Not *a family*, so to speak, but family connections. I want to feel some meaning in what I do and who I do it with."

"You don't want kids?"

"No," he said, unhesitatingly. "Never did, never will. You?"

"Nope. I'm not a mother. I can't handle the idea of little humans who rely on you for everything. It's too much. I couldn't keep myself safe. How can I keep a kid safe in this fucked-up world? Objects are easier to deal with, and I find my meaning in restoring these old places."

"I think you could do what you do successfully in any city," he said, tentatively.

Alex looked at him, fearfully contemplating the implications, although she played along for the moment.

"Lots of old buildings, I guess."

"Yes." His body tensed beside her, and his breathing changed as he anticipated her next words.

"Your job," she said. "I bet you work crazy long hours, right?"

"Yeah," he admitted.

"Weekends, of course."

"Yeah." He waited for her to finish her thought.

"Mine, too. I work hard. Sometimes too hard. But now I ask myself why. Why have I worked such a crazy schedule all this time? Because I had nothing else. Nothing, Blake. Nothing and no one, and no reason not to work. Work filled the void."

He inhaled, still tense, and looked pensive. "Me too. It's exactly the reason I took the job I have. It's so easy to put all your energy into your work when you have nothing else."

"Blake," Alex leaned up on her elbow and faced him, "I guess my question is, do we have to work so hard? What if we both detonated our lives and built one together from scratch? Someplace new? I don't know, like Maine or something. Could we do that?"

He went silent for a moment. "Jesus, I don't know." His expression grew apprehensive. "I've controlled every aspect of my life since I left Dwight's. I've worked so fucking hard to get where I am. It would be like giving up a part of myself. Plus, it would be almost impossible to find another job with a pro team. Maine doesn't even have a pro team, do they?"

"I used Maine as an example." Her enthusiasm deflated. "Besides, it was only an idea. Never mind."

"Alex, I built my entire life from nothing. So did you, I can see that. Wouldn't it be hard to give it all up for the unknown?"

"Yes, it would. Like I said, never mind. Please forget I asked. Of course you don't want to leave your life in Chicago. I'm sorry."

"Don't be sorry. I don't have an answer right now. I want us to be together. I'm not sure how yet."

"Well, I'm not sure I could live in Chicago. Or any big city, for that matter," she said, emphatically. "I would be such a fish out of water in a city. I'm a beaver, through and through."

"Alex, I'm not asking you to move to Chicago."

"Wow," she said, feeling as though the breath had been knocked from her lungs. She couldn't catch it back up. It was like drowning. Forcing herself to calm down, Alex faced the ugly truth, Blake didn't want her with him in Chicago. He wasn't asking her to come with him, and he hated it here. This really was a dead end. Realization settled in like an elephant stepping on her solar plexus. What was she thinking?

Before Blake could see how upset she was, Alex said, "Okay. I'm going to head downstairs and get dressed."

"Wait, Alex," Blake said, sitting up as she stood. "That came out wrong. It's not that I wouldn't ask you to move with me. It's that we haven't gotten there yet, and I didn't think you'd want to."

Everything went quiet. Remorse engulfed her. Why had she started this disaster of a conversation in the first place? Did she really want to give up everything she'd worked for? Of course not. So why should he? Now she had put him on the spot twice in two minutes, asking him questions neither of them was ready for.

Knowing he might've revealed his true feelings was hard to take. She wasn't used to dealing with someone else's emotions in such close proximity. Relationships weren't her strong suit. A flood of ancient insecurity rushed into her. This was a shitty situation, and she had made it infinitely worse. Now that she knew what attachment felt like, though, she knew it would be awful to be apart from Blake when this inevitably ended.

———

Alex walked away. "You should call Jacob," she said over her shoulder as she headed towards the stairs.

"I guess so," he agreed. He watched her withdraw.

She stopped and stood at the top of the stairs, ready to descend, and looked back at him for a moment. With her muscular body, her beautiful skin, and her sexy curves, she was absolutely flawless. A vision of pure feminine strength and radiance. The sadness in her face, however, destroyed Blake. He hadn't meant to hurt her. Why couldn't he tell her he'd blow up his life in Chicago for her? A big part of him wanted to, but that was insane. He wasn't ready. Neither of them was. He respected Alex enough not to lie.

"Angel," he said, softly, smiling at her.

Obviously holding back tears, she mustered a wistful smile in return and headed down the stairs.

He lay back as the emotion of the moment washed over him. The sensation was startlingly unfamiliar, as he was so unused to having an emotional tussle with a woman. It was painful and awkward. He wanted it to be easier, but of course that wasn't the way with love. He had no idea what to do and no modeling for this kind of situation. All he'd seen was how people hurt each other. He had vowed not to hurt Alex, but he also knew that any rash decisions would affect the entire trajectory of his life.

Blake needed time to think. He hadn't spent any time away from Alex in weeks—working, eating, and now sleeping side by side. Although he didn't want to be apart from her, as he found that idea painful, mightn't he need some time alone to sort things out, for perspective? Would telling her this hurt her even more? They had promised to be honest with each other, so shouldn't he tell her what he was thinking? His head spun with the confusion of it all. He had no idea what he was doing.

The whole time he spent getting dressed, he worried. Maybe he could tell Alex he was going for a drive. It sounded stupid, though, even in his head. It was too late in the evening to go for a run, but maybe he would tomorrow. Exercise was as good a reason as any to get some time away without hurting her feelings. He smiled at himself for finally figuring it out. Maybe the solution to their future relationship would happen like that—naturally, with a good amount of thinking it through.

Downstairs, he found Alex reading a book by the window. A glass of wine stood tall on the side table, the afternoon light hitting it directly, lighting it up blood-red.

"Wine's in the kitchen if you want some," she said, without looking up from her book.

"Thanks. I'm good. Do you want to be in on the call with Jacob?"

"No. You go ahead. You guys have a lot to talk about. In fact, maybe you should drive together to the DA's, and I'll get some work done tomorrow. That way, you have time alone with your dad."

"That's thoughtful, Alex," Blake replied. "Are you sure?"

"Yep. I'll start on the roof."

"No, please don't do the roof until I'm there with you. I don't like the idea of you up there all alone."

"Blake, I've been doing it alone for years. I'll be fine. Please don't worry about me."

Alex's fierce independence was one of the reasons he loved her. He didn't want to change who she was. "I wouldn't dare tell you what to do," he said, gently. "I'll go call Jacob and see if he's free."

————

Looking rather excited, Blake went to the kitchen, retrieved his phone, and headed upstairs to make the call. As Alex sipped her wine, and as Blake left, her sadness intensified. He thought everything was okay between them. Or he was pretending it was. He had taken the easy way out of being with her tomorrow. Well, to be fair, he did, and he didn't. Spending time with his biological father was a good idea. And maybe he needed some space. It was still hard to swallow. Regretfully, Alex knew she shouldn't have pushed him.

Fighting back tears wasn't easy, but she did. Fighting back the desperate heartache consuming her, however, was impossible. She would've given up everything to go and forge a new life with him somewhere neutral. But was that the best option? Why should she give up her whole world for a guy she'd only met a few weeks ago? It seemed foolish now that she contemplated it more fully. She had no experience with love or with meshing her life with another person's, and neither did Blake. It was so complicated. There was no good solution.

Moments later, he returned, exuberantly stating that Jacob would join him. They would drive to the DA's office and deliver the material together. He would also mail the package of evidence to the Attorney General of New York, and email Freddie's phone confession to them both.

"That should cover our bases," he said.

"Good." Alex tried to sound upbeat, but inside she was drowning.

They spent the remainder of the night quietly, gathering their strength for the coming Monday. Alex slept uneasily as Freddie's stories about the war came to life in her nightmares. When she finally woke up, she couldn't help but wonder how it all fit together. Like a thousand-piece puzzle of a tangled jungle and its innumerable, indistinguishable shades of green, Alex was sure the pieces would fit, but she couldn't find the connections.

The morning dawned gray and melancholy, finally allowing the wakeful Alex an excuse to get out of bed. While the coffee brewed, she put on her work clothes and ate an apple. As Blake came down, the separation between them was obvious and painfully uncomfortable. The unfamiliarity of an attachment sundered, whether temporarily or otherwise, was beyond her realm of experience.

"I'm going for a quick run." He left before she could ask any questions.

Standing alone with two coffees, in the middle of her kitchen, Alex was stunned.

"Fuck it," she spat, letting anger subsume her sadness.

She left his cup of coffee on the breakfast bar, along with a note that said, *Good luck today*.

At the camp, she set up the ladder, perched herself on the roof, and started prying off shingles. It was the end of May, and the black flies were coming out. A copious layer of bug spray formed a veritable oil slick on her body beneath her long-sleeved shirt and a baseball cap, but it didn't prevent the occasional fly from finding its way onto her skin for a meal. By the time she realized they were biting her, it was too late.

By noon, she was pissed off, covered in bites, and had only stripped three quarters of the roof. It was going to be a long day. She climbed down the ladder, ate a quick sandwich, and clambered back up. The black flies would only be worse tomorrow. Furiously, she finished stripping the shingles, started laying the roof felt, and then began re-shingling.

Around three, between blasts of her nail gun, she heard the distinct sound of a vehicle on the road. It didn't sound like Blake's car. It sounded more like a truck. Her heart froze. Out of instinct, she pulled up the ladder and balanced it across the chimney. She crouched on the far side of the roof, straddling a dormer. Cradled in one arm, she held her nail gun, and with her other hand she held her phone, ready to face any motherfucker that might show up. She had a distinct feeling, however, that she knew exactly which motherfuckers it would be. She was right.

A black pickup crunched up amidst a billow of gravel dust, and out of it stepped Dan Arquette and Vinny. They looked around for a moment but didn't notice her. Her truck was parked out of sight on the other side of the house. They wandered onto the porch, went inside, checked the scene, and headed back out. The sound of the screen door slapping the frame made her jump. Her subconscious, which kept a running to-do list, took a mental note—fix the screen door.

Steadying herself, she set her phone to silent, snapped a few pictures of the truck, and then a few of the men. Thankfully, they still hadn't noticed her. Then, at Dan's gesture, Vinny got a can of gasoline from the back of the truck and headed toward the camp. Alex's heart froze as she switched her phone from camera mode to video.

Holy shit. They're going to torch the fucking place so that Blake has no reason to be here. They want him gone. She kept videoing Vinny with the gas can as he stopped to talk to Dan and then realized that she needed to get off the roof before he lit the place up.

After mustering her courage, Alex shouted, "Put the fucking gas can down, asshole."

Vinny and Dan actually looked around themselves like slapstick cartoon characters, to the left, then to the right, then to the left again before they thought to look up. The sight of her aiming the nail gun at his heart froze Vinny in his tracks. Dan, however, moved forward slightly.

"Well, hello there, Miss Taylor. Would you mind getting down, please? We'd love to have a little conversation."

"Tell your gas man to put the napalm back in the truck, and we'll see about it."

"Vin, put it back."

Vinny did as he was told, scowling all the while.

"There. Now you can come on down and we will talk like nice, normal people. We have a couple questions for you."

"Questions for me? I don't have anything to say to you guys." She kept her voice steady. "What do you want with me?"

"You heard me," Dan said. "We want to go for a little ride and ask you some questions."

"Well, you can fuck off, then. I'm not going anywhere with you two." Alex, still perched atop one of the dormer windows, readjusted her aim at Vinny. "This is private property, and you are trespassing."

"Then call the cops, sweetheart."

"I already did." She brandished her phone.

"Bullshit. There's no cell reception here and you know it."

Her heart was racing. Dan had called her bluff, and she was terrified. "You guys should spend more time covering your tracks than committing new crimes," she spat.

It was a stab in the dark, but it was all she had.

"What are you talking about, Alex?" Dan's tone was low and dangerous, his eyes narrowed.

"I'm talking about you and your crime ring. You trafficked Vietnamese women into the country for mail order brides. You covered up the fact that Dwight Anderson killed his wife. You committed enough horrible crimes in Vietnam to lock your ass up for the next three hundred years. You should be more interested in saving your own skin at this point than asking me any stupid questions. Get the fuck out of here."

She used her free hand to make sure her phone was recording video of Dan's response.

"You can't prove any of those claims you made, honey. Now come on down and play nice."

"No, I don't think I will. And actually, I do have proof. Dwight kept a folder about you guys and all your awful shit. In the folder, he confessed to killing Caroline, showed evidence of your illicit business, and had photographs of all the horrible shit you did in Nam. Blake is with the DA right now, handing it all over. Game's up, asshole."

Dan Arquette looked at Alex with deepening malice. His soul was utterly black. Before her was the face of an extremely dangerous man and she needed to watch her step.

"You're lying," he said. "Dwight didn't give a shit about anybody but himself. You're bluffing."

"Whatever. Wait and see. He had a box under his kitchen sink, with all sorts of info on you and your little lap dog there." She gestured to the glowering Vinny. "Dwight had been collecting evidence of your crimes for years, in case he needed it. You're finally going to pay for everything."

"Vinny, on second thought, torch the place. This little girl is lying about Dwight, but I think I know where she got her info."

And with that, Dan Arquette got into the truck. Vinny grabbed the gas can from the tailgate and lumbered toward the camp once more. Alex, who had maintained relative calm up to this point, fired the nail gun at Vinny's leg. Thank God she had tricked out the safety mechanism on the nail gun.

He howled in pain, "You fucking bitch!"

"Dump out a drop of that gas and you'll get it between the eyes, asshole." She shot him again, this time in the arm. "I have excellent aim."

He dropped the gas can and got into the truck. She

could see Dan yelling at Vinny and gesturing to the camp. Then he seemed to give up and change his mind, and they sped away.

Alex succumbed to the terror she had so bravely held at bay. She had no idea how she was going to get away, to get safe, but at least she wouldn't be burned alive. She needed to get to Helena as fast as she could. Once she was sure the men's truck was gone, she shakily clambered back down the ladder, got into her truck, locked the doors, and sped back to town. Her whole body was shuddering from the adrenaline charging through her veins. Queasy and light-headed, she was terrified she was going to pass out. *Just drive. Just fucking drive.*

She pulled up to the police station and ran inside, praying Helena was there. She was.

"Jesus, Alex. Are you okay?"

With eyebrows raised and eyes wide, Helena looked shocked to see her friend burst through the doors in such panic.

Alex's hair was a wild mess, her face betrayed her terror, and she trembled from head to toe as she tried to explain to Helena what had happened.

"You are not going to believe this shit. I've got the video to prove everything I'm about to tell you. Vinny and Dan tried to set Blake's camp on fire, with me on the roof."

"What?"

"Look at this."

Alex texted Blake the video of the horrible encounter, in case something happened to it or to her before she could show him. Her hands were shaking so badly she almost dropped the phone. Then she showed it to Helena, who watched in horror and slammed both hands on her desk.

"That's fucking it. He was literally going to set you on fire. What a complete psychopath. I'm going to arrest him right now. Listen to me, Alex. You need to get somewhere safe. Go to Ricky's and wait for me. Do not leave until I come back for you. Do you understand?"

"Yes. Please be careful."

"Always."

The women left together, got into their separate vehicles and drove away.

Alex's phone buzzed, scaring the living daylights out of her. It was Blake.

"Alex? Oh, my God. Are you okay?"

"Yes."

"I saw that crazy video. What the fuck happened?"

"I'll explain it when I see you. Where are you?"

"Twenty minutes away. Where are you?"

"I'm heading to Ricky's. Helena told me to wait there because it's public and I'll be safe."

"Jesus. You sure you're okay?" Blake's voice was desperate.

"I am."

"I'll get to you as fast as I can, Alex. I'll meet you at Ricky's."

"Thank you, Blake. Drive safely."

As she pulled up to Ricky's, though, her thoughts turned to Freddie. In all the insanity of the afternoon, she had forgotten his role in all this. Her stomach seized up as she remembered mentioning his photographs to Dan, and even though she'd said they were Dwight's, Dan had somehow known she was lying. He knew it was Freddie who'd given him away. Putting Freddie into extreme danger drove Alex deeper into panic. She prayed she was wrong.

She stormed into the pizza joint and marched through,

to the bar out back. "Have you guys seen Freddie?" she called.

"Not today."

"Did you see him yesterday?"

"Come to think of it, it's been a few. Why? Is everything okay?"

"No, everything is not okay," Alex snapped. "There has been some awful shit going on in this town for the past thirty years and no one has done anything about it. Now I think Freddie is in danger and I need to take care of him. He doesn't deserve for Dan Arquette and Vinny Frazier to set him on fire."

With that, she dashed out the door, got back in her truck, and sped to Freddie's house. His tiny shack of a cabin was set back in the woods, far enough out of town to be a long walk home on a cold night after drinking himself stupid. How many nights like that had there been, when this man had drowned his sorrows, guilt, and fear in plain view of an entire town of silent bystanders? Alex was furious.

When she pulled up, Dan's truck was parked outside Freddie's shack. Her heart beat rapidly, like a wild animal sensing the danger ahead. She knew full well she was walking right into the middle of a clusterfuck. This time, she didn't even have a nail gun. After pulling out her phone once more, she texted Helena, praying the reception was good enough to send it.

Dan's here at Freddie's. Shit is going down. Bring guns.

Beating back panic, she turned off her truck, stealthily snuck around the side of the building, and looked in through the grimy window. Freddie was sitting at a table, and Vinny and Dan were circling him like predators, yelling and shaking their fists. Dan leaned forward and punched poor Freddie in the face. The old man crumpled to the floor. Vinny picked him up and hit him again. Alex videoed the brutal scene for a moment, but she had to intervene.

She crept into the camp through the backdoor, grabbed a cast iron skillet from the stove, and stole forward toward the front room where all the action was. Peeking around the doorframe, she scanned the space. Dan was closest to where she stood, with Vinny to his right. Their backs were to her, and they eclipsed her view of Freddie, who sat at an old Formica table. At the other side of the room there lay a ratty couch and a wood stove. Terror clawed at her chest, but she couldn't let Freddie suffer for telling her the truth. She needed to put an end to the madness.

Then Dan took a gun from a holster concealed beneath his jacket and held the barrel to Freddie's head.

"I should've put you out of your misery long ago, old man. You're the only one left to link us to all that stuff in Nam, so it must have been you. You're the canary. You told that girl about everything."

"No, Dan, I didn't. I never betrayed you guys. All your sins are your own." Freddie's voice sounded strong, and if he was scared, he didn't let it show.

"You were complicit in all of it, don't you ever forget that. No one will be surprised that you finally killed yourself, 'cause that's what it'll look like. Like you finally had enough and did it. Any last words, old buddy?" Dan's tone was mocking and cruel.

"You've always been a bastard, Dan."

"Nice, Freddie. Very eloquent." Dan kept the gun leveled at Freddie's head.

Alex burst through the doorway and swung the cast iron pan into Dan's arm with all her strength. The gun went off, but the bullet hit the table. The weight of the pan, coupled with the momentum she'd built up by rushing forward, knocked her off balance. Struggling to regain her footing slowed her down long enough for Vinny to grab her from behind. She swung the skillet backwards and hit him squarely on the head, with a sickening crack. His grip loosened as he slumped to the floor. She spun around to find that Dan had retrieved his gun and taken a few steps back in the small room.

"You're a real pain in the ass, Alex. I deeply regret not killing you earlier when I had the chance. Didn't anyone tell you not to go digging up the past around here?"

"I believe I was told that dead horses like to stay dead, actually."

"Well, you should've listened."

Malevolence glinted in Dan's eyes as he turned the gun on Alex, aiming straight for her heart. Being confronted with the distinct possibility of death was surreal. She didn't know what to do. Time seemed to slow down and stretch out as her perceptions sharpened.

Then, from somewhere deep within her core self, the most shocking emotion arose. She had expected fear or sadness or regret. Instead, she was taken with a sudden swell of gratitude in the midst of all the chaos. Gratitude for having experienced something of love before she died. Thinking of Blake brought a lump to Alex's throat and a smile to her lips.

She steeled herself with that gratitude as she ferociously stared down the barrel of Dan Arquette's handgun.

FOURTEEN

Jacob and Blake had been having an interesting day together, until Alex's text gate-crashed the party. The DA had quietly examined the evidence, considering their story with an expression of ill-controlled fury. As she simmered to a boil, she informed them that they had given her all the information she would need to begin an investigation of Dan Arquette and company. Feeling incredibly successful, the father and son had grabbed a burger for lunch and driven back to Edison, chatting about their lives and discovering that they enjoyed each other's company. They were starting to get to know each other.

When they pulled over to watch the video of Alex fending off Dan and Vinny, they came together as a new force. Blake's wild, protective anger and Jacob's analytical, intellectual powers were instantly charged with the task of ensuring Alex's safety. Blake sped the last fifteen miles back to Edison, desperate to see her.

Blake had barely parked the car before he jumped out

and ran into Ricky's. After bursting into the restaurant, he scanned the place for Alex.

Then he sprinted to the back and asked the room at large, "Where is she?"

"Alex went to Freddie's," Stan replied.

"Where the fuck is that?"

"Just down the street a bit, son. Take it easy. Freddie's a good man. He's not about to steal your girl."

"Maybe not, but Dan Arquette might try. I need an exact address. Where is she?" He was growing more agitated with every second.

Jacob followed Blake into the bar a moment later, trying to make sense of what was happening.

"Where is she, Blake? She was supposed to wait here."

"She *was* supposed to wait here, but she didn't," Blake said, a flurry of panic blinding him.

Knowing Alex had left a place of relative safety only to throw herself into extreme danger, Jacob and Blake sprang once more to action. With directions to Freddie's, they sprinted back to the car and peeled out. Blake's hands were sweaty, barely able to grip the steering wheel, and his heart was racing.

Only that morning, he had unceremoniously walked out on Alex and gone for a run, offering no explanation. She, in turn, had left him a terse note and a cold cup of coffee. They hadn't even said goodbye. After their uncomfortable conversation last night, a schism had formed between them, and Blake desperately needed to put things back together. He wanted her. He needed her. Nothing else in the universe mattered, yet he was powerless to mend the rift.

Alex was so good at putting things back together, but Blake could only tear them apart. A monstrous guilt arose within him, consuming him. This wasn't who he wanted to be. Alex had only been trying to figure out a solution to the problem of them living far away from each other after Blake had told her he couldn't live without her. Hadn't he been the first one to say I love you?

That love now gripped his heart with fear for Alex's safety. His hands shook with fury as he gripped the steering wheel even harder, plowing forward into the unknown. One thing was crystal clear, he would fucking kill Dan Arquette if he hurt one hair on Alex's precious head.

He pounded the steering wheel in frustration. "Fuck."

"Calm down, Blake. We need to keep calm."

"Listen. Alex is in mortal danger. You saw what Dan is capable of. We need to get there. I need to help her."

"I know. Don't kill us on the way, though, because that won't help anybody," Jacob said.

They sped out of town and skidded onto the dirt road Freddie's camp was on. There was Alex's truck parked to the side, and Dan's truck parked right up front.

"Jesus, they're all here," Blake breathed.

The nightmare was already unfolding inside without him. He was too late.

He parked and scrambled out of the car and up the porch steps, in time to hear a gunshot and Alex's blood-curdling cry. He froze. His heart stopped. *No!* His chest felt like it caged a wild tiger, clawing at its confines. *Please don't let her be hurt.*

He erupted through the front door to find Dan still holding the gun, pointing it at Alex. Alex and Freddie were in a heap on the floor across the room, covered in blood. Blake's entrance had startled Dan, who turned, shifting his aim to Blake's heart. On autopilot, Blake roundhouse kicked the gun out of Dan's hand and surged forward. He punched Dan in the face, knocking him out cold.

In that moment, through the commotion, the sirens of Helena's police car sounded. As she pulled up, Jacob ran back out to tell her what had happened and that she should radio for the medics. Inside, Blake leaped over Dan's limp body and rushed to Alex, trying to make sense of what he was seeing, all the while praying she was okay.

Sobbing and covered in blood, Alex held the lifeless body of Freddie Cormack. His cloudy blue eyes were open wide, frozen in an expression of shock. His withered, weathered face had drained of color, contrasting starkly with the livid crimson river spilling from his chest.

"No. No. God. Oh, Freddie." Alex wailed, rocking back and forth with Freddie cradled in her arms.

"Jesus," Blake whispered, trying to suppress his blazing panic.

"I tried to help him, but he threw himself in front of me. Oh, Blake, I'm so sorry I couldn't help him. I'm so sorry. I was too late." Alex cried, racked with emotion. They hadn't been able to stop Dan from committing this one final act of cruelty.

Crouching, Blake reached forward to feel for a pulse. Finding none, he closed Freddie's eyelids. He knelt powerless before Alex, with Freddie's body contorted between them, until Helena came in.

"Goddamn it," she muttered.

She felt for a pulse on Freddie's neck but gave up when she found none. She pulled out handcuffs from her back pocket and cuffed the groggy Dan Arquette. She repeated the process for Vinny.

"What a fucking disaster," she said.

She looked down at Alex, who now met her gaze.

"I couldn't save him."

"I see that." Helena took off her police cap, rubbed her head and put her cap back on. "I thought I told you to go to Ricky's."

"You did. Are you in with these fuckers?" Alex screamed, wild with rage and sadness. "Tell me."

Helena hesitated, looking hurt. "No, Alex. I've had a feeling for years that there'd been a lot of corruption in the past, but until you came around asking questions and stirring shit up, I didn't know for sure. Then once I started putting pieces together, it all added up. I helped you guys the best I could, but I still need to have a job in the morning, you know?"

"I know but look at Freddie. He's dead now, Helena. He's dead. He threw himself between Dan's gun and my body, or this would be me on the floor and my blood spilled, my life ebbing out of me."

"Fuck, I'm sorry, Alex. I'm so sorry. I should have known sooner. I should've started digging ages ago. I had no idea it would end up like this, though."

The backup unit and medics showed up, cutting through the emotional moment. They checked Freddie's body for vital signs, and finding none, they left the scene untouched for the investigators.

Alex was wrecked. Jacob, however, was a practical man. He had called the DA, who was on her way. She would meet them at the station to question Dan and Vinny, who were finally regaining consciousness. Dan's expression, as he blearily grasped the circumstances, was one of furious resignation. It was clear that he knew his time was up.

———

Reluctant to release Freddie's lifeless body, Alex resisted as Blake and Helena tried to help her up. Separating from him seemed so final. If she could hold him for a little while longer, wouldn't he come back?

Eventually, Blake coaxed her to her feet, and with soothing words he led her to the kitchen. Together at the sink, they washed her crimson hands. Freddie's blood mixed with the stream of water, swirling pink against the stained, cracked porcelain as it swirled down the drain. Feeling disconnected from her own body, Alex almost passed out at the sight of it. Diluted and powerless, it was the remains of her vain effort to save a lost soul.

In her strain to remain upright, she diverted her gaze to the other objects in Freddie's home. His pots and pans. The tattered, yellowing wallpaper. The shabby surroundings he wore like a hair shirt. Why? Because he thought he deserved to suffer. *Poor Freddie. Poor Freddie.*

"Let's get these assholes down to the station," Helena said to the other cops, looking disgusted.

They helped Helena walk the groggy, cuffed men to the cruiser, all the while reading them their rights. Helena returned, looped her thumbs through her heavy belt and assessed Alex.

"What?" Alex asked, in annoyance, feeling dazed and spent.

"I need to take your statement down at the station. Do you think you can make it?"

The cop's gentle tone was so unfamiliar, so incongruous to the Helena Alex knew that Alex involuntarily frowned. The pity on Helena's face and in Blake's gaze sickened her. She wanted no part of it and the rejection emboldened her.

"Fuck yeah," Alex replied, her feistiness returning in force. "I want to see those bastards serve time."

"This has been one crazy ride, you two. Can't say I won't be happy to put it all in the past." Helena shook her head as she walked out.

"Jacob, do you mind driving my car? I'm going to drive Alex." Blake stood tall, looking mammoth in the tiny house.

Jacob, looming every bit as large and twice as uncomfortable replied, "Sure, Blake. See you at the station."

Blake tossed his dad the keys and took Alex around the waist to lead her out.

"Don't." She swatted his hand. "I'm fine. I can walk myself out."

She had managed this long on her own. Blake's offer of help now just made Alex mad. Without a further backwards glance at the devastation, Alex strode out the door and down the steps, alone.

———

Chalking it up to Alex's shock and the harrowing experience she had faced utterly alone, Blake tried not to take her off-putting tone personally. Alex drove the mile to the station, in silence.

When they arrived, she got out of the truck, slammed the door behind her, kicked the tire and screamed, "Fuck. Why are people so awful? Why did Dan have to kill him? What was he thinking? I don't get it."

Blake stood by, in silent solidarity, while Alex raged and pounded the hood of her truck. He desperately wanted to join her, but if he let loose with his feelings now, he would never regain control. She could scream for both of them.

Finally, Alex collected herself once more, took a deep

breath and strode into the police station, where Helena was waiting to take her statement.

The DA showed up moments later. "Mr. Anderson, Mr. Blackwell. Long time no see." She shook their hands, her expression grave. Then, noticing Alex, her eyes widened. "You must be Alex. You've been through it today, from what I understand. I'm sorry to hear about the man who was killed," she added, examining Alex's bloodstained clothes. "Let's get these assholes locked up for good. Looks like they've deserved it for decades."

"My pleasure," Alex said.

Since the station was comprised of a single large room, the DA sat Vinny across from her at the far desk. Therefore, Alex and Blake overheard everything as they patiently awaited their turns to provide statements. Jeanne Weathers was a hard-ass, and by the time the sun set, she had squeezed out a full confession from Vinny, offering him a plea deal if he spilled everything about Dan Arquette's criminal actions spanning the past five decades. Vinny was only too happy to try and save himself, and since he wasn't the one who had pulled the trigger on Freddie or tried to set Alex on fire, he was an extremely helpful witness.

Dan had immediately demanded his attorney, who arrived and conferred with his client in his cell. When they received a copy of Vinny's confession, coupled with the evidence at Freddie's house and the video of Dan telling Vinny to set Dwight's cabin on fire, the attorney must have whispered to Dan that he didn't have a leg to stand on. Dan reluctantly told the DA everything.

First, he confessed to killing the old man to keep him quiet. Freddie had known everything Dan and Vinny had done in the war, and although they never brought him into their business stateside, he had been suspicious of their actions. When Helena had come asking questions, Dan immediately suspected Freddie of divulging their secrets. Freddie had known enough to see Dan put away for good. Alex had gotten in the way right as everything had gone down.

When Weathers questioned Dan about his dealings with Dwight in Vietnam, he grew somber. He told a tale of exploitation and crime, admitting that Dwight had run a human trafficking racket back then, and that he and Vinny had been Dwight's henchmen. He said he'd made enough contacts in Vietnam to continue trafficking women long after the war, and no one ever suspected a thing. He said Dwight had continued with contacts in the states, but after a few years he didn't want to do the work anymore. He wanted out. Dan paid him off, but it wasn't enough. He started blackmailing them, threatening to expose their illegal dealings, promising to ruin Dan's career and marriage by disclosing his past violence in Vietnam.

In exchange for Dwight's silence, Dan had covered up all the accusations against Dwight for violent domestic crimes, including the murder of his wife. Dan paid Dwight a handsome sum in bribe money over the years.

When DA Weathers asked about Caroline, Dan shook his head and said, "Of course Dwight killed her. The bastard killed her in cold blood and didn't even bother to hide it. We covered it all up. You have to understand, I knew he'd ruin me if I didn't do everything he asked. He even threatened to kill my wife and kids if I didn't protect him. Vin and me might be bastards, but Dwight was the king."

As Blake overheard Jeanne Weathers question Dan, and the explicit confession he gave to covering up Caroline's murder, Blake's body responded involuntarily. His hands shook with fury as he absorbed Dan's cold description of her death. This man didn't care that he'd ruined countless lives and aided a violent psychopath. He only cared that he'd been caught.

But Blake's true anger could now rest squarely on Dwight. The man had murdered his wife. Blake had finally routed out the truth for his mother and could now begin to transcend his own rage at the past. Maybe his mom would rest in peace now, knowing that some form of justice would finally be served.

Then Blake pictured Freddie lying dead in Alex's arms, and his heart constricted again. He was desperately sorry that discovering the truth had to be at the cost of poor Freddie's life. Without Freddie's taped confession and the incriminating photographs he'd carried around for five decades, they wouldn't have had much of a case. But Freddie's betrayal of Dan and Vinny had been the tipping point. Dan had become sloppy and irrational, gripped by fear that their actions would finally be revealed. Dan had decided to kill Freddie to tie up loose ends. He had gone to Dwight's camp to ascertain how much information Blake had, never expecting to see Alex. His idea of setting the place on fire had seemed like a good way to solve the problem of having Blake and Alex sniffing around asking questions, digging up the past. Dan had figured if Blake was gone because the camp was demolished, everyone would stop snooping around. Dan never expected Alex to be in either of the places he'd headed that day. It was uncanny.

Afterwards, Alex and Blake gave full statements to the DA. The entire process took hours. By the time they were done, DA Weathers assured them they had nothing to worry about. With the confessions in place, Dan would serve the rest of his life in prison, and despite Vinny's plea deal, he would still do a good chunk of time.

Blake and Alex left the station in a daze. The stars hung in the sky, twinkling peacefully overhead as though nothing had happened. It was time to get the exhausted Alex home.

Although Blake had been beside her for hours, she was on an island—isolated, emotionally too far away to reach. He understood. When his own pain had grown too deep over the years, he'd walled himself off from all emotional contact as a matter of survival. Alex was traumatized by Freddie's death and Blake feared she would push him away in response. Panic swelled in him once more, for he didn't know how to stop her from slipping away. He needed to pull her back to him now, or he would lose her forever.

"Alex, I'm not going to insult you by asking if you're okay. I know you're not. I also won't try to tell you something comforting, because nothing on earth will touch the pain you're in. What I will say is this, when I heard that gunshot today, I thought I'd lost you. I died in that moment. My heart stopped, I swear. The thought of losing you was too much to bear. Please, angel. Please don't leave me now."

"Blake, I'm not going anywhere. What are you talking about?" Alex's voice was thin and exasperated.

"I'm talking about the separation between us since last night when I was too selfish to tell you what I now know I should've said. I'll go anywhere and do anything with you, Alex. I never, ever want to feel like that again."

"Like what?"

"Like the better half of my heart had been ripped out of me. I love you, Alex. And that love means I'll do anything for you. Name it."

"Okay. Take me home."

Blake looked into her face. Bone-tired and bereft, she

still managed a weak smile. Her clothes had long since gone stiff with Freddie's dried blood. She had faced violence and death and had come out on the side of the living, but only by a crazy twist of fate. Freddie's sacrifice had scarred her in the way that only loving and losing can scar someone. But she would be okay. After all, Alex was the strongest person he had ever met.

She tossed Blake her keys, and for the first time since they'd met, he drove her truck.

He took her home.

FIFTEEN

A lex was almost catatonic, as the adrenaline-fueled action of the day ebbed away. Blake brought her home, led her upstairs, undressed her and guided her into the shower, leaving her side only long enough to take her blood-soaked clothes downstairs and put them in a garbage bag. They were beyond saving.

After returning, he scrubbed Freddie's sacrificial blood from Alex's skin and hair and dressed her in sweatpants and a sweatshirt. He made her a fire and fed her a bowl of hot soup. Although she ate little of it, he was satisfied she'd at least eaten something. As he fed her, Alex stared into the fire.

Blake was acutely aware of how the tables had turned. His whole life, Blake had carried the pain of his mother's death alone. Today, however, his quest for the truth had spiraled out into the universe and had cost a life. It had also cost Alex her peace of mind. For now. He would see her through it.

The revelations of the day had also precipitated another outcome. Blake had finally been able to release the burden he had always carried. It was as though the experience had followed the First Law of Thermodynamics—energy in a closed system can be neither created nor destroyed—but it can be transformed. Grief and pain, which had gripped him so tight for so long, had slipped away so easily when replaced by the truth. He was so thankful to Alex for her deep bravery and for her willingness to throw herself into his fight without a thought for her own safety.

She fell asleep before the dying embers of the fire. Blake took a moment to call his dad.

"Jacob, I wanted to call and say thank you for your help today."

"Nothing to thank me for, son. Is Alex okay?"

"No," Blake said, rubbing his face, "but she will be. I hope."

"She's fierce. I have every confidence she'll be better in time. Did you tell her how you feel?"

"I did. Thank you for your advice. Talking to you on our trip today helped me see things more clearly."

"Take it from someone who loved a woman, only to lose her to my own fear and insecurity. I never want you to make the same mistake. I was lucky and got a second chance at love, but not everyone is so fortunate."

Blake got off the phone and found himself deeply thankful for the gift of his real father. They may not know each other well and they may not end up best friends, but Jacob was an honest, kind man. Alex was still asleep on the sofa when Blake returned, so he carried her upstairs, put her to bed, and lay next to her. Sleep took him soon after and he dreamed of a tall, white lighthouse set upon a cliff beside a calm, sapphire sea.

In another first, Blake awoke before Alex. In the dim light of her bedroom, Alex's face was lovely in repose. Her eyelids fluttered. Her skin was drained of color. Her beauty was so natural he could stare at her all day. When Alex stirred, she slowly awoke into a blissful, blank mindscape before the crash of memories folded in on her. Blake knew that liminal moment well, for in the interstice between dreams and consciousness had always lay this beloved moment of peace. He had cherished that moment all his life, and recognizing it, he now capitalized on it. He would fill Alex's heart with as much of his love as he could before she remembered everything from the day before.

She woke to Blake's warm, loving smile.

"Good morning, angel." He kissed her forehead.

She blearily smiled back at him, still ensconced in the gossamer threads of her dreams. Blake was banking on it.

"I dreamed of a lighthouse last night, Alex. It seemed to be calling me, this beautiful beacon slicing through so much darkness. Who knows, maybe it's a sign. Can I take you on a trip to Maine?"

Alex was still smiling. "That sounds great, Blake."

"I love you, Alex. I love you."

"I love you, too, Blake."

Then Alex's face darkened as reality's dreadful weight settled upon her, a furrow creasing her brow. Her tranquility dissipated like morning's mist in sunlight, replaced by anguish. Crushed as all her memories surfaced at once, she let out a cry of pain and closed her eyes again.

"Come here, babe. Let yourself feel it. I'm here. It's okay."

———

Alex wept as Blake held her close. His heat filled her with comfort, her desperate scrabble for survival the day before having left her bereft. She cried into his chest, balling her fists as the raw power of fresh grief charged through her, scraping her emotional energy down to the quick.

Still, Blake held her and whispered, "It's okay. You're so strong, Alex. You'll get through this. You're like the heartwood you told me about. You're forged so much stronger than you know."

"Oh, Blake," she sobbed, "I don't know about that."

"You're the strongest person I've ever known. You've struggled for survival and won. You'll get through this, too, in time."

When all her tears had come and gone, Alex was drained. Nestled in Blake's embrace, she never wanted to leave. The scent of him bolstered her as she sought strength in his presence. Then the disconnect they had been struggling with only twenty-four hours ago surfaced once more between them. She needed him to understand how she had felt the day before.

"When you ran out the door yesterday without saying goodbye, it was like you'd slapped me across the face. I couldn't believe it. It hurt so much. I know you need to run, and we can all use space sometimes, but considering our conversation the night before, it felt like you were running away. From me."

"I'm so sorry, Alex. I regretted it all day. I didn't think about it before I left, and I should have. All I could think about was running as hard as I could, as fast as I could. I needed to feel my body's power, to push myself, so that I could clear my head. I should have said goodbye. I should've come over to you and held you and told you I love you before I left. All I could think about all day was that I was an asshole for not saying goodbye. Then you sent me that video and I thought, if I never saw you again the last memory I have of us is the look on your face when

I left. The look of betrayal. It killed me. I couldn't have lived with myself if you had died. I'm so thankful you're here with me right now and I never want to let you go. I am so thankful to Freddie. I promise to be the best man I can be to honor his sacrifice. To honor you."

"Thank you, Blake. I appreciate the apology, but we're still back at the place we started. Nothing has changed. We still need to figure out what we want, where we want to be, and if we want to be together."

———

Frozen, Blake stared at her, praying she wasn't going to leave him.

But instead of saying so, he forced himself to ask, "What do you need?" His voice was barely audible.

"I don't know. I think I'm going to drive up to my parents' house today, to clear my head. I think they deserve to hear about yesterday in person rather than over the phone. Besides, I need to see them after everything that's happened."

"I understand. Do you want me to come?"

"No," she replied, miserably. "I need some time alone to think."

Blake tried his hardest to be courageous but knew he was losing the battle. She might be leaving him for good, and he didn't know what to do. He was a panicked child again. His mother had died, and he was all alone in the world.

No! Never again. "Alex, whatever you say, wherever you go, I'm going to love you. Take the time you need, but I'll be waiting for you when you get back."

"Thank you, Blake."

Less than an hour later, she set out for Lake Placid to

see her folks. Blake was left alone with his reeling mind. Unable to sit still, he went for a long run, cleaned Alex's house, searched the Internet for jobs in Maine, and went for another run. The trouble was his thoughts were choking him. Fear was overriding his common sense. He couldn't settle to anything. It was going to be a long day.

Eventually, he called Sal to tell her everything. Grateful to finally know the truth of her sister's death, she sobbed throughout the revelation. Then she grew furious that it had taken decades and an innocent man's murder to see justice served.

"I can't believe that man died saving Alex," Sal said.

"It was horrible. I'm having a really hard time accepting any of it and I was there."

"I'm so thankful Alex is okay. She's an incredible person."

"She honestly is, Sal. I thank my lucky stars she survived yesterday. I hope she still wants to be with me." His voice betrayed his desperation.

"Why wouldn't she want to be with you?"

"It's a long story, but we had a fight before this all went down. We hadn't made-up yet and then the shit hit the fan."

"Did you tell her how you feel?" Concern radiated from Sal's voice.

Unsure how to deal with her genuine empathy, Blake paused. "I did. I love her."

"One thing I know for sure, she's good for you, Blake."

"I know she is. Jesus, Sal. This is completely unfamiliar territory. I have no idea what I'm doing."

"You have to start somewhere. Have faith in her. Listen to her. Keep your heart open. She'll come around."

"God, I hope so. Listen, I gotta' go. See you soon, Sal."

"Call if you need anything at all. And thank you for finding out the truth. I love you, Blake."

He only hesitated a moment. "I love you too, Aunt Sal."

———

Alex drove the hour to her parents' craftsman-style lake house set outside the cutest town in the Adirondack Park. When they bought it in the eighties, they had never dreamed that they'd be sitting on a goldmine years later. The house was full of the kind of period detail that had germinated Alex's early love of architecture and antiques. It was a lovely place set on the quiet side of Lake Placid, where it was actually still placid.

As Alex drove through the familiar mountains, her heart grew lighter. Going home to the people who had always loved her most in the world would help. They would know what to say. They would know what to do. And their relationship, with all its flaws and tensions over the years, had withstood the test of time. She could look to them for some sorely needed guidance.

"Alex?" her mother gasped when she opened the door.

"Sorry I didn't call. Sort of a spur-of-the-moment trip."

"Something's happened, baby. What's going on?"

Her mother's look of concern had always made her uncomfortable. It was part of why she had learned to put up a stolid, strong front early in her life. Her father, however, always had the opposite effect on her. As he rounded the corner to see who was at the door, Alex burst into tears.

"Come in, come in," he said.

"Sorry. I'm okay. It's good to see you guys. I've got a

lot to tell you." Alex walked through the house and sat in the airy kitchen.

Years ago, her dad had remodeled the back half of the place, opening the kitchen and dining room so the whole space overlooked a wide deck with the lake and mountains beyond, through picture windows and French doors. It was Alex's favorite part of the house.

Her mother didn't even bother to ask if she preferred coffee or tea. She made a fresh pot of coffee and poured Alex a cup, adding sugar and milk, and sat next to her. Her dad stood across the marble island, trying not to look concerned and failing spectacularly.

"I've had an interesting couple of weeks. I've met someone and I like him, and we've been investigating his mother's death, and we uncovered a crime-ring, and I was almost killed and an elderly veteran named Freddie saved my life."

There was a short pause, during which Alex noted her mother's blanched face and her father's shocked expression.

"You're going to have to give us some of the details, honey," her dad said, patiently. "Let's start with the part about you almost being killed."

Her mother's blue eyes were wide and afraid as she squeezed Alex's hand, but she maintained her composure.

Alex took a breath and started over. She told them everything. When she got to the part about Blake, and how much they cared for each other, she begged her parents to tell her how to handle it.

"You guys know why I've never had a steady guy in my life. After Foster, I didn't want to get hurt again, so I put up a boundary against any possibility of love. But Blake is so...I don't know, so different. He's been hurt, too. We understand each other in a way I never expected to find. But we live so far apart. I want to know what to do."

Alex's dad looked at her mom before answering, as though to ask permission. Her mother nodded almost imperceptibly.

"Alex, we're so happy for you. We've always hoped you would find someone special, and after what happened, well, we wanted you to be able to know the good parts of being in a loving relationship. But it's never easy. You guys could live down the street from each other and it still wouldn't be easy. Loving someone takes work and faith. But if he's as great a guy as you say, be patient and give it time. Don't make any rash decisions, but don't close yourself off either."

"Yes," her mother said, "this is what we've hoped for you for so long. Your dad and I have each other, and knowing the kind of love and support you can find in a real relationship makes all the little pains and uncertainties of life worth it. Do you love him?"

"I do," Alex replied, miserably. "He's wonderful."

"Then go figure out a way to be together," her mom said. "Trust each other, be honest, and it'll be okay."

After a moment of silence, her dad asked, "A crime-ring?" His eyebrows were raised.

"Yes. An actual crime-ring."

"I'm so thankful to Freddie," her mom said, "whomever he was. What a brave man. We owe him so much." She shook her head and held her daughter's hand, fighting back tears. "We're so lucky to have you, sweetheart. And we're incredibly proud of the woman you've become. We only want you to be happy."

After lunch with her mom and dad, Alex drove back to Edison. She loved her parents so much. As a younger person, she hadn't always wanted or appreciated their advice. Now, though, as she grew older and more objective, she was deeply thankful for them and for their wisdom.

She pulled up to her house. It looked so solid standing there, tall and stately and all hers, and full of newfound love. An apprehensive, fidgety Blake awaited her inside. Alex looked around in disbelief at her impeccably clean home.

"This looks incredible. You're hired." She smiled at him.

"Thanks. How was your visit?" Blake was on tenterhooks.

His nervousness was a living thing, crouching in the room with them.

Alex couldn't bear to see him looking so miserable. Reaching out to hold Blake's hands, she looked into his face, searching for the love she knew was in there.

"Are you okay?" she asked.

"I'm, um, I don't know. It physically hurt to be apart, and I've been worried about you."

Alex regarded him, thoughtfully. His words were a balm to her wounded heart.

Finally, she said, "I didn't tell you this yesterday, but as I stared at the gun Dan pointed at my heart, something happened. My mind emptied, but for one thing. In this moment of crystal clarity, deep gratitude flooded me, Blake. Because of you, at least I would die knowing what it meant to love and to be loved. It was a revelation, and peace settled into my heart, quelling the fear. I'm so thankful for that, Blake. I am. Whatever else happens, we made it through yesterday alive. Let's face today together."

Blake, who'd been holding his breath as Alex spoke, obviously praying she wouldn't tell him to take a hike, exhaled in relief. His expression softened, and his eyes, which had been so sad a moment before, lit up with relief and joy.

He kissed her on the head and squeezed her in a hug. "Thank you, Alex."

"For what?"

"For being my angel."

Blake picked her up and swung her around, kissing her vehemently. When his exuberance settled and he had returned her to the ground, Alex smiled at him.

"We need to do something kind for Freddie," she said, sadly. "In his honor. Should we have a memorial for him after his funeral service?"

"That's a great idea. Let's plan it together. He was a good man who was put in a horrible position. What he did yesterday was an act of true nobility. Maybe he felt like he needed to do something honorable in the end, even if it meant his death."

"I am so thankful to him. It was so hard to watch him die, Blake, right there in my arms."

"I can't even imagine."

"He died for me, and I need to live to honor him, like you said this morning. We need to live in the moment, Blake, with each other, finding happiness. We deserve it."

She threw her arms around Blake. They stayed locked in their embrace, feeling each other's heat and life and steady heartbeat melt into their own.

Alex mustered the courage to say what she had held silent in her heart all day. "I love you, Blake."

"I am so relieved to hear you say it. I love you too, Alex."

After dinner, they walked to the water to watch the sky exsanguinate from florid pinks and oranges into grayed purples and blues. As they sat at the end of the public dock, arm in arm, the serene beauty beyond held them captive.

Blake asked, "Do you remember what Freddie said—something about how the truth doesn't always set you free?"

"Yeah. He said it can sometimes drag you under."

"He was wrong, I think. He's free now. Free of a lifetime of pain and lies. And I think knowing the truth is going to help me be happier."

"I hope so," Alex said, leaning her head on his arm. "You seem different already."

"I feel different. Like I said, when I heard that gunshot, everything changed. My pain didn't matter anymore. Nothing mattered anymore. Nothing but you."

Alex processed this statement for a moment, feeling the gravity of it. "It's weird how we can go through our lives so bound by our experiences, only to then let them go in an instant. It proves that we can make our own happiness."

"You, my darling, make me happy."

Blake squeezed her to him, and she held him back. Somehow knowing the past was in the past had landed them, however unlikely, together in the now. There was no place Alex would rather be.

As the sky darkened across the lake, reflections of camp lights glimmered in the rippling water like stars. It reminded her of a Van Gogh painting.

"What are you thinking about, Alex?" Blake asked, breaking the silence.

"I was thinking of art and beauty and nature, of the stars. Of how all those things transcend daily human endeavors and suffering. Like Van Gogh's paintings, for instance. He suffered and died. And even though he's gone, he'll never be forgotten. The work he created has transcended time."

"He was a visionary."

"He was. They've studied his paintings, and there's actually a mathematical formula hidden in them that eluded mathematicians and scientists for ages. It's the formula for turbulent flow. His artwork follows it almost exactly."

Blake kissed the top of her head.

"Have you ever seen pictures of Jupiter," she said, "all full of wild storms? It looks like a Van Gogh painting, too. But how did he know?"

"Maybe there was something connecting him to the universe, deepening his understanding. Maybe that's what drove him mad."

"Maybe. But the nature of the universe, that vast energy out there with all its patterns and mysteries, it makes me feel wonderfully small and perfectly unimportant."

"Well, you're important to *me*," Blake said. "That kind of meaning transcends time, too, I think. Love, like beauty, knows no place in time. Time is a construct. Love is a force."

"I like that. You're pretty philosophical for a sporto, you know. You might've liked art school better."

"No doubt," Blake laughed sadly. "What would you do if you could start over?"

Alex considered this question before answering, staring out over the glittering water to the silhouette of the far-off trees against the inky sky.

"It's too hard a question. If I changed even one thing in my life—even the most painful thing—I wouldn't have met you. I would not be sitting here with you right now."

"I should've asked a different question. What would you do if you could do anything?"

"Travel," Alex said, without hesitating. "I would see the whole fucking world. I want to see Machu Picchu. I want to see Angkor Watt. I want to see ruins in Scotland and Ireland, tile work in Morocco, paintings at Museé D'Orsay in Paris. That's what I'd do. I'd draw pictures of all of it and write children's books about the art of human endeavor. What would you do?"

"Wow. That actually sounds pretty good. Can we start in Maine?"

"Man. I never thought mentioning a random state as a possibility for starting over would get you this obsessed. That lighthouse from your dream still on your mind?"

"Yeah. I can't get it out of my head. I've never been there. In fact, I don't think I've ever even seen a lighthouse that wasn't on a calendar or in an advertisement. But I can't seem to let go of the image of the one from my dream. It's white and tall and has this little house in front of it. It's set way up on the cliffs, with rocks jutting out, and beyond it is this glittering sea. I want to see if it's real."

"In search of a mythical lighthouse. I like it. We can make a children's book out of that, too." Alex smiled her widest, most genuine smile at Blake.

"Now we have a plan."

———

DA Weathers called the following day. She had done some digging, subpoenaing Dwight Anderson's medical records on a hunch. It hadn't made sense to her why Dwight had suddenly gotten angry enough with his wife to kill her.

"Get this," Weathers said. "It turns out Dwight had had some medical tests run because of problems he was having from exposure to Agent Orange. He had a sperm count of zero. He must have realized that it didn't make sense how he could have a kid unless his wife had slept with someone else. The timeline adds up. It wasn't long after those test results were relayed to him that he killed your mom."

Chills went down Blake's spine as he considered this new evidence. "This means it was premeditated murder, not a sporadic act of violence. Dwight knew exactly what he was doing." Blake was floored.

"Does knowing this make it easier or harder to absorb?" Weathers asked, her cold voice warming in a moment of concern.

"Nothing can make the past easier to swallow, but I'm so thankful to know the truth. Finally. Thank you so much."

"Well, you guys did the bulk of the work on this. I'm trying to fill in some of the missing pieces."

"That was the one thing Alex and I couldn't figure out. What had finally put Dwight over the edge."

"His record showed a long list of concerns expressed by his doctors over the years regarding his stability, starting with his first exam to get into the army. The treatment of mental illness in the armed services back then was less than stellar, but it looks like he was a violent psychopath before he ever even joined the army. He had several misdemeanor charges for assault during his teens."

"I wish my mom had seen him for what he was before it was too late," Blake said, sadly.

"Me too. You've been so courageous throughout this

process. And without Alex's particular brand of heroism, this might have gone differently. Dan Arquette might have slipped past the net of the law yet again."

SIXTEEN

The number of people who showed up at Ricky's to honor Freddie's memory astounded Alex. The bar was full. The TVs were off. The whole place buzzed with conversation. Alex talked with Stan, who knew Freddie best, judging that if Stan approved of the gathering, then they'd done right by Freddie. The VA had put the word out, and a lot of Freddie's buddies from there showed up as well.

It had been over thirty years since Sal and Jacob had seen each other. When Jacob walked in and saw Sal, the exact image of his beloved Caroline, his face betrayed his deep sadness.

Alex went to him immediately. "I'm glad you're here." She gave him a hug.

"I wouldn't have missed it. How are you holding up?" Jacob's baritone voice was so similar to Blake's.

"I'm sad and still a little traumatized, but I think honoring Freddie like this is going to help. I didn't realize how many people knew and loved him."

"This is a really good turnout." Jacob's gaze wandered back to Sal.

"Twins," Alex said, wistfully, looking at her as well. "I'm so sorry. It's gotta be really hard to see her. I know Blake's always had a rough time with it."

"I don't know what I expected to feel, but this is hard. It's surreal. I can't imagine how Blake dealt with it as a kid."

"It wasn't easy. None of this has been easy. But we can't undo what's been done, can we? It's all about moving forward. Come on, I'll reintroduce you guys."

Blake, Sam, and Sal were at the bar talking when Alex brought Jacob over.

"Well, holy shit." Sal looked at him and smiled sadly. "You haven't changed at all in how many years? Thirty? More? How old are you, Blake?"

"Sal." Blake elbowed her, looking mortified.

"It's good to see you, Sal," Jacob said, stretching out his hand, which Sal roundly ignored, going in for the hug instead.

"I'm sorry about everything," Sal said. "I didn't know you loved her. She never told me anything. I lost Caroline long before that bastard Dwight got his hands on her, and by then it was too late. Everything I ever tried to do to help only made her life worse."

"I should've tried harder to help her. I let my own insecurity get in the way. I'm sorry." Jacob's voice was thick, his face was full of pain.

"Please don't apologize. You're going to be the father Blake never had. That is a gift I accept on behalf of my sister."

"Thank you," Jacob said, stoically.

"Jacob, this is Sam, my husband."

The men shook hands, and Sam said, "Good to meet

you."

Alex squeezed Blake's hand tightly and he bent down to kiss her on the head.

"Thank you, Alex," he whispered into her hair. "You brought my family together."

"I love you, Blake," she whispered back.

After a few moments, the guys got wrapped up in sports talk and Sal took Alex aside.

"I wanted you to know how thankful I am to you. You brought Blake back to me. After so long, I didn't think I'd ever be able to let him know how much I care for him."

"People in pain close themselves off. They put up walls and shut out everyone, even the people who love them. But he knows it now. He loves you, too."

"His dad's a hunk, huh?"

Alex choked on her beer. She looked at Sal and they both burst into giggles.

Alex eventually called everyone to attention, chiming a fork against her beer glass. Then, gathering her courage, she stood on a stool and addressed the room.

"I would like to make a toast to Freddie," she said, trying to keep her voice strong.

Everyone raised their glasses in silent unison.

"Freddie Cormack didn't owe me anything. We didn't know each other well. Yet this man gave his life for mine, in the face of violence. His bravery and self-sacrifice are why I'm able to stand before you today. I'll never forget Freddie's heroism, nor will I ever take his gift to me for granted. To Freddie."

"To Freddie," the room called back.

Over the next few weeks, Alex and Blake finished the work on the cabin, which was finally out of probate. Thankfully, the title had automatically transferred to Blake, as he was Dwight's only legal relative. A realtor put the camp on the market and scheduled an open house for the following Sunday. Blake already had two offers, both over asking price. He could hardly believe that it was the last he'd ever have to see of the place he'd grown up in.

When he signed the paperwork accepting the highest offer, which had exceeded his wildest expectations, he and Alex visited the camp one last time to say goodbye and to admire their hard work. She pulled the truck up the gravel driveway and stopped. They got out and looked down at the lake, which had suddenly taken on the joyful characteristics of summer, with its strong light glimmering on the water. A party barge full of revelers putted by, leaving laughter in its wake.

Hand in hand, Blake and Alex walked all the way around the cabin, surveying their work. The cabin looked like a different place altogether. It shone proudly with its new porch, new paint, new roof, and renewed energy.

"We did a good job, Blake," she said, softly.

"It's astounding. The place is unrecognizable. Speaking of which, I owe you some money, Alex. This is a job well done."

"You don't owe me anything."

"What are you talking about? We had a contract. Half down, half at completion. I owe you fifteen thousand dollars."

"Jesus, Blake, I was overcharging you because I was mad at your shitty attitude when we met. You were so surprised I was a woman."

"You brat."

"You bet. We're settled, Blake. You did half the work, anyway. You owe me nothing."

Blake looked at her and smiled. "You're something, Alex Taylor. Thank you, but I will be paying you for the job you did. That's final."

"Well, you're wildly overpaying."

Laughing, they strolled into the cabin, arm in arm. They walked through every room downstairs. The new appliances and countertops made the kitchen look clean and bright. The freshly polyurethaned floors gleamed throughout. The bathroom was still shabby, but the next owner could deal with it.

When they reached the bottom of the steps leading to the upstairs dormer, Alex hesitated.

"We don't have to go up there," she said. "I made sure it was clean and tidy."

"I want to. I need to close this chapter with bravery, babe. I need to look Dwight's cruelty in the eye and tell him that he lost. In the end, he lost it all."

Blake climbed the stairs with a determined gait. At the top of the stairs, he pushed open the door and forged his way into his childhood bedroom. The ghosts were thin as cobwebs though, and he easily brushed them aside.

"Well, fuck you, Dwight," he said, quietly. Then louder, he repeated, "Fuck you. You were a horrible bastard and no one loved you. I feel sorry for you, man, being that fucked up."

Alex put her hand on his back.

"Do you see this woman? This is what love looks like. And love will always trump hate. I can't hate you anymore, Dwight. Hate's what's wrong with this world and we don't need any more of it. Now I just pity you and I'm thankful you'll never hurt anyone ever again." He turned to Alex, holding back tears of emotion. "May I kiss you, angel?"

"You may." Her gaze was full of love and pride.

They kissed each other deeply, in utter defiance of the agony of their tortured histories, to prove that their love was stronger than the pain that had been inflicted upon them. Their kiss was full of passion and love, tapping into the great energy of the universe. Swirls of turbulence followed their mystical trajectories, projecting Blake and Alex's feelings for each other into new territory as they transcended sorrow and loss, grief and suffering.

As they parted lips, they looked at each other with deep understanding.

Smiling, Alex said, "That should leave some better energy in this place."

Together, they left the camp. As they drove away, a cloud of gravel dust billowed up, obscuring all they had left behind. The way forward, however, was perfectly clear.

ACKNOWLEDGMENTS

Writing a book is a labor of love. It's also a deeply emotional experience. An author puts herself into the treacherous riptide of imagined worlds, fully understanding the risk of being sucked under. Because of the steadfast support of family and friends, I always know when to step back from the water and breathe.

Thank you to my kind husband and two sweet children for their continued patience and support as I send my stories spinning off into the universe. My family grounds me. They inspire me. They love me unconditionally. They remind me of everything that is important in this life. For that gift, I am eternally grateful.

Thank you as well to my talented editor, Carly Hayward. Her clear thinking and skill helped transform this book, polishing its many rough edges. I couldn't be happier, and that's saying something. Thank you to Caroline Akervik for her sharp editorial eye and positive feedback. And to Nancy Schumacher, thanks for always being willing to take a chance on me. Your support means so much.

Lastly, because the topics addressed in this book are so serious, I urge anyone who has experienced domestic abuse or sexual assault to seek the help they deserve. The National Domestic Violence Hotline is 1-800-799-7233. The National Sexual Assault Hotline is 1-800-656-4673.

Be safe, stay strong, and remember—love will only win if we let it.

THANK YOU FOR READING

Did you enjoy this book?

We invite you to leave a review at your favorite book site, such as Goodreads, Amazon, Barnes & Noble, etc.

DID YOU KNOW THAT LEAVING A REVIEW...

- Helps other readers find books they may enjoy.
- Gives you a chance to let your voice be heard.
- Gives authors recognition for their hard work.
- Doesn't have to be long. A sentence or two about why you liked the book will do.

ABOUT THE AUTHOR

Emma Hartley is an author and artist living in picturesque Maine. She has been writing and making art since childhood and has been insatiably curious and industrious her whole life. Emma was a double major in English and Fine Arts and holds a Masters in Art and Design Education. Emma has also won a literary award for her short story, *The Baking*  *Lesson* (2021), and an honorable mention for her short story, *The Factory* (2022). Her novels center the lives of strong women and their artistic work, and include themes ranging from overcoming trauma, grief, and loss, to finding the perfection in every-day moments. Emma's other interests include playing drums, gardening, and exploring every square inch of the Maine coastline. Her published novels include *The Beauty of Fragile Things* (2020), *The Annealing of Aliza Bennett* (2018), and *The Nature of Entangled Hearts* (2017).

www.emmahartleyauthor.com

facebook.com/emmahartleyauthor

instagram.com/emmahartleyauthor

ALSO BY EMMA HARTLEY
WITH SATIN ROMANCE

The Nature of Entangled Hearts
The Annealing of Aliza Bennett
The Beauty of Fragile Things
Heartwood

www.ingramcontent.com/pod-product-compliance
Lightning Source LLC
Chambersburg PA
CBHW021519240626
47154CB00002B/698